PRAISE FOR THE NOVELS OF RUTH GLICK
(WRITING AS REBECCA YORK)

"Rebecca York's writing is fast-paced, suspenseful, and loaded with tension." —Jayne Ann Krentz

"A compulsive read." —*Publishers Weekly*

"Rebecca York delivers page-turning suspense." —Nora Roberts

"York has penned a convincing and sensual paranormal romance, and readers who fell in love with the characters in . . . *Killing Moon* will be glad to meet them again." —*Booklist*

"Mesmerizing action and passions that leap from the pages with the power of a wolf's coiled spring." —*BookPage*

"*Killing Moon* is a delightful, supernatural private-investigator romance starring two charming lead characters." —*Midwest Book Review*

continued . . .

"Glick's prose is smooth, literate, and fast moving; her love scenes are tender yet erotic; and there's always a happy ending."   —*The Washington Post Book World*

"A true master of intrigue."   —*Rave Reviews*

"No one sends more chills down your spine than the very creative and imaginative Ms. York!"   —*Romantic Times*

"She writes a fast-paced, satisfying thriller."   —*UPI*

"*Edge of the Moon* is clever and a great read. I can't wait to read the final book in this wonderful series."
          —*ParaNormal Romance Reviews*

BEYOND
FEARLESS

REBECCA YORK

BERKLEY SENSATION, NEW YORK

THE BERKLEY PUBLISHING GROUP
Published by the Penguin Group
Penguin Group (USA) Inc.
375 Hudson Street, New York, New York 10014, USA
Penguin Group (Canada), 90 Eglinton Avenue East, Suite 700, Toronto, Ontario M4P 2Y3, Canada
(a division of Pearson Penguin Canada Inc.)
Penguin Books Ltd., 80 Strand, London WC2R 0RL, England
Penguin Group Ireland, 25 St. Stephen's Green, Dublin 2, Ireland (a division of Penguin Books Ltd.)
Penguin Group (Australia), 250 Camberwell Road, Camberwell, Victoria 3124, Australia
(a division of Pearson Australia Group Pty. Ltd.)
Penguin Books India Pvt. Ltd., 11 Community Centre, Panchsheel Park, New Delhi—110 017, India
Penguin Group (NZ), 67 Apollo Drive, Rosedale, North Shore 0632, New Zealand
(a division of Pearson New Zealand Ltd.)
Penguin Books (South Africa) (Pty.) Ltd., 24 Sturdee Avenue, Rosebank, Johannesburg 2196,
South Africa

Penguin Books Ltd., Registered Offices: 80 Strand, London WC2R 0RL, England

This is a work of fiction. Names, characters, places, and incidents either are the product of the author's imagination or are used fictitiously, and any resemblance to actual persons, living or dead, business establishments, events, or locales is entirely coincidental. The publisher does not have any control over and does not assume any responsibility for author or third-party websites or their content.

BEYOND FEARLESS

A Berkley Sensation Book / published by arrangement with the author

PRINTING HISTORY
Berkley Sensation mass-market edition / December 2007

ISBN: 978-0-425-21866-2

BERKLEY® SENSATION
Berkley Sensation Books are published by The Berkley Publishing Group,
a division of Penguin Group (USA) Inc.,
375 Hudson Street, New York, New York 10014.
BERKLEY SENSATION and the "B" design are trademarks belonging to Penguin Group (USA) Inc.

PRINTED IN THE UNITED STATES OF AMERICA

10 9 8 7 6 5 4 3 2 1

BEYOND
FEARLESS

CHAPTER
ONE

THE COOL BLUE silence of the sea swallowed Zachary
Robinson as he dove toward the luxury yacht that rested on
a coral reef sixty feet below the surface of the Caribbean.

Colorful tropical fish and a small shark swam lazily
around the wreck. The predator would have sent a less experienced diver kicking for the surface. But Zach wasn't
worried. Sharks might have a bad reputation, but they rarely
attacked divers, unless you did something stupid. And Zach
always calculated the risks before going into any situation.

He was taking a risk today—using local guys instead of
the crew that had been with him for the past two years. But
they were back in the States, on a well-deserved vacation.
Zach had stayed on Grand Fernandino, a Caribbean island
east of Jamaica, where French, Spanish, English, and
African influences combined to create a richly unique cul-
ture.

The day after Barry and Simon had left for California
and Georgia, respectively, he'd been offered a job too lu-
crative to turn down. A millionaire from Palm Beach, Terrance Sanford, was looking for his missing brother and his
brother's ship, the *Blue Heron*.

So Zach had hired José, a certified diver, and Claude, an experienced sailor capable of handling the *Odysseus*, his sixty-five-foot converted work boat.

That morning, Zach had thought he'd located the missing craft with his onboard sonar. But when they'd dived down to the ship in question, he'd realized they'd found an older junker, already picked clean by other divers.

Now he and José were going down for the second time in one day. It was not recommended procedure, since their tissues would still carry nitrogen from the last dive, but they'd be okay if they added an extra safety stop on the way up.

Propelling himself downward, Zach reached the yacht, which was resting on its side on a reef. Swimming to the stern, he felt a thrill of elation when he saw the name *Blue Heron* through the aqua water.

According to Terrance Sanford, the boat had gone down ten days ago on an ill-advised trip from Grand Fernandino to Jamaica, piloted by his sixty-year-old brother, William, who had ignored storm warnings when he'd left port.

Terrance wanted to recover his brother's body, as well as some valuables from the yacht. Apparently, he'd heard of Zach's talent for finding wrecks. He hired him by e-mail, with an advance wire-transferred payment.

While Zach was confirming the ship's identity, José swam to the front deck, then slipped through the hatch into the cockpit.

Zach had just reached the deck when the other diver burst through the hatch.

With the swift insights that often came to him in an emergency, Zach sensed that José was planning to do something very stupid: strike out directly for the surface. Without making the necessary decompression stops, he was looking at a case of the bends, a painful and sometimes fatal condition caused by rising too quickly.

As the lithe shape shot past, Zach caught one of José's swim fins.

The man kicked out, the blow muted by the clear blue water around them. When he couldn't free himself, he whipped around. Launching himself forward, he made a grab for Zach's air hose. Zach's only choice was to block the grasping fingers, then turn the attacker so that he faced away.

Holding José in place, Zach kept the man from fighting free.

Stop trying to kill both of us, he shouted in his mind. *What the hell is wrong with you?*

But there was no way to speak in the watery environment, so he could only hold the diver still, praying that he'd settle down before they both used up their oxygen in the fight.

When José stopped struggling, Zach kicked upward to the first decompression stop, forcing himself to wait while they both adjusted to the decreased pressure.

José had gone limp in his arms. He wanted to turn the diver toward him and find out if the guy's eyes were still wild, but he had to content himself with knowing that the man seemed to be cooperating.

At the last stop, Zach realized he'd been lulled into dropping his guard. José broke away from him and shot toward the surface like a torpedo released from a submarine.

Shit!

Zach's silent curse followed the other diver. He ached to swim after him, but there was no way he could catch up. And he'd seen what happened to divers with nitrogen bubbles in their bloodstreams. It wasn't pretty, and he wasn't willing to risk it. Not when José was almost at the surface.

So he waited the required minute at the decompression stop, then kicked upward again. As soon as he broke the surface, he struck out for the diving platform of the *Odysseus,* spitting out the mouthpiece of his air hose as he swam.

On the platform, he shook the water from his sun-streaked hair and kicked off his fins before scrambling onto the deck, where Claude was crouched over a sprawled limp form.

Claude looked up, his island drawl turned accusing. "What in hellfire happen, mon? He look like he came up too fast."

"He did! When we got to the wreck, something in the cockpit spooked him," Zach bit out. "I tried to stop him, but he fought me off."

José stared at him, his dark skin turned dull gray, his eyes vacant, and his breathing raspy.

Containing his anger, Zach said, "We'd better get him to the hospital. Call ahead and start the engine."

Claude went to the wheel so Zach could tend to the injured man.

As he sat down beside José, he demanded. "What the hell did you see down there?"

José looked away.

Zach reached down and brought the man's face back. "What was worth killing yourself for? And maybe me?"

José looked like he was struggling for coherence, but he managed to give Zach a defiant look. "Pagor."

"Huh?"

"Kill me dead. I see Pagor down der," he whispered.

Zach recognized the name. He'd done some reading before he came to Grand Fernandino, and he knew that the island had its own unique version of the Caribbean religions, called Vadiana. Pagor was one of the Vadiana deities, or saints.

"Pagor? The god of war?" he demanded.

"Yeah, mon" José whispered. "He send that boat—the *Blue Heron*—to the bottom. And he don't want nobody to see."

"Christ!" Zach wanted to inform José that Pagor was no more real than the boogeyman.

He had been raised by a mother and father who went to church on Christmas and Easter. On official forms that asked for his religion, he said he was a Christian. But religion had never played a big role in his life.

On the other hand, José was a true believer. The man had about killed himself trying to get away from what he thought was an angry god.

Zach gritted his teeth. He wasn't going to talk the islander out of his beliefs. Even if they'd almost killed him.

Especially if they'd almost killed him.

He looked toward the horizon, watching the blue mountains of Grand Fernandino draw closer.

He wanted to turn around and head back to the dive site and find out what the hell José had really seen down in the cockpit of the *Blue Heron*. But he'd already been pushing safe limits with the afternoon dive, and there was no way he could go down again until twenty-four hours had passed.

CHAPTER
TWO

WITH THE SUN hovering just above the ocean's western horizon, the alley was shady and cool, a relief from the heat of the Caribbean day.

Yet as Anna Ridgeway hurried along the cobblestone passage between the pastel green, blue, and yellow buildings of Palmiro, she felt the fine hairs on her arms prickle.

She'd thought she'd found a refuge on Grand Fernandino—five hundred miles from the mainland United States. Now she suspected that danger had followed her from Denver.

Her eyes probed the shadows for signs of anyone following—or someone who had circled around and gotten in front of her.

The sights and sounds of the port city enveloped her. No one who lived in the old quarter had air-conditioning. That modern luxury was only available in the high-rise hotels along the strip of sand known as Five Mile Beach or at some of the bed-and-breakfast inns dotting the city and the surrounding hills.

Through open doorways and windows along the alley, she glimpsed rooms with five beds crowded together; heard voices speaking in a mixture of French, Spanish, and English; and smelled the aroma of fried bread, spicy beans and rice, and fish baking in banana leaves.

In some of the rooms she saw shrines to various Vadiana saints. The Blessed Ones—the gods that seemed to dominate the religious life of the island. They appeared to be an important part of everyday existence. And she supposed the people here hoped the saints could make their lives better.

A rattling sound made her fumble for the Mace she carried in her purse. Then she saw a skinny black cat slip from behind a trash can and prepare to streak across the alley.

They both stopped short. The cat had encountered her before and looked up hopefully.

"Here you go, sweetie."

Instead of the Mace, she took out the plastic bag of dry cat food she'd started carrying with her and spilled some on the ground at the side of the alley. The cat waited until she moved away before starting to eat hungrily.

Feeding it was probably a useless gesture. There were thousands of stray cats on the island. But she'd decided to try and make life a little less miserable for some of them.

She'd come here last week on the invitation of Etienne Bertrand, who'd contacted her agent several months ago about booking her into his Sugar Cane Club in Palmiro.

At first the timing had seemed perfect. She'd thought the island represented escape, a place to relax during the day before going out to wow the customers at night.

But she'd been uncomfortable here since the first night she'd arrived. And not just because Bertrand turned out to be a giant of a man who served as his own bouncer.

She'd been on her own for ten years, and she was a pretty good judge of people. There was something "off" about Bertrand, but she didn't know what.

Or what, exactly, was going wrong in her personal universe. Everything had been fine until her engagement in

Denver, when she felt like someone was watching her—getting closer. Getting ready to spring. Too bad the feeling was worse on Grand Fernandino.

She'd thought about breaking her contract, but she'd already discovered that Bertrand was well connected here. She was sure that if she tried to change her plane ticket, the island grapevine would inform him. And he could turn out to be more dangerous than whoever was following her.

"Stop it!" she muttered. Maybe nobody was following her. Maybe she just needed a long vacation after nine straight months on the road.

She sighed. Mostly, she'd been satisfied with the life she'd made for herself.

Now she couldn't shake the conviction that outside forces were messing with her destiny.

She reached the back door of the Sugar Cane Club. From the alley it looked like a dump, with peeling paint and smelly garbage cans lined up along the wall.

But she knew the front facade sported a bright green and yellow paint job, designed to attract the tourists who were the lifeblood of the island. Without the foreign currency, everybody here would be living at the poverty level.

She stepped inside, breathing in the smell of stale smoke and liquor. But it looked okay—unless you saw it with all the lights on.

The biggest point in its favor was that Bertrand was paying her more than she'd made in her Denver gig. And with the low cost of living down here, she could save some money while she was on Grand Fernandino.

After closing the door of her dressing room, she pulled off her lime green T-shirt, navy cropped pants, and tennis shoes, then quickly donned the black dress and strappy black high-heeled sandals she wore during her performance.

Methodically, she began applying makeup, accenting her blue eyes with beige and gray shadow, stroking some color over her high cheekbones, and making her upper lip as full as the bottom.

But she didn't spend too much time on her appearance. It wasn't the important part of her act. She could have looked like Grandma Moses and it wouldn't have mattered. In fact, sometimes she wished she could take on the disguise of an old lady—and hide behind it.

FAR away from Grand Fernandino, in a former hunting lodge near Cumberland, Maryland, a man pushed his wheelchair away from the computer. Once he'd been named Jim Swift. He'd worked for an organization called the Crandall Consortium, and he'd been paid well for his skills at stalking human prey and killing with stunning efficiency. Always for a good cause, of course.

Now that he was homebound, he was reduced to sending others out to handle the vital job he ached to do himself.

In the endless hours of pain when he'd lain in the hospital burn unit, he'd come to understand that if he survived, he would start a new phase of his life. God or fate or whatever controlled the universe had spared him for a reason—given him a mission in life.

Twenty dead and more than two hundred to go. And every time he sent another one of the monsters to hell, he felt a profound sense of satisfaction.

He must get them all, before they destroyed the human race—the way they'd destroyed the Crandall Consortium.

He turned to stare out the window into the darkness, feeling the winter cold penetrate his now-fragile skin. All the way to his bones.

In his previous life, his home base had been a converted mansion on the bluffs above the Potomac River, where he'd worked for the powerful Kurt MacArthur.

Officially MacArthur had run a think tank with ties to

Congress, the military, and the CIA. Unofficially, his consortium had taken on jobs no one else had wanted to touch—whether they were legal or not. Until one stupid decision had destroyed everything.

When their headquarters building had gone up in flames, Jim had been lucky to escape with his life. And lucky he had the connections to take on a new identity. Now he was Jim Stone. And nobody knew he had been the Crandall Consortium's most trusted operative.

Too bad MacArthur's secret records had been wiped out in the fire. If Jim had had a list of names, he could have proceeded more quickly. Instead, he was reduced to research—and probabilities. Which meant he might make the wrong call.

But he'd long ago decided that it was better to kill ten innocents by mistake than to allow the guilty to escape. Like in the Middle Ages, when some sinless women had been burned at the stake along with the witches.

The computer beeped, and he spun his wheelchair back to the desk. The message was from Bill Cody. Wild Bill. His operative on Grand Fernandino.

While Jim ran the message through the decoding program, he poured a cup of coffee, then sipped the Kona blend as he read the text.

By the time he was finished, he was 90 percent sure he would order a kill.

ZACH waited for a horse-drawn carriage and a motorcycle to clear the intersection. Then he stepped onto the cobblestone street, careful not to get horse manure on his deck shoes as he crossed to the row of shops and bars across from the city square.

A rotund man standing next to four trained parrots on perches called to him.

"You wanna picture with Ozzie, Harriet, Ricky, and David?"

"No thanks," he answered. He needed a drink, not a souvenir photograph.

He'd intended to go back to the *Blue Heron* as soon as possible. But the day after the diving mishap, he'd quickly found that his plan wasn't going to be so easy.

José and Claude had both been busy spreading the Pagor story, in the island patois. But the message was clear in any language—"stay away from that American, Zach Robinson. He'll get you on the wrong side of Pagor."

So was this whole thing a setup? Had someone paid off José and Claude to make sure he couldn't hire anyone? And why? Had William Sanford been murdered? And the murderer didn't want the *Blue Heron* investigated?

He might have put José and Claude in the middle of a conspiracy—until he remembered the look of sheer terror in José's eyes. The man hadn't been faking his fear. He had been trying to escape the wrath of a supernatural being.

Unfortunately, since then, José had been talking about it to everyone who would listen.

With no other alternative, Zach had put in a call to his regular crew, but they couldn't get there for a couple of days. So he was stuck until they made it to the island.

Which was why he was looking for a dark, quiet place that matched his current mood, where he could have a few beers and silently curse the trio of José, Claude, and Pagor.

As he passed a nightclub painted a garish green and yellow, a publicity poster in a glass case stopped him in his tracks.

The top of the frame said, "Now Appearing at the Sugar Cane Club." Below it, the picture showed a very attractive young woman with wavy dark hair that hung around her shoulders. She was holding a silver tray in one hand and stretching out her other hand toward him as though waiting for him to give her something. The caption at the bottom of the poster said, "Magic Anna: the woman who knows you better than you know yourself."

His first thought was *that's ridiculous hype*. Yet he had always believed in magic, at least in some hidden corner of his soul.

Or he had wanted to believe. You could call it magic if you wanted. Or psychic talent. He wasn't sure which was the better term. He'd read dozens of books about people who were supposed to possess abilities denied to the likes of ordinary humanity.

Sometimes he'd felt like he was on the edge of possessing magic powers himself. He had fantastic intuition when it came to finding shipwrecks and other lost objects.

And yesterday afternoon, that sixth sense had made him whip out his hand and prevent José from shooting to the surface and killing himself.

But that was the extent of his talent. And maybe it hadn't been extrasensory perception that had helped him catch José. Maybe it had been a flash of movement at the corner of his vision.

His attention turned back to the woman who called herself Magic Anna. He liked her body, liked her slender waist, gently rounded hips, and high breasts.

He'd been drawn to her face, then deliberately focused on the rest of the package to give himself a little breathing room. Now he slowly raised his eyes. She looked to be a few years younger than he was. Her lips were sensual. Her nose was short and straight. But her eyes were her best feature, their blue depths fringed by dark lashes—a very attractive combination.

Yet he wasn't just staring at a good-looking woman. The longer he regarded her, the more he thought she really could look into his mind and . . . what?

Connect with him on a level he'd never experienced with

any other human being? Even as the notion flitted through his mind, he stifled a laugh—and gave himself points for a vivid imagination. He thought he was going to find the thing he'd been looking for all his life in a nightclub in Palmiro?

Sure.

With a mental shrug, he walked down the block to a bar where the main activity was drinking.

A soft knock at the door of her dressing room made Anna jump.

"Twenty minutes, sweetheart," Bertrand called in his soft island accent.

She'd come to think of that accent as part of a disguise, along with his short-sleeved button-down shirts covered with tropical flowers. On the surface he seemed like a laid-back dude—drifting along on an island breeze. In reality, he had the sharp teeth of a jungle cat.

When he walked away, she breathed out a little sigh.

From almost the moment she'd arrived in Palmiro, she'd known that Bertrand wanted something from her.

It had started with the long, speculative look he'd given her while they were waiting at the airport for her luggage to be unloaded. Although he hadn't made any moves on her, his hidden agenda added to her tension level.

So what was going on? Did he want her to read his palm? Did he think she could put him in touch with a dead relative—or a dead lover? If so, he was going to be disappointed. Because her powers were limited to what she did in her act. That was it.

She hadn't figured him out. Just the way she hadn't figured out a lot of things that other women seemed to know instinctively about the opposite sex.

Too bad her psychic abilities couldn't help her in that department.

She'd had a few relationships. But nothing deep. Nothing that didn't lead to a disappointing dead end. Because she'd never been able to really open up with anyone. And more than once she'd thought that fate had granted her a mental power that few other people possessed—and left her with a crippling emotional disability as payment.

CHAPTER
THREE

ANNA DRAGGED IN a breath and let it out slowly, wishing her talent hadn't brought her to this place and this time. It had started off as a childhood game, picking up things that belonged to other people and tapping into their memories.

She'd turned the game into a profession after Mom and Dad had died in a car crash during her sophomore year in college. Dad had been trying to pull off one of his big real estate deals at the time, so he'd left her with a boatload of debts.

Vowing to pay them off, Anna had started looking for a way to make some money. And she'd never gone back for her degree because she'd been too busy supporting herself. Her first job had been in the nightclub of a hotel owned by one of her father's creditors, who'd probably figured he had nothing to lose by hiring her. She'd impressed him with her talent, and he'd helped her get hooked up with an agent who had booked her into clubs in several cities. That first agent had given her the name Magic Anna. It didn't exactly fit. When she'd done some research, she'd found out what she did was called psychometry. But by then she was stuck with the Magic Anna name. And if people came in expecting a magic act, they quickly found out the real deal.

To be honest, her nightclub act had given her a sense of secret power—until the first jolt of alarm had cut through her like a knife stabbing into her soul.

She'd found herself facing a man she knew was a rapist. At least she'd clicked onto the picture of a rape when she'd picked up his money clip. And there was nothing she could do about it because she had no proof of what he'd done.

Damn. Why was she thinking of that *now*?

A block away from the Sugar Cane Club, Raoul San Donato watched a customer studying a display of wood carvings in his native arts gallery.

That's a live one, he thought from his desk at the back of the shop.

She was obviously a tourist, with badly sunburned shoulders and a few wisps of dyed brown hair escaping from under the crown of her wide-brimmed straw hat. She looked to be in her midforties, about ten years older than he. The kind of lady who might like some afternoon fun in bed.

Briskly, he switched his mind from sex to a more practical topic—making a sale.

He gave her a few minutes to examine the beautiful objects he had assembled in his gallery, then walked over and asked in his most cultured voice, "May I help you?"

Without bothering to glance up, she gave the standard tourist answer: "I'm just looking."

"We have some wonderful buys on works by talented local artists." He gestured toward a trio of dolphins leaping from waves. "Pablo Ramos is just coming into his own. In a few years, his sculptures will be collector's items." As he spoke, he exercised one of his special talents and sent her a silent message urging her to buy something. When he felt a subtle change in her attitude, he smiled inwardly.

"Really?" she asked, looking him full in the face. He knew she was taking in his island good looks—the combination of Caucasian and African features that had blended so well to make him a striking man with a coffee-and-cream complexion, a Roman nose, and sensual lips.

He kept speaking smoothly as he silently encouraged her desire to buy, using the talent he'd had since he was a boy. "Or you might consider the work of Thomas Avery. He's a bit more established, but his prices start off very low, so you can still get in on a good deal."

She nodded, considering a black onyx cat sitting with its nose pointed toward the sky.

"For you, a special price. Three hundred dollars," he said, knowing he could tip her over the edge if he only had the time.

She came back with an immediate counteroffer.

"One hundred and fifty." Not so low as to be insulting, but low enough to let him know she understood the game.

"Two hundred."

"I don't know . . ." she murmured. "How about one eighty?"

"At that price, I'll have to give Thomas less. And I know he's supporting his wife and children on his earnings."

"All right. Two hundred."

"I'll include a certificate telling about the artist and his work."

Just as he was about to clinch the deal, a man wearing an orange T-shirt stretched over a jiggling belly that hung over khaki cargo shorts came in.

"Honey, come on. I'm hot and tired. And the ship is sailing in an hour."

She held up the cat. "I'm buying this. It will look fantastic on the shelves in the living room."

When the man started to nix the transaction, Raoul

repressed a curse. Instead, he acted quickly, blocking the husband's negative comment with a quick jab of mental energy.

The fat man closed his mouth and went back outside while Mrs. Pam Birmingham of Bridgeport, Connecticut, bought a tchotchke from Grand Fernandino.

After walking her to the door, he stood staring around his gallery with satisfaction. For the first eight years of his life, he'd thought that everyone lived in a dirt-floored hovel, ate rice and beans for breakfast, and crapped out back. Then his aunt had come home from Palmiro to brag about the high life in the port city, where she made solid money in the big hotels—cleaning the rooms of the rich tourists.

Momma had followed her. And she'd taken Raoul and a couple of the other kids with her. At first, he'd been bug-eyed at Palmiro's grandeur. In the island's capital, too many people might squeeze into one room at night, but life was nothing like in his village.

And when he helped Momma clean up after the rich folks in the big hotels, he saw how they lived. Sometimes they left wonderful things behind when they flew back to their homes—candies nestled in crinkly brown paper cups, soft drinks, magazines with pictures of naked women.

He enjoyed the booty. When he ran errands for the tourists, their tips seemed like a fortune. And he vowed that he would do what it took to live like them.

He'd started with his speech, imitating their grammar and vocabulary but keeping the soft island tone of his voice and just enough "native" turns of phrase to make himself seem charming.

Some island kids quit school early. He stayed through tenth grade. And after class every day, he joined the hordes of higglas—street vendors—saving his earnings until he could rent a stall in the marketplace.

It was about that time that he began talking seriously to Joseph Hondino, one of the local Vadiana priests.

Old Joe had taught him about the pull toward complete-
ness and divinity in the universe. He'd taught his young
disciple that reality is a world of forces in continual process, of energy moving at different rates of speed. Raoul
had zoned out on the deep background stuff, but he understood that men and spirits interacted. And if you courted
their help, they might be on your side. Or they might not.

When he'd done a little reading on his own, Raoul discovered something even better—that nothing is completely
"good" or completely "evil." And as far as the universe is
concerned, no action is completely "wrong" or "right."
Which meant, in his mind, that the end justified the means.

Of course, when he talked to Hondino about it, Old Joe
was horrified at that interpretation. He'd lectured Raoul on
right and wrong. On the proper use of Vadiana and the for-
bidden.

Although Raoul pretended to listen, he was already making his own plans. He'd long ago discovered he had special
powers—way before he had heard of the Vadiana gods.
Hooking up with the Blessed Ones simply added to what
he already had. And, he figured, the proof of a course of
action was in how well it worked.

So far, it was working very very well for him.

A lot of islanders had tied their fortunes to his. More
and more people came to the private compound on the
other side of the island, where he held his very potent ceremonies on Friday nights.

With a little smile, he strode to the door of the gallery to
flip the lock and then the Open sign to Closed. As he was
about to pull down the shade, he stopped short.

Speak of the devil.

Joseph Hondino was standing across the street, staring at
him. The dark skin of his bald head gleamed like he'd
rubbed it with palm oil. His white beard was neatly trimmed.
And his eyes were sleepy-looking. But everybody on the island knew that he missed very little. If you were stealing

goodies from the tourists' rooms, he knew it. And if you needed a pair of decent shoes so you could get a job as a waiter, he knew that, too.

Raoul went stock-still. For just a moment he felt like a street kid caught with his hand in a tourist's pocket.

He recovered quickly. Manufacturing a grin, he gave the priest a jaunty wave.

They stood regarding each other for several heartbeats, across an enormous gulf. Raoul broke the spell and turned away.

Hondino had told him he was perverting the principles of Vadiana, but he didn't care what old Joe thought. Because he was getting ready to make his big move. And when he did, Hondino was out as the big cheese on the island. And Raoul San Donato was in.

He pulled the shade, then went back to his cash drawer to count the day's receipts. Two thousand dollars. Excellent!

He left the credit card slips in the drawer and hid the money behind a loose board in the shop's back room. Business over for the day, he stepped into the small rear yard, where the darkness and a high wooden fence gave him privacy.

In a building that had once been a storage shed, he had set up a small shrine to Ibena. She was one of the Blessed Ones, the deities who ruled over every force of nature and every aspect of human life. To please her, he had decorated the shrine with rich gold, red, and coral. And he had carefully collected some of her favorite objects—fans, tortoiseshell combs, peacock feathers, and a small boat floating in a tub of water because she was the deity of rivers.

She was also the goddess of love and of sexuality, of marriage and fertility. And she would bring him a woman who was his equal, a woman to share the bounty they would create together.

Some people expected a strong man to make Pagor his patron saint, but Raoul had found a better focus for his prayers.

He took off his shirt and hung it on a hook by the door. He was offering himself to the goddess. Offering her the tattoo that he kept hidden from the tourists. It started at his right shoulder, snaked partway down his arm, and spread across his chest. He had gotten an artist to depict the Blessed Ones, with Ibena in the middle, her brown hair spread out like a fan and her eyes a dramatic shade of turquoise that drew people's attention to her power.

He loved that tattoo. And his followers did, too. It was the living symbol on his body of what he had made himself into. And what he would become. When he married, he would add his wife's face to the mix. But on his back, because he would never offend the gods by placing her among them.

Shirtless, he walked past the shrine and stepped to the cage where he held the chickens that he used in his rituals.

All of the saints required sacrifices, to renew their life force, and he had dedicated himself to renewing and pleasing his special saint. His diligence was working, even if Old Joe didn't approve of his goals or his vision.

He knew that the term "saint" had first been used by the early Vadiana worshippers to hide their practices from the slave owners who wanted to wipe out their native traditions. So the slaves had let themselves be converted to the Catholic faith—at least on the surface—while secretly giving the new saints the attributes of their old deities. He didn't know which saint Ibena had stood for, because she was so sensual and so womanly. Not like the dried-up old nuns who ran a convent at the edge of town.

Opening the cage, he quickly pulled out a chicken, then ignored its squalling as he brought it into the shrine. As he chanted a prayer to his patron saint, he expertly wrung the chicken's neck, making a quick kill. Then with his knife he made a cut in the throat and let a few drops of its blood drip onto the altar and the rest into a bowl. Later, he would give the chicken to a poor family that would appreciate the meal.

Straightening his shoulders and speaking in the formal tones of a priest, he said, "Bring my future wife to the right man. The man she was meant to join with in love and power." He made the request in a clear, loud voice. "Help her realize that her own abilities can be greater than she knows. Help her find her destiny."

As he spoke to Ibena, he pictured himself stepping onto a windswept plain, away from the world of men, where he could meet the woman he had chosen as his bride. He would introduce himself to her there. Later they would unite their bodies in sexual ecstasy and their minds in power. And together they would rule this island.

A small doubt tugged at him. Perhaps he was moving too fast, calling her to him now. And in this way. But he wanted to test his power over her. And give her a taste of how much they would mean to each other.

He pictured her stepping into the reality he had created. She would be wearing only a gauzy green dress. Green like the island jungle.

As the image grew in his mind, he felt his own spirit expand, flowing out to meet hers.

ZACH had drunk his bottle of beer slowly, enjoying the taste of the island brew, but he couldn't get the woman on the poster out of his mind. It was as though she was calling him back. And finally, he left the bar and returned to the Sugar Cane Club.

Instead of going inside, he stood on the street, staring at the poster. At Anna. Taking in her striking good looks again, then focusing on her shimmering blue eyes.

A sense of expectation gathered inside him. Like the change in the air before a powerful storm. Only it was something different. Something he couldn't name.

Then suddenly—unaccountably—he was lost to the port town around him. From one instant to the next, the heat and noise and smells of the Caribbean city disappeared. Instead he had the sensation that he was standing on an immense plain that he couldn't see, because the light was low and the view was obscured by swirling clouds and mist.

He should've been frightened. Instead he felt his blood pumping through his veins in exhilaration—like the times he'd jumped out of a plane and felt the rush of wind before his parachute opened.

RAOUL was winging toward his meeting with his destiny, when suddenly he came up against an unexpected barrier.

In that instant, he went sick and fuzzy in the head. His hands pressed against his temples as he fought the sudden stab of pain that had replaced his sense of anticipation.

What!

When he realized the barrier was the spirit of another man, his anger flared.

In that terrible moment, he knew that he had a rival. A man who had come to steal what was his.

Raoul made an animal sound deep in his throat, layers of civilization peeling away as he struggled to push the other man away. Not physically, but with his mental powers.

But the viper had stepped into the scene as though he were the one who belonged there!

Who was he?

"Devil! Turn your face to me."

The man did not respond. He didn't seem to hear the order. And Raoul's clearest sight of him was a head of thick, sun-streaked hair.

Even as he shouted the words, he felt the scene waver, felt himself pulled back into the reality of Grand Fernandino.

He was left standing before the altar, his heart pounding.

He blinked, bloodlust rising in his soul like a dark curtain that cut him off from the light. He wanted to scream in rage, but he must not let fear and anger overcome good sense. He willed himself to silence, the telltale sound of his anguish locked behind his lips.

Calling on every scrap of discipline he possessed, he ordered himself to calm down. A priest should always keep his cool. Like Old Joe.

Once Raoul found his imperturbable center, he knew what was happening. Ibena was testing him—making him work for the sweet pleasure of joining his body and soul with the woman who should be his by rights. And he would show the deity he was worthy of that honor.

With fingers that weren't quite steady, he stroked the tattoo on his chest, tracing the familiar lines of Ibena's face, willing himself back into the world he had created, struggling to make himself the master of the fantasy scene again and send the other man plunging into hellfire.

CHAPTER
FOUR

ANNA HAD PUT herself into a light trance the way she always did before her performance.

She let the familiar detached feeling flow over her, welcomed the little buzz in her head.

And then from one instant to the next, everything changed. The shabby dressing room disappeared, and she was standing on a high, windswept plain, gasping in shock.

She reached out to touch something familiar, to touch *anything*. But the world had gone away, and she was in another reality.

She struggled to draw back as she fought to return to the safety of her dressing room. But it had vanished, and she knew that the only way she could go was forward. So she took a cautious step, then another, feeling the strange springy surface beneath her feet. Her bare feet, she realized suddenly.

In the world, she had been dressed in black. Here in this new reality, she was wearing only a gauzy green dress. Green like a field in springtime.

* * *

ZACH stared at the woman walking toward him. A light wind blew, lifting her hair and swirling the insubstantial skirt around her shapely legs.

He could see the curves of her body through the thin fabric. Her high breasts, her sweetly rounded hips. The shadows of her nipples and a triangle of dark hair at the juncture of her legs.

This is it. The real thing. What you've been waiting for all your life.

Even as the thought flitted through his mind, he wondered what it meant.

The woman had stopped walking, her features tense as he closed the space between them, reaching his hand toward her.

When her lips moved, he heard no sound. But he knew she had said, *Who are you?*

Zach, he silently answered.

He wanted her to know him. Want him. Trust him. Complete him.

He grasped her shoulder and folded her close, drawing in a sharp breath as he felt her breasts flatten against his chest—his naked chest, because somehow he was wearing only a pair of faded jeans, unsnapped at the waist.

A jolt of arousal shot through him, and he tightened his hold on her as a whirlwind of sensations swamped him. The brush of her raven hair against his cheek. Her slender body pressed to his. The buzz of sound in his brain as she spoke voiceless words he couldn't quite catch.

He wanted her to raise her head.

As if she'd heard his thoughts, she lifted her face to his.

He felt a shock of awareness go through him. Strange. This was strange. And at the same time so right that it made his insides ache.

Though he longed to kiss her, he held himself still, because some part of him knew that if he did anything that intimate, nothing in his life would ever be the same. Yet the thought of her pulling away made his insides go cold.

He held his breath, willing her to make the decision. She stayed where she was, her lips slightly parted, as though she were having the same thoughts as he. And she didn't want to be the one to make the first move.

Finally, because that was his only choice, he lowered his head to hers. The first contact of their mouths was like an explosion in his brain, in his body.

He had never tasted anything so rich, so totally tempting as this woman's mouth.

She made a small needy sound that sizzled through him. Accepting her invitation, he tipped his head first one way and then the other, changing the angle, changing the pressure, changing the very terms of his existence.

Desperate to satisfy his craving for intimate contact with her, he slid one hand down her body, pulling her hips against his erection.

She moaned, moving against him in a way that told him she was as aroused as he.

Thank God.

His other hand moved between them, cupping one of her breasts, then stroking his fingers across the hardened crest.

He needed to be on top of her, needed to plunge inside her.

And she kissed him with the same desperation.

He was about to drag her down to the horizontal surface under their feet when another voice cut through the vivid daydream, or whatever it was.

"Go on. Git! You got no place here."

A man was speaking to him, and he fought an instant feeling of disorientation as he was pulled back into the heat of a tropical night.

* * *

ANNA blinked. From far away, she heard the calypso band playing a little fanfare.

Reaching out, she grabbed the edge of the table in front of her, pressing her fingers against the hard surface, anchoring herself to the world.

She had been sitting there, getting ready to go out and do her show. Then she had been . . . in another place. Somewhere else. Somewhere she didn't want to be. With a man who wanted her. A man whose voice spoke inside her head.

Alarm zinged along her nerve endings.

What had happened to her?

She had no reference point to describe the strange experience. And she couldn't afford the luxury of dealing with it now.

Yeah, right.

She didn't *want* to deal with it.

And she had a perfect excuse for thrusting it away with an almost physical effort; she had a job to do. And she was too well disciplined to let this strange experience interfere.

To give herself more distance from the past few minutes, she stood, almost knocking over her chair. She righted it, gripping the back until she felt steady enough to walk.

She had learned to push her own feelings to the background and focus on other people with a single-minded concentration. She did something like that now, imagining the whole audience out in the show room, waiting for her. They would be disappointed if she didn't go out there and give them the performance that they'd paid to see.

But she was still fighting for every scrap of self-control she could muster as she held on to the chair and breathed the stale air inside the club, grounding herself in the world around her.

"Think about what you have to do now," she ordered herself.

When she felt steady enough to let go of the wooden rungs, she turned and opened the door, then hurried down the hall toward the stage. Toward reality. And sanity.

ZACH struggled to pull himself back to reality. Someone was speaking to him. A man.

The man from the dream? The guy who had made it clear with a few angry words that they were bitter enemies?

He got ready to defend himself, then realized the nemesis from the dream had vanished. Or maybe he'd never been there.

No. The man speaking now was someone . . . out here on the street.

Zach was back in front of the Sugar Cane Club, staring at the poster of Anna.

"Come in, mon. Twenty dollar cover charge. You have a good time here," an islander wearing a brilliant white T-shirt said. He was standing beside the door, gesturing toward the interior.

"What?" Zach croaked.

"Come in, mon. We put on a great show here. Magic Anna. She amazing."

Magic Anna.

Zach swallowed, pressing the soles of his shoes into the sidewalk and trying to figure out what had just happened to him.

In the daydream, or whatever it was, he had been aroused—ready for sex with the woman in his arms. The woman on the poster. Apparently the effects were only in his mind, thank God.

And he could still walk away from whatever had happened in that out-of-body experience. Maybe he *should* walk away. Or more likely, run as fast as he could in the other direction.

Instead, he heard himself say, "Sure," as he dug into his pocket for his wallet. Twenty dollars. Cheap by standards in the States.

When he'd paid for the show, the man swept aside a curtain made of two-inch bamboo pieces strung between round fishing corks.

Still struggling to regain his sense of balance, Zach stepped into a small reception area lined with bamboo posts. He was fighting to stay detached. Yet he felt a breathless anticipation coursing through his veins as he walked into a show room that held perhaps thirty small varnished tables facing a brightly lit stage where a four-piece island-style band commanded one corner.

About three-fourths of the spaces were occupied, and Zach slipped into a bentwood chair at the back of the room, where he ordered a bottle of local beer from a waitress wearing a sarong that looked more appropriate for the South Pacific.

A large man in a flowered shirt and white linen slacks was on the stage, talking.

"I'm Etienne Bertrand and I welcome you to my Sugar Cane Club. We got a treat for you tonight. Magic Anna, all de way from Denver," he said in a softly accented voice. "A real talented lady. I could talk her up big time. But you see for yourselves soon."

Several long seconds passed. Zach felt his pulse pound in anticipation.

It speeded up when Anna stepped lightly from the wings. His fantasy had primed him to see her in the green dress. Instead, she wore a simple black sheath like the one on the poster. It set off her slender body and long legs.

He wasn't the only one who was reacting. And not just the men. He felt electricity crackle in the room—a mixture of tension and expectation. The poster outside had promised something special, and the audience was waiting to see if she could deliver.

"Thank you," she said in a low, musical voice, yet there was a look of uncertainty on her face that she quickly wiped away.

She must have walked onstage hundreds of times. Maybe thousands. She shouldn't be nervous about facing the audience. So what was wrong with her? Had she really been in that fantasy with him? Had some force pulled them into that other world together? Or had she been the one who had done it?

Both alternatives seemed impossible.

The woman had been intriguing-looking on the poster. More intriguing in his fantasy. In person she took his breath away—literally. As he struggled to fill his lungs, he felt as though his chest were tightened by iron bands, preventing him from drawing a full breath.

She stood calmly onstage, smiling into the lights. He suspected she couldn't really see anything beyond shadowy shapes. Yet she turned toward her right, focusing on him. And for a moment it felt like they were the only two people in the room. Just as they'd been the only two people on that windswept plain. Until the other guy had broken the spell.

Zach hadn't seen him. But he had heard the anger in his voice.

He tried to put the daydream out of his mind. But the feeling of connection with Anna tugged at him. In a moment of madness, he almost climbed out of his chair and started for the stage. Then he forced himself to simply sit there and watch her.

"Thank you for coming," she said, making it feel like she was speaking only to him. "I hope you had a wonderful time on Grand Fernandino today."

He closed his eyes, struggling for distance, thinking that his life had started going off the rails yesterday, when José had thought he'd come face-to-face with Pagor down in the *Blue Heron*.

CHAPTER
FIVE

WITH THE SPOTLIGHTS in her eyes, Anna could see only vague outlines of the people sitting in the audience. But she felt a presence at the back of the room. A man so focused on her that his gaze was almost like a physical touch.

She took a calming breath and stretched her arm toward the wings, making a theatrical gesture. "Lights, please."

At her command, the house lights came up about halfway, bathing the room in a warm glow that was not enough to reveal the dirt on the floor.

In the illumination, she knew where to look for the man who was watching her. She intended to flick her gaze right by him. Instead, she stopped abruptly, taking him in.

He was sitting at a table in the back, dressed in a dark T-shirt and jeans, one of his legs stretched out at the side of the table. He looked tall and tanned, with brown hair streaked by the sun. His eyes were large and dark—watching her with an intensity that made her throat tighten. Yet at the same time, she saw something vulnerable in his gaze, as though he was as wary of her as she was of him.

Unbidden, an image swam into her mind—the two of them standing together on that broad, windswept plain, the only two living beings in an uninhabited world. She wore a gauzy green dress. And he was naked to the waist, his broad chest covered by a mat of sun-bleached hair. When he pulled her body against his, the contact was electric.

Stop it, she ordered herself. With a mental shake, she banished the fantasy from her mind before it could suck her under and break the concentration she needed to get through her act.

A woman in the audience shifted in her seat, and Anna realized she had been standing mute for several seconds. Clearing her throat, she said to the room in general, "Thank you for joining me. I see some of you have been here before. Welcome back." She smiled, hoping that the facial expression looked genuine.

She had delivered this patter a thousand times. And she was good at it. Smooth. And lucky she could function on automatic pilot.

"If you're just joining the show, you're probably wondering what the hype on that poster outside is all about. Of course it was designed to lure you inside so you could enjoy the island drinks the Sugar Cane Club serves. But now that you're here, let's boogie."

Appreciative laughter rippled thorough the small show room, and she knew that the vacationers gathered in front of the stage were on her side. They'd give her the benefit of the doubt—until she screwed up.

"This is an audience participation event. So I'm going to ask you to do some of the heavy lifting. If you'd like to volunteer to be part of my act, I can tell you things about yourself. It works like this: My assistant will walk around with a tray. If you like, you can put some personal item on it. Something that you've owned for a while. Like a watch or a ring or a key chain. Don't worry, I'm not using my act as an excuse to take possession of your property. But if you'd like to leave something behind, make it appealing. Diamond rings are always good."

Once again laughter rippled, and she smiled. "I'll pick up some of the objects from the tray. And when I do, I'll be able to share some of your memories. It's as simple as that. So if you'd like to give it a try, pass me those rings and watches."

Etienne took the tray from her, then stepped down to the level of the audience and began to walk among the tables.

At first, nobody responded, but she was used to a bit of reluctance.

"Don't be shy," she encouraged, knowing that it would take only one man or woman to get the ball rolling.

A woman handed over a scarf patterned with green leaves. After that, a flood of earrings, watches, and key chains followed.

Anna watched closely. Instead of participating, the man with the sun-streaked hair kept his hand clenched around a bottle of local beer.

Etienne returned to Anna and set the tray down on a bar stool he had brought to the stage.

She stared down at the collection spread before her, feeling a ripple travel over her skin. Something bad was in that pile of stuff. Something she didn't want to face. But she couldn't be sure what it was.

The scarf appeared harmless enough. It was lying curled in a circle at the side of the tray. She glanced at the woman who had set it there, a redhead who looked to be in her early thirties. She was with a man, probably her husband, and she smiled when Anna picked up the scarf.

"We've never met—right?" Anna murmured.

"Right."

"And you haven't filled out any personal questionnaires since you came to the island."

"That's right," the woman confirmed.

Anna closed her eyes, focusing on what the silky fabric had to tell her, then grinned.

"You two are in Grand Fernandino on your honeymoon, aren't you?" she asked.

The woman blinked, glancing down at the impressive diamond ring on her left hand, then back at Anna. "Yes."

Enjoying herself now, Anna ran her thumb over a bright green leaf in the silk pattern. "You were married in Boston. Well, in the suburbs—at Don's country club." She gave the woman a warm look. "This is your second marriage, and your little girl, Grace, was your maid of honor."

The woman looked astonished. "How . . . how do you know all that?"

"I can pick up impressions from the objects you leave on the tray." She continued to finger the silk as she spoke. "Like . . . I know Don proposed to you on the golf course. At the eighteenth hole. When he picked up his ball, he slipped something into the cup—that beautiful engagement ring you're wearing. Very romantic, Don."

The audience was staring at her with respect, now that she'd proved her worth.

She returned the scarf. "Thank you, Melinda, for sharing such nice memories," she said.

Etienne began to clap, and the audience joined in. She flicked her gaze to the man in the corner and saw he was still holding on to his beer bottle and staring at her.

She picked up a man's watch—an expensive model, with real gold links in the band, she was sure. Immediately she got a picture of a small boy, huddling in the dark, in a shed. Outside, the wind howled, and the boy curled up in the corner, wrapped in several empty feed sacks to keep warm.

She wished she hadn't been attracted to the watch. She wanted to slam it back onto the tray. Instead, she squeezed her fingers around the metal, striving for closer contact.

"You're sorry you broke the pitcher, Teddy," she whispered.

In the audience, a large man with a high-domed forehead sat up straighter, then leaned toward her.

She hadn't known who put down the watch. As she turned toward him, the room fading around her. In a quiet voice, she spoke only to him. "You didn't mean to break the pitcher," she said again, her voice low and far away. "And you know your momma is going to be sad. She doesn't have the money to replace it. But she's worried about you now. You have to go back in the house. Because she doesn't know you're in the shed. And a storm is coming. You don't want her going out in the storm."

"You can't know anything about that! How do you know my mom used to call me Teddy?"

Ignoring the outburst, she continued. "It was a long time ago. The next week, you went out and got a job after school." She paused for a minute. "Sweeping up the store for old Mr. Winslow. He gave you an employee discount—and you bought your momma another pitcher."

"Yes."

Tears gathered in her eyes. "And now she lives in a nice apartment that you bought her. And she has the best of everything."

"I never knew why I went back in the house," he said in a hoarse voice. "Were you really there?"

"I . . . don't know," she answered honestly. She thought she was simply viewing the past. But she'd talked to him as she saw him hiding in that shed. Had he actually heard her? Sometimes when she was in the midst of a session, it seemed that way. But was that reality?

It was the kind of question she'd asked herself dozens of times—and never been able to answer. Maybe someday.

She returned the watch to its owner, knowing the audience was waiting for her to amaze them again. Quickly, she reached toward the tray, and her hand collided with a stainless steel ring that had a plastic sea horse at one end and a set of keys at the other. Instantly, her fingers began to burn, and she heard the sound of a woman screaming in terror.

"No," she breathed, wondering if she'd spoken aloud.

CHAPTER
SIX

ZACH WATCHED ANNA turn pale. When she swayed on her feet, he tensed, prepared to leap from his chair and charge up there to steady her. But before he could move, she straightened her shoulders and pulled her hand back from the tray, wiping it against the fabric of her skirt as though she were trying to clean it.

Then her hand darted out again and quickly picked up an earring.

She squeezed it in her fist. Then after long seconds she said, "Patty? This is your aunt's earring, isn't it?"

A woman in the second row of tables moved in her seat. "Yes."

The conversation went on, with Anna telling the woman details of her life. He looked around, seeing the audience hanging on her words. They were fascinated with her. So was he.

But he was interested in the other people there, too. The man who had introduced Anna was looking at her with a lot more than casual interest. Actually, for a moment he looked like he wanted to eat her alive. Then he straightened and turned away, as though he was aware that he'd better keep his emotions in check.

Zach noted that Anna had grown more cautious about which objects she picked up. She stayed on stage for almost an hour, then passed the tray back to the audience, returning the items still there.

She left the stage to thunderous applause. She'd turned the crowd from skeptics to believers. And Zach was among the converts.

He started to stand, then sat down again, wondering what he'd intended to do. Charge into her dressing room and grab her hand?

The image in his mind was very strong, but Zach forced himself to settle back in his chair and look relaxed while the band played a forty-minute set of calypso tunes mixed with disco. Some of the patrons danced to the loud music. Others left the club.

Zach ordered another beer and leaned back, listening to the music and watching the action. Some of the dancers looked like married couples. Others were single men and women tourists who appeared to have hooked up at the bar. And some were men dancing with island women who had materialized out of the shadows. Probably Bertrand charged them a fee for coming in here. Maybe he even took a cut of any business they drummed up.

ANNA closed the door behind her and leaned against it. She needed fresh air, not the stale atmosphere of the club. But she didn't want to go outside, so she paced back and forth in the tiny dressing room.

A knock on the door made her jump.

"You all right?" Bertrand called.

"Yes. Fine."

"You looked a little nervous."

"I've got an upset stomach," she answered. That was the truth, but not because of anything she'd eaten.

"You need anything?"

"I'll take an antacid. I'll be fine."

To her vast relief, the club owner went away. In the next second, she thought she could have used the distraction, because she was left with her fantasy—the place outside the world, where she'd met another man.

No. Two men. There had been two of them, she reminded herself. The one holding her in his arms and the one in the distance, who had called her there.

She might be making that part up, but she was pretty sure that he had broken her and the other guy apart and sent her hurtling back to the world. At least that's what it seemed like.

She wanted to know what it meant. At the same time, she didn't want to know. And she wasn't sure which need was stronger.

She sat down in the chair, thinking that she would put herself into a light trance to relax herself before the next show. But the fantasy had swept her away the last time she had done that.

With a shake of her head, she closed her eyes, struggling to calm the pounding of her heart as she waited to go out on stage again.

Or could she say she was sick, and just go back to her hotel?

Of course not!

But her stomach was churning. Because one of them was out there. The man who had been holding her, kissing her. She had seen him sitting in the corner, watching her.

She clenched her teeth. She was building a hell of a lot of assumptions on one daydream.

Maybe it came from this club. Some other woman had sat in this chair and touched the dressing table, and Anna was picking up memories from her, just the way she did in her act. Only this was bigger, more full-blown. Because . . .

She fumbled for a reason and decided that maybe the woman was a psychic. Yes, that was it. Bertrand had hired another psychic, and she'd left her energy here.

The explanation didn't make perfect sense, but it was enough to calm her. Enough to make sure she went out there and did her second set.

And what about the man in the corner? Well, he was an attractive guy. Obviously intrigued by her abilities. Which was why he was so focused on her.

WHEN the band finally stopped playing, Zach breathed out a small sigh. Looking around, he saw that half the audience for the second show had already sat through the first. So that meant he wasn't obsessed. Right? Other people were just as interested in Anna.

When Anna took the floor again, she kept her gaze away from him. But when she called for volunteers, he was tempted to put something on the tray the big guy carried through the audience. If she picked up something of his, she'd have to admit he was there.

Yet he held back. Although he wanted to make contact with her, he didn't want to do it through a key ring or a watch. He wanted it to be personal. And private.

Yeah. Good luck.

During this second performance, Zach paid more attention to the subtle cues Anna gave off. As she spoke to the owner of each object, she seemed totally involved with the person. Yet as soon as she put the item down, she withdrew behind an invisible barrier, firmly giving the message that the intimate contact had ended.

After the show, he told himself he might as well go back to his hotel. Instead, when he'd stepped out of the club he started down the block, wondering if he could find the stage door.

And do what? Ask questions? No. Not ask, exactly.

He wanted to know if she had pulled him onto that windswept plain with her. And he knew the way to find out was to touch her.

The craving for physical contact surprised him. Not just for sex. Something more. Something he couldn't name.

He stopped short. What the hell was wrong with him? He prided himself on calculating the risks before he went into any unknown situation. Now he was throwing caution out the window.

But that didn't stop him from rounding the corner and turning into a narrow alley that smelled of garbage.

He walked a few feet farther, his eyes probing the shadows, thinking it was an excellent location for an assault.

Was that why he was feeling the back of his neck tingle?

He'd learned to pay attention to his intuition. Treading softly, he listened for the sound of footsteps behind him. Two men were following him, judging from the echoes on the cobblestones.

Did this have something to do with yesterday? Were they out to get the guy who had made José confront Pagor down in the *Blue Heron*?

Or could Terrance Sanford have sent them? That would be an interesting twist. What if the man didn't want his brother found? And first he'd set up the Pagor scam to scare away the island diver. Now he was after Zach.

Or was it simpler than that? Had these guys been waiting around, hoping to surprise some unfortunate tourist in the alley?

The men behind him drew closer.

Still, it could be innocent, he knew—two guys coming home after a night on the town.

He kept walking, planing his next move. When he

reached the back of a house where a couple of empty trash cans partly blocked the alley, he picked up one of the cans, turned, and saw two men with island features, dressed in jeans and dark T-shirts.

Both of them held knives, and Zach figured they weren't planning on using the weapons to pick their teeth.

He raised the can above his head, then hurled it at the closer man. It hit the assailant square in the midsection, and he sank to his knees.

Both men cried out, the one who'd been hit howling in pain.

The other charged around his friend, knife at the ready. "Bad mistake, mon."

Zach had spent a lot of his life in port cities and had learned his street-fighting techniques the hard way.

He dodged to the side, then aimed a kick at the guy's gut, sending the man sprawling on the ground, out of the action for the time being.

In one of the houses down the alley, a light went on. But nobody came out, and Zach was pretty sure that the local residents weren't going to get involved in the fight. Would they call the cops? Probably not.

The man on the ground lay without moving. But there was still his companion to contend with, the one who'd taken the trash can in the gut. He climbed to his feet and dragged in several shallow breaths, then started forward on legs that weren't entirely steady. He was hurting, but the murderous look in his eyes told Zach that the injury had only made him more deadly.

"Come on, you bastard," Zach called.

The man grunted and looked Zach up and down. Then he charged, slashing with the knife as he came.

Zach dodged back, then lashed out with his foot again, connecting with the man's hip. He'd been aiming for the crotch, but the guy had better instincts than his friend; anticipating the move, he turned at the last minute.

When Zach took another step back, he found his shoulders pressed to the wall.

Both men were on their feet, facing him. They might have set out to rob him, but the stakes were higher now. He'd offended their honor, and he saw murder in their eyes.

Well, he wasn't going down if he could help it. Looking around for a weapon, he spotted a broom handle sticking out of a trash can beside him. He pulled it out and swished it through the air, pleased with the whistling sound it made. Too bad it wasn't an old-fashioned broadsword.

The two men eyed the stick, staying well back. They knew he was a competent fighter, but they still thought they could take him.

"Come and get it," he taunted. "Aren't the odds good enough for you?"

He hoped the insult would knock them off their stride. But before they could charge, a door to his right opened.

Company.

The man who stepped out was Etienne Bertrand.

Unfortunately, Anna was right behind him.

CHAPTER
SEVEN

ZACH SWORE, BUT Bertrand acted quickly, pushing Anna back into the hallway and closing the door before turning to survey the dangerous scene.

As he stepped forward, he reached down to his boot, and a knife appeared in his hand.

"You wanna fight me, you hot steppas?" he asked, his voice calm, his speech island slow as he addressed the two would-be muggers.

"We wasn't doin' nothin'."

"Liar. You wanna tess me?

"No, mon."

The two punks looked at each other, then turned and ran, leaving Zach and Bertrand in the alley.

Zach lowered his weapon, half wishing he'd gotten the chance to beat the crap out of them.

Still, he wasn't going to challenge the big man for putting himself at risk. Turning to the club owner, he said, "Thanks. You evened up the odds."

Bertrand gave him a long gaze. "What you doing back here, mon?"

Zach shrugged, looking around as though he had just realized where he was.

Bertrand tipped his head to one side, studying Zach's face with narrowed eyes. "You was in the club tonight. Both shows."

"So?"

"If you come back here to talk to Anna, she don't converse with guys from the audience."

"You make the rules for her?"

"She make her own rules."

Before Zach could reply, the door opened, and the woman in question looked out. In the light from over the doorway, her face was pale and drawn.

She went still as she caught sight of Zach, and he heard her breath hitch. "You were watching me," she said accusingly. "During the show."

She could have said a lot more than that, but he focused on her statement.

"Everybody was watching you," he answered. "Your act is very impressive."

This wasn't the way he had planned to meet her. But nothing in the past two days had gone the way he'd planned.

"If you were so interested, why didn't you put something on the tray?" she challenged.

"I didn't want to be part of the act," he said, the answer true as far as it went.

Neither one of them had mentioned the daydream. It was like the elephant in the room that they were both ignoring. Was it possible she didn't know she'd been there with him?

Had it all been his fantasy? Like a guy calling up a picture of a beautiful woman when he wanted to jack off?

His stomach muscles clenched. It hadn't been like that. Not at all. It hadn't come from his head—unless maybe he was going crazy.

Every instinct urged him to cross the space between them and touch her. His hand on her arm or her shoulder. Then, in some unaccountable way, he'd *know*!

He gave himself a mental shake. What was he thinking? That touching each other would be the key to some private communication? Right here in front of the club owner?

It helped his mental state that she was looking at him expectantly—like she really had been there with him in that fantasy experience. Or was he grasping at straws?

He stayed where he was and kept his lips pressed together, because Bertrand was standing between them.

Still, he couldn't stop himself from speaking to her. In his mind.

I'm Zachary Robinson. You and I have to talk. Zachary Robinson. I'm staying at the Sea Breeze Hotel.

She stared at him, blinking. And he wondered if he actually had sent her a private message.

If so, it didn't look like the contact had done him any good. She wasn't going to respond. Or maybe the silent communication only went one way. Could she receive his thoughts the way she picked up memories from the objects she touched? But not talk back to him?

She licked her lips, drawing his gaze to the slight movement. In the daydream he had kissed her. And he wanted her to acknowledge that.

He thought she was going to respond. Give him some clue. Something. But her next words dashed his hopes. "I don't have private conversations with patrons. That's an absolute rule."

Bertrand gave him a satisfied smirk.

Zach would have argued if he'd thought that it would do him any good.

I'll see you later, he silently vowed, then turned and walked away, his back straight and his arms swinging easily at his sides.

* * *

ANNA stood staring at the man's departing back, ordering her pulse to stop pounding. In the club, she'd felt his interest like heat coming off a blast furnace. Not just in the club—in the fantasy.

Then she and Bertrand had stepped into the alley—and there was the guy. In the middle of a fight with two island punks.

A name leaped into her mind. Zachary Robinson. He had told her he was Zachary Robinson. And along with the name came an image of him dressed in diving gear, standing on the deck of a handsome boat. The water scene vanished, and she saw them together the way they had been in the fantasy. She and Zachary Robinson were holding each other tightly. She felt his hard-muscled body, his erection pressed to her middle.

The sensation was so strong that she expected him to turn around, come running back down the alley, and pull her into his arms.

But he kept walking—around the corner and out of her sight. Because she had sent him away.

No. Yes.

She made a small sound as she fought to separate fantasy and reality. Truth from imagination.

"Everything's rosy," Bertrand said. "Nothin' bad is gonna happen."

She knew he was wrong. She could feel the danger like lightning crackling in the clouds. A few miles away, but rolling inexorably closer.

Bertrand spoke again, breaking into her thoughts. "You know that guy?"

"No," she said quickly. "I just saw him in the audience." She certainly wasn't going to admit anything else. Not when she hadn't worked her way through it herself.

"You want I should take care of him?"

"You mean hurt him?"

The club owner shrugged.

"No. Just take me home."

"Mos def," he answered easily. "Maybe you been workin' too hard. Maybe you need to relax a little. Take a vacation on the island when you finish this gig."

Her head snapped toward him. "A vacation . . . here?"

"Just a suggestion. Let's get you to your hotel. You relax tonight. Sleep late."

"Yes. Thanks," she answered, but her mind was racing again. He wanted her to stay *here*? Why?

They walked through the midnight streets, then through the empty marketplace, and she knew she was safe from robbers. Nobody was coming after Etienne Bertrand. At least, nobody in his right mind.

But robbers weren't her main concern. Not now.

"Have you hired a psychic before?" she asked.

"Yeah. Once. Why?"

"I was just wondering." Relief flooded through her. So maybe her theory was right.

Maybe.

Bertand watched her walk into her hotel, the Palm Court, and she was grateful that he didn't try to follow. She'd heard some of the girls who worked in the club talking about the way he took advantage of them.

But not her. It was almost as though he'd labeled her off limits.

That should be reassuring. But somehow it wasn't.

ETIENNE waited until he saw the light come on in Anna's room. He saw her walk to the window and pull down the shade, and he knew she was tucked in for the night.

Bon. It was his responsibility to keep her safe. So walking out of the club with her and into the middle of a street fight had set his teeth on edge. And he didn't much like finding one of his patrons heading for the stage door.

He'd instinctively reacted to the fight scene, letting the two islanders know they'd better crawl back under the rock where they'd come from. But if he'd been alone, he would have made sure that the tourist guy stayed away from Anna in the future.

He hurried back the way he'd come, the street lights giving the town a romantic look that he had always liked.

When he stepped into his office, which was furnished with comfortable chairs and a desk purchased from a small hotel going out of business, Raoul San Donato was waiting for him.

The two of them went way back. He'd been a ten-year-old living in his momma's hut when Raoul had come back home with tales of life in Palmiro. And when Etienne's aunt had decided to look for work in the city, he'd begged to go with her.

Once he'd gotten to the city, he'd never looked back.

Raoul, who was a few years older, had shown him the ropes. They'd been street vendors together. Then Etienne had worked as a waiter in one of the hotels, saving as much money as he could, until Raoul had clued him in that Eddie Morgan, the owner of the Sugar Cane Club, had been murdered right behind the stage by a guy who'd found out Eddie was boinking his wife.

That had put a hex on the place, as far as most of the locals were concerned. But Etienne hadn't cared about the hex. He'd gotten a sweet deal from the widow when he'd leased the space. Then he'd used all his savings to put a down payment on the club.

Now he owned one of the premier nightspots in the city. And other properties around town.

Raoul had asked him to hire Anna, and he'd done it for his old pal. Well, Raoul was more than a friend now.

His guest was already sipping a rum and Coke.

Etienne fixed one for himself.

Then, instead of sitting behind his desk, he took one of the guest chairs and stretched out his long legs, crossing them at the ankles.

Raoul gestured toward the video player and monitor on the sideboard. "I watched the tape of her act—from last night and the night before." His friend swirled liquid and ice cubes in the glass, then took a sip. "No bull. She amazing."

"Yeah. Exactly what I wanted. I owe you for getting her here."

Etienne shifted in his seat, and his friend immediately picked up on the movement.

"You got a problem?" Raoul asked sharply.

"Maybe nothin'," he said, relaxing into their childhood dialect. "I come out the back way to take her home, and I run into two hot steppas tryin' to put a knife in some guy."

"Bad for business," Raoul murmured.

"I tink the guy was lookin' for the stage door when he caught it."

Raoul sat forward. "The stage door? Why?"

"Maybe to see Anna."

"Oh yeah?" Raoul asked sharply.

"Happens sometimes, you know. Dey see what she can do, and dey want a private session."

Raoul got up and paced to the door, then turned. "What he look like?"

"A dude from the States. But not a tourist." Etienne tried to recall the man's features, silently cursing himself for not paying attention to the guy when he'd been in the club. But back then he'd just been another paying customer. "Tall, good muscles. Tanned, like he works outside. Sun-streaked hair. And he had dem boat shoes on."

"Okay. Den go down to the docks tomorrow. See if you can spot him."

"Sure," Etienne quickly agreed. He was hoping that would be the end of it, but Raoul had more to say.

"And I got plans for Anna tomorrow." In a quiet voice, he began to outline what he had in mind.

Etienne didn't like it. But he wasn't going to say so. He owed Raoul too much.

CHAPTER
EIGHT

RAOUL FINISHED HIS drink and left the club. He'd gone there to reassure himself that everything was okay after the nasty episode when he'd lost control of his own vision. Now he was more worried than ever.

And he knew that his own arrogance had brought on the trouble. He'd moved too fast with Anna. He should have picked a more normal way to meet her. Let her see how important he was on Grand Fernandino. How much she'd benefit from getting hooked up with him.

Etienne had brought Anna to the island for him. He'd thought that once she was here, everything would fall into place. Now he knew he needed stronger magic than a simple chicken blood ceremony asking for Ibena's blessing.

There was too much at stake to lose his bride to another man.

She had the magic. He had seen it for himself on the videotapes from the club. And once he joined his power with hers, his place would be secure.

When he'd come to the city from the backcountry, he'd learned that he had a knack for making money. Then he'd added a whole new dimension to his life when he'd begun studying with Old Joe.

He'd started as a lowly convert, trembling before the priest—and even the men and women of the congregation. Raoul could still remember the ceremony where Joe had shaved the new boy's head, dripped the blood of a young chicken on him, then stripped him naked and washed his body as part of his initiation.

He'd thought at first that just being a member of the group would secure his future.

But as he'd gotten to understand the way things worked in the congregation, he'd realized that the priest held the real power. People brought him tributes, gave him a special place in their lives, because he asked the Blessed Ones to favor them.

Raoul wanted that big up. And he'd started making plans for how to get it. He'd gotten a pile of good stuff. But a whole lot more was almost within his grasp. He could feel it. Taste it. And he wasn't going to let some viper snatch it away. Certainly not when he'd already gone to so much trouble.

He walked rapidly toward one of the houses he owned in old town, his anticipation growing.

As a kid, he'd thought that he was like everyone else. But it wasn't true. He had powers that other people only dreamed of. And when he'd learned about Vadiana, he'd realized that, since boyhood, he'd had a special connection with the saints.

With his power, he had served many of his people. Like Etienne. He had held a ceremony, asking the saints to help his friend prosper. And they had obliged him with the untimely death of Eddie Morgan.

There were other proofs of his favor with the saints. Like when he'd snagged a rich husband for Maria Delgado. When the man's wife had died in childbirth, he'd needed someone to take care of the child, and Maria had filled the position—then married the father.

Raoul knew he had rare abilities. And he had invented creative rituals to bring him closer to the Blessed Ones. Rituals that the other island priests, like Joe Hondino, would never have condoned. But he needed something more—a bride as powerful as himself.

At first he'd searched for the right woman close to home. It hadn't taken long to realize that no suitable mate for a man such as himself lived on Grand Fernandino. So he'd started using modern tools—like the Internet—to search for the right partner. He had focused on many psychics. And the one who felt right to him was the woman named Magic Anna.

Earlier he had sacrificed a chicken to Ibena to bring her to him in a place outside the world. Tonight he would use a different mojo to strengthen his position with her.

Ibena was the goddess of eroticism and pleasure. He must give the saint pleasure as well as animal sacrifices. And she would bless his plans for tomorrow.

He reached the little house and climbed the backstairs, unlocking the door with his key.

Inside, he looked around the kitchen. It was large by island standards and furnished with a modern stove and refrigerator. When he saw the dishes neatly stacked in the drying rack, he smiled. Nadine had started off leaving them in the sink. He'd told her that if she wanted to live in this house, she had to keep it clean.

She was capable of learning. And, if she continued to please him, she could stay in this house, in his life, even after he married Anna and took his bride to live in the compound on the other side of the island, where his followers could keep an eye on her.

He stopped at a locked cabinet in the hallway and inserted the key. Inside was a small bottle of lotion—a sexual aid he'd first gotten from a witch woman a few years ago.

Not that he had any trouble with his cock. This was his gift to Nadine.

When he had poured some into his hands and rubbed them together, he strode through the silent rooms, furnished with pieces he had taken from a house the owners had abandoned during the threat of a hurricane. After the couple left, Raoul prayed to the saints, sweetening his request with many animal offerings. And the gods changed the course of the hurricane, sparing the island.

In the bedroom, Nadine was sleeping, her golden hair brushed out and spread seductively across the pillow. The sheet was pulled down to her waist, giving him a view of her generous breasts through the silky fabric of her gown.

She had come to Grand Fernandino on a luxury yacht, crewing for a rich man who liked to watch nimble young women at work on his craft. He also liked to take two of them to bed with him at one time—and watch them make love to each other before he fucked them, a practice that Nadine hated.

She had jumped ship in Grand Fernandino and disappeared into old town.

The cops had found her sleeping in a warehouse, hiding from the man who wanted her back on his boat. The saints had sent Raoul there at the right time. He'd paid off the cops and offered her a job in his shop—and a place in his bed. Where she'd stayed for the past year.

He moved into the room, stopping at the side of the bed, admiring her sleep-smoothed features before reaching to run his dark hand over her pale shoulder with his lotion-slick hand.

She gave him a sleepy smile.

"Let's go into the altar room," he murmured.

"You want to worship Ibena with me?"

"Yes."

"I'm honored," she answered, but he knew it might have been a lie. She had come from the mainland, where his religion was an oddity. And she tolerated his practices because she liked the life he could give her.

He didn't care what she thought about his deities. He only needed her cooperation and her pleasure. Ibena would not honor him if he failed to bring Nadine to climax.

He knew men who believed that sex was only for their own enjoyment. For Raoul, pleasuring a woman was an important skill that any self-respecting man must possess.

When he connected with Anna, he would bring her to ecstasy. He would make her understand the advantages of joining with him. And he would show her what wonders they could work together.

But tonight he and Nadine would worship the goddess to ensure his success in his quest.

He reached out, stroking her collarbones, then slid lower, under the bodice of her gown, lifting one of her generous breasts in his palm, stroking her softness until he could see her nipple harden through the thin fabric.

Pleased with her response, he squeezed the tight bud, watching her heat up from his knowing touch—and from the lotion. He had it specially made for him now, in this form and as a scented soap. A little gave you a pleasant sexual buzz. A lot sent you into a sexual frenzy.

But he didn't need to make Nadine frantic. He had learned what she liked, learned the best ways to please her. As he fondled her now, he closed his eyes, imagining that he was already with Anna, touching her, arousing her. As he let the fantasy grow, his breath quickened.

"Raoul?"

His eyes snapped open. "Right here, sweetheart."

Taking her hand, he helped her off the bed, then pulled her gown over her head and tossed it onto the iron footrail. He leaned to suck one nipple into his mouth while he unbuttoned his own shirt and dropped it on the floor. Nadine could pick it up later.

When he was naked, he dragged his lover's body against

his, stroking his hands down the curve of her back and over her rounded bottom, loving the feel of her feminine skin as he rubbed his tattooed chest against her breasts, knowing that Ibena would like the contact.

He wanted Anna, but he kept his focus on Nadine, kissing her neck the way he knew she'd liked, then nibbling at her earlobes and making his tongue into a point so he could probe the sensitive canal above it.

She softened in his arms, leaning against him, and he stroked between her butt cheeks, and farther down, feeling her folds. She was juicy and ready for him, and he moved his hips, sliding his erection against her middle.

Then he broke away, turning to drape an arm around her waist as he led her down the hall to his private sanctuary.

The room was decorated much like the shrine behind his shop. The main colors were gold, coral, and red, with favorite objects of the goddess on display. Fans, peacock feathers. At one side was a fountain where a stream of water shot from a turtle's mouth into a shell-shaped basin. The animal's head looked a lot like a penis.

The altar opposite the door was draped with gold and coral cloth.

At the doorway, he stopped and kissed her deeply before lifting her into his arms and carrying her to the worship table.

He lay her onto the padded surface so that her head rested on a red silk pillow near the altar and her legs dangled off the other end. Standing between her legs, he could look up and worship Ibena or look down and see Nadine.

He stepped to the end of the table and opened her thighs, lifting her feet onto the wooden pedestals on either side, comfortably supporting her legs.

He loved to view a woman that way. It gave him a feeling of power over her. Standing between her thighs, he looked down at her hidden female parts spread out before him so trustingly.

"Look at my tattoo," he said, his voice thick.

She did as he asked. "The faces look like they're alive," she whispered.

"They are. When I worship here, they are."

Delicately, he caressed her knees and then slid down to her thighs, stroking his hands inward toward her pussy. He loved the deep coral color of her intimate flesh, the delicate dewy sheen that told him she was aroused.

He stroked his fingers to the sensitive line where her thighs met her body, then moved inward, playing with her labia, then dipping one finger inside her, slipping it in and out, before stroking up to her clit, watching what he was doing, smiling as he saw that she was hot and ready for anything he wanted to do next.

She moved restlessly on the table, lifting her hips toward him in supplication.

"Play with your breasts," he said in a husky voice. "Twist your nipples, pull on them." She did as he asked, moaning as he bent to stiffen his tongue and probe the sensitive bud of her clit, before stroking down between her lips, tasting her juices as he lapped his way back to her clit. As he focused there, he slipped two fingers inside her, finger fucking her as he pushed her to climax.

He felt her orgasm gathering, heard her cry out as her pleasure exploded from her clit to the rest of her body. He kept lapping at her, stroking her until she climbed over the peak and screamed in ecstasy. When she started down, he stood and thrust his cock inside her, pumping in and out as he pushed to reach his own climax, feeling the skin under his tattoo tingling.

His pleasure burst from him as he directed his gaze toward the altar, asking Ibena to bless him as he shot his juice into the vessel spread before him.

When he lowered his gaze, Nadine was smiling up at him.

"That was good."

"Wonderful," he answered, meaning it. "Your turn to do the work," he said, reaching for her hand.

She nodded, letting him help her up, then standing beside the table while he reversed the pedestals and the pillow.

Then he lay down, smiling at Nadine as she looked down at him.

She leaned over, stroking her breasts against his face, allowing him to capture first one nipple and then the other in his mouth.

When she stepped away, he was hard again. And this time he let her suck him off.

Afterward, he slid his lips to her cheek, then stroked back her damp hair so he could nibble at her ear. He had gotten what he wanted, and in their bed, he let her choose the way they pleasured each other one more time before finally falling asleep.

ANNA tossed in her bed for a long time. Finally she fell into a relaxing sleep, until a dream captured her.

She was standing onstage, about to start her act. Nothing strange about that, until Zachary Robinson walked up beside her. Zachary Robinson, the man who had told her his name in the alley.

He looked at her expectantly, then started pulling things out of his pockets and plopping them onto the tray, so fast she couldn't see each one until he was finished.

Her stomach muscles knotted as she stared down at the collection he'd given her. Her eyes were drawn to a gold coin that looked very old, an Indian arrowhead, a child's alphabet block, a metal button, an old spoon, a worn piece of tooled leather that she was sure had come from a saddle, a red toothbrush, a crumpled cigarette pack, and a set of car keys.

And she knew that they all belonged to him. For long

moments, she stared at the tray. She wanted to know about him, yet she had to steel herself to take the plunge.

Finally, she picked up the arrowhead and stroked her thumb over the chipped edge, then looked at him.

"You're from the West—the mountains."

She saw him swallow. "You can tell that from holding an arrowhead in your hand?"

"Yes." Still clutching the chipped stone, she murmured, "You grew up on a ranch."

"Uh-huh."

Feeling a sense of power gathering inside her, she reached for the red toothbrush, seeing a little boy leaning over a sink, brushing his teeth. This was like her act. Sort of. On stage she touched one thing from each patron. Now she had a whole tray of objects—from one man. And she could learn so much more.

"Your mother was your father's second wife. She was so happy to have a baby. But your older brother—"

"Didn't agree," he finished for her.

"That's putting it mildly." She scrambled for a name and came up with, "Craig. He hated you, right?"

He raised one shoulder, and she figured he didn't want to talk about his brother. So she picked up the piece of leather and squeezed it in her fist, getting another image. "As soon as you were old enough, you'd saddle a horse and go off into the mountains."

"Yeah."

On a roll, she kept speaking. "You had a cave that you fixed up with a blanket and a metal box for food—to keep the bears away. You called it your fort."

His expectant gaze stayed fixed on her, and she knew he was waiting for more, so she reached for the cigarette pack.

The image from it was strong. "You took the cigarettes to your fort and tried to smoke them. But they made you sick."

He grimaced, remembering. "As a dog."

"So you crumpled them up and threw them away."

"That was an expensive mistake for a kid who had to earn his allowance by doing chores."

She picked up a metal button faced with mother-of-pearl and held it between her thumb and finger, seeing him clinging to a mean-looking horse that was trying to buck him off. "You were in a rodeo."

"A few of them."

She had left the keys for last. But finally she picked them up and weighed them in her hand, instantly overwhelmed by a feeling of sadness.

"You went away to college. And you never came back."

He nodded.

"You hated to leave the mountains."

His face turned defiant. "I did okay for myself."

"Yes. But that's not the point."

"What is?"

They stared at each other across three feet of charged space.

"You're the mind reader," he challenged.

She lifted the tray. "I need more than this."

"What?"

She felt herself start to tremble. Deep inside, she knew the answer. But she didn't want to tell him. Or admit it to herself.

Shaking her head, she took a step back and then another, until her shoulders were against a wall. When he took a step toward her, she knew there was only one way to escape.

Clawing herself from sleep, she woke with her heart pounding, remembering the collection of things on the tray and the conversation. And the feeling of panic at the end.

That was real. But what about the rest of it? Had she tapped into Zachary Robinson's life story? It felt like it.

But she could have made it all up because she wanted to be close to him.

She lay in bed, holding on to a handful of the sheet as one more question circled round and round in her head.

Why did some of it—the early years of his life—seem strangely familiar?

CHAPTER
NINE

ZACH'S EYES BLINKED open, and he turned his head toward the window. It was very early, just after dawn. But a dream had awakened him.

First he'd been in the Sugar Cane Club watching Anna do her act. Then he'd been up on stage with her. He'd started reaching into his pockets and putting things on the tray. Things from his life. He hadn't even known what they were going to be. And as each one hit the tray, a memory zinged into his brain.

Then Anna had begun picking them up. As she did, he felt her right along with him, watching his life unfold.

So what was the dream trying to tell him? That Anna could pull his memories out of his head?

Unable to deal with the direction his thoughts were taking, he showered and pulled on his clothes, then checked his e-mail for an answer to the message he'd sent to Terrance Sanford, explaining that he had found the wreck, but he couldn't get back to it immediately.

There was no reply. Maybe Sanford was going to cut him loose and hire someone else. Damn.

He wanted to find out what exactly had happened on

that yacht. It didn't look like he'd get a chance until his crew arrived.

But that wasn't the main frustration eating at him. He needed to contact Anna.

Needed? The urgency of the desire was startling. And alarming. Since his childhood, he hadn't relied on anyone besides himself.

So what was different about Anna? The question sent him back to the theory that she had powers beyond the ones she had demonstrated the night before in her act. She was a witch—and she had gotten her hooks into him. She had made him think he'd known her for years, that they hadn't just met last night.

Of course, there was a serious problem with that scenario. In the alley, the look on her face had said she was as confused as he.

Did that mean some outside force was working on both of them?

He laughed. Sure. Like maybe the Vadiana Blessed Ones? They were supposed to be powerful here, weren't they? Maybe they wanted him and Anna together for some reason.

He snorted. What was he thinking now—that in the Caribbean the old religions held sway? And the gods were playing with him and Anna?

Angry with himself for letting his mind drift toward the supernatural, and too restless to stay around his hotel room, he walked to a nearby coffee shop for a latte and a cheese croissant. It was hard to sit still and sip the coffee; he wanted to start prowling through old town, looking for Anna's hotel.

He should have followed her last night. And he would have if Bertrand hadn't been there.

Jesus! What did that make him? A stalker?

No!

He just needed to think. And the best place for that was

the water. Not on the *Odysseus*, which would be hard to handle on his own. Something smaller.

After taking a final sip of coffee, he strode down to the docks, rented a motor launch, and cast off.

As he steered the small boat into the wind, he felt the rush of pleasure he always got when he reached the open water. At the same time, his thoughts returned to the dream. To the details of his life that had come flooding back as Anna had picked up each possession.

He'd acquired a lot of nautical know-how in college. And after graduation he'd gotten a chance to sign on to a treasure hunting expedition off Hispaniola. That was when he discovered his knack for diving in the right place.

He was the one who had led the more experienced men to the wreck of the *Santa Inez*. They came up with a chest of Spanish doubloons and a boatload of museum-quality artifacts.

Zach had gotten to be friends with James Foster, the man who financed the expedition. They struck up a business deal where Foster set Zach up with a boat of his own in exchange for 25 percent of the profits. Zach worked under that arrangement for four years, until he had enough money to buy his own rig. By that time, he'd also acquired a reputation that led to a string of customers lined up to hire him for jobs.

He'd dived for ancient treasure and modern wrecks. And in between, he sometimes took tourists out on diving expeditions.

The salvage jobs had led him to Grand Fernandino. Maybe he and Anna had both arrived here about the same time. He didn't even know her last name or where she was staying. And maybe that was good.

Last night he'd been under the spell of Magic Anna. Now that he was thinking more clearly, maybe he should go back to his hotel, get his gear, and leave the island. Before he got into serious trouble.

Or maybe he should stop focusing on Anna and start trying to figure out who had put that image of Pagor on the *Blue Heron*.

NADINE Linzer opened her eyes. Slowly she turned her head. When she saw that Raoul was gone, she breathed out a little sigh. She had the house to herself for the rest of the day. Maybe the rest of the night. Or he might not be back for a few days. Sometimes he'd drop in unannounced. Other times, he'd send a message. Like yesterday evening. So she'd washed her hair and made herself pretty for him.

She stretched, her muscles sore from the kinky sex of the night before.

After the man had rescued her from what amounted to slavery, she'd been grateful. Then as she'd gotten to know him better, she'd wondered if she'd jumped from the frying pan into the fire.

Raoul had set her up in this nice little house, and she'd thought all she had to do to earn her keep was make love with him. It was a couple of months before she found out what was in the locked room down the hall.

Her benefactor had strange tastes, starting with his tattoo. And progressing to fucking and sucking on a table in what looked like a religious shrine. She'd come to realize that he was serious about what they were doing in there. The sex was part of worshipping his goddess, Ibena.

At first that had creeped her out, but she'd learned how to deal with it. And they usually ended up in bed, where they could finish off with his doing something spectacular to her.

She got up, pulled on a silk dressing gown, and padded down the hall to the kitchen. He'd made coffee and left a pot on the warming pad in the coffee machine. She sniffed the dark liquid. French roast. The good stuff.

She poured herself a cup and added cream and sugar,

then thumbed through the stack of cash he'd left on the counter. A hundred dollars. Not as payment for the sex, but for the household expenses.

As she showered, she planned her day. She'd go to the market and buy some supplies. Fruit. Cheese. A chicken. Alive and flapping a minute before they wrung its neck.

Since she'd learned to shop the way the island women did, she'd put away at least thirty-five or forty dollars out of every hundred. Her little stash was adding up. And she had more money, too. Money Raoul thought he'd hidden under a floorboard behind the sofa.

She knew where it was, and she had no compunctions about using it. Raoul was using her. That was the ugly secret of their relationship.

He thought he was in control. But if she needed to get away from him, she had the money to do it. Not just travel expenses; enough to live on while she found a paying job.

Transportation was a problem, though. She'd have to find someone willing to take her away. Someone who wasn't afraid of Ibena and Pagor and the other saints Raoul worshipped.

Meanwhile, she had a pretty good deal with Raoul. Except that the bastard wasn't satisfied with a mistress; he wanted to add a wife to the mix, and she knew the kind of woman he wanted. Someone with psychic powers to juice up his mojo.

He strutted around, acting like he could do the Vulcan mind-meld or something. Although she wasn't so sure his beetle-browed look had any effect on reality, she had learned to live with the religious mumbo jumbo.

Now there was that other woman to consider. One night Nadine had walked down to the art gallery and heard Raoul and his friend Etienne discussing business. He'd asked the club owner to hire the woman, and now she was here, working a "mind reading" act down at the Sugar Cane Club.

Maybe it was Nadine's duty to save the woman from Raoul. Or maybe she'd better keep the hell out of it—if she didn't want to end up like one of those chickens with its neck wrung.

When she'd dressed modestly in white capris and a loose-fitting white shirt, she left the house and headed for the marketplace.

She had reached the corner when she saw a dark-skinned, bald-headed man with a neatly trimmed beard walking toward her. Going stock-still, she wondered what she was going to do or say.

She knew who he was.

Joseph Hondino, the most influential Vadiana priest on the island. Raoul had pointed him out and talked about Hondino from time to time. He'd sneered at the old man because he had a completely different view of the religion.

But there were aspects of the worship practices that gave Nadine the creeps. No matter who was sacrificing chickens and goats for whatever reasons, she didn't go for that kind of stuff. In her mind, it was worse to kill them than to have sex on the altar—the way Raoul liked to worship with her.

Probably Hondino had the opposite opinion. Still, from what she gathered, the older man had a sense of morality that Raoul completely lacked. And in Raoul's mind, that made the priest a chump. He should be out for what he could get. He should be consolidating his power and getting ready to rule the island.

But maybe he couldn't. Maybe Pagor and Ibena and the other saints were on Raoul's side.

All that flashed through her mind before the man said, "How are you?"

"I'm fine."

"Maybe I can help you."

"How?"

"Are you frightened?"

"No!"

He gave her a considering look, and she felt like he could see into her head.

"I think you're lying to me—or to yourself."

As the priest studied her, she struggled not to squirm.

"I see you're not ready to ask for my help. But you will be. I think you'll know when the time is right. You know where to find me?"

"I . . ."

"My house is the yellow one with the purple bougain-villea in the front yard. And the old stone altar—made from ships' ballast. You know the one?"

She answered with a tight nod.

"Don't be afraid to come to me when you feel the world closing in on you."

She swallowed and looked furtively around to make sure nobody was watching them. If Raoul found out she'd said anything at all to this guy, he'd be furious. Without another word, she walked quickly toward the market, praying that nobody was going to report this meeting on the street to Raoul.

ANNA had vowed to sleep late, but once she woke from the dream about Zachary Robinson, it was impossible to go back to sleep. She lay in bed, thinking about him, adding details about his life—and then pondering the strange fantasy she'd experienced just before she'd gone on stage last night. When the two of them had been together.

Yes, the two of them. Because when she dared to be honest with herself, she knew that he had been the man holding her in his arms. But he hadn't been the only one there. Another man had been hovering in the background, watching them, his anger simmering. And he had yanked them back to reality.

She grabbed two wads of sheets to keep her hands from shaking.

What did it mean?

The fantasy—and the dream?

She'd felt like she'd been dragged into the first encounter against her will. But in the dream, she'd been in charge.

Or was she kidding herself?

She wanted to scream in frustration. Instead, she got up and pulled on cotton shorts and a T-shirt so she could go down and get a cup of coffee and some fruit, which was about all she could handle that morning, even though the hotel provided wonderful baked goods, eggs, and bacon.

The breakfast was served in a charming courtyard where orange and magenta bougainvillea climbed the walls and pink and white geraniums bloomed in island-manufactured clay pots.

While she was still sitting at the Spanish tile and wrought iron breakfast table, an island boy arrived with a note. Etienne Bertrand needed to see her at the club.

She'd rather take care of whatever it was over the phone, but there was no phone in her room. She'd have to talk to him in the hotel parlor, and he probably wanted to have a private conversation.

So she told the boy who'd brought the message that she'd go to the club in an hour, then gave him a tip for delivering the message, although she was pretty sure Bertrand had already paid him. But she'd seen the poverty on the island. And if she could feed stray cats, she could give kids money, too.

She took her time showering and washing her hair. Last night Bertrand had told her to sleep late. This morning he was sending for her. So had something changed?

She put on loose-fitting white cotton pants and an aqua shirt with a sea plant pattern, along with comfortable sandals.

Maybe on the way back she could stop at a couple of the market stalls and buy some more of the comfortable cotton clothing that was a specialty of the island.

As she took the route along the waterfront, a dozen children and teenagers materialized in front of her, blocking her way.

When she tried to skirt around them, they held out their hands, pulling at her clothing, and one of them tried to grab her shoulder bag.

"Lady. Lady," some of them shouted.

"Please. Don't crowd me," she begged. But the young people just pressed in closer.

She had never seen anything like this on the island. It felt like someone was directing an attack on her.

WILD Bill Cody tugged at his straw hat, pulling it lower over his eyes. He was dressed like an island kid, with a torn T-shirt and faded shorts.

But even without the disguise, he didn't look like a killer. He came across more like a teenager. In this case, a kid hanging around the docks. Even so, he'd already had several years of heavy-duty surveillance and dirty tricks under his belt before hiring on to work for Jim Stone.

His appearance was an advantage—the Ted Bundy, nice-guy look. Which made it easy to get close to his mark.

A couple of times he'd stood a few feet away from Anna Ridgeway—in a crowd of children—and she hadn't known who he was.

He had been on duty when she went to bed. And he knew she wasn't going to leave the island. So he'd broken off his surveillance during the night, then checked his e-mail in the morning.

He had new orders. He was supposed to get rid of her. And he was thinking about the best way to do it.

He hardly ever killed in broad daylight. But the night was going to be a problem here—with the big bruiser of a club owner walking her home after every gig.

Bill was always flexible. Minimizing his height, he darted forward, moving rapidly. He could kill her now. Right here across from the dock. And it would look like one of the kids had done it.

He had almost reached his goal, when a man pushed through the crowd, heading for Anna.

The assassin hesitated, then took a step back. The equation had shifted, and he didn't like the balance now.

AS she tried to fight her way clear, Anna's heart threatened to block her windpipe. Then, from the edge of the throng, a man materialized. A man with a very pleasing combination of African and Caucasian features.

"Aright," he shouted. "Leave the sista be." As he spoke, he pulled some coins from his pocket and threw them onto the cracked sidewalk. Immediately the kids charged after the money, pushing and shoving as they scrambled to pick up the booty.

The man took her arm protectively, moving her into the shade of an awning at the front of a candy shop.

"Thank you," she said, taking in more details. He was wearing a white linen shirt and neatly pressed tan slacks.

He gave her a broad smile, revealing even white teeth. "I could see you were in trouble." He had spoken to the kids in the patois of the island. He spoke to her with a cultured American accent.

"I haven't had any problems like this before," she murmured.

"Sometimes the kids get aggressive. It's a sad fact of life here."

"Yes."

"I'm Raoul San Donato," he said. "I own an art gallery down the street. I was just going to open up when I saw you."

She nodded. Was he waiting for her to tell him her name? She wasn't sure she should.

"I have an appointment . . ." she tried.

"Let me escort you. So you don't run into any other trouble."

She would have liked to refuse, but she didn't want to be impolite. He had rescued her, and maybe it was safer to walk with him.

"You're Anna Ridgeway," he said, shocking her.

"How . . . how do you know?"

"I told you, my gallery is only a block away. I pass the Sugar Cane Club on my way to work. I saw you on the poster."

She stopped short, a shiver traveling up her spine. "But the poster doesn't have my last name on it."

He shrugged. "I'm a friend of Etienne. We sometimes talk about the acts he's planning to hire. I told him you would be a good choice."

"I was on my way to meet him," she said, feeling awkward. Etienne had discussed her with this man? Before he'd even hired her?

"I know a lot about Palmiro. What works here and what doesn't," he said, as though he had read her mind and answered the unspoken question.

She picked up her pace, hurrying toward the club. There were more people on the streets now, taking advantage of the cooler morning air.

San Donato was speaking again, and she struggled to focus on his words, and not his wolfish expression.

"I'm sure if I stopped in the club with you, Etienne would let you leave soon. I could show you the scenery up in the hills. The view is spectacular from up there."

"No, thank you," she answered quickly. She didn't want to go anywhere with him—certainly not where the two of them would be alone.

As she declined his invitation, she saw a shadow pass across his face. Maybe he wasn't used to people turning him down.

But when he spoke, his voice was mild. "Another time," he said, as though he knew that the two of them were going to meet again. She heard something in his tone. Something. But she couldn't bring it into focus.

"Thank you," she repeated.

They had reached the club. Quickly she stepped inside, then found Etienne in his office. He was supposed to be waiting for her, yet when she walked in the door, he seemed surprised to see her.

"You wanted to talk to me?" she said.

He put down the piece of paper he was holding. "Yes. Thanks for coming." Leaning back in his seat, he gave her a closer inspection. "You look a little pale."

"On the way over here, some kids crowded me on the street."

"Sometimes they get pushy."

She nodded.

"Everything okay?"

"Yes."

He was silent, and he looked like he was waiting for her to say more. When she didn't, he said, "Sit down."

She lowered herself to one of the comfortable chairs across from the desk.

"Thanks for coming. I'd like to talk to you about adding an extra show Saturday night."

She blinked. "Last night you told me I was working too hard."

"Yeah, well, I see an opportunity—for both of us. And I'm willing to pay you a nice bonus."

"How nice?" she shot back.

"A day's pay just for the one extra show."

She kept her voice cool. "A day and a half."

The request was outrageous, and she expected him to come back with a lower figure. But he waited a beat, then nodded. "Okay."

Surprised, she raised her eyes to his.

"You're worth it," he said. "We've been doing fantastic business since you arrived."

"Thank you." She started to stand. She had to . . .

There was nothing she had to do. She'd been anxious to get inside the club. Now the feeling of needing to get back outside was strong.

"Thank you. It will be good for the club. And good for you," Etienne was saying.

She didn't think it would do much for her personally, since she wasn't planning to stay on Grand Fernandino after her contract was up, but she was willing to give Etienne the extra time—to keep their relationship smooth.

When he went back to the papers on his desk, she exited the club through the front door.

She'd had a frightening experience on her way there, and maybe she should go directly back to her hotel.

And what? Hide out?

It was tempting, but she wasn't going to run her life that way. And what could happen in broad daylight?

Another gang of street kids assaulting her. Probably not now, with so many tourists prowling the streets.

When a picture of the docks flashed into her mind, she let the image guide her footsteps, even if she did look over her shoulder a couple of times to make sure nobody was right behind her.

Ahead of her, the sea was an unbelievable shade of blue. When she came to the edge of the sidewalk, she stepped onto the worn boards of the dock and kept going, feeling the wind blowing through her hair.

In the harbor, a motor launch was speeding toward shore,

and as she watched it come closer, she felt anticipation tightening her throat.

The launch reached the dock, and a man threw a rope over one of the pilings. When she saw his face, her breath caught.

It was Zachary Robinson. If that was really his name.

As though he knew she was watching him, he looked up. And when he walked toward her along the wooden dock, she wasn't able to turn away.

A sound from under the shadow of a rowboat made her startle. Then she looked down and saw a gray cat staring hopefully up at her.

Fumbling in her purse, she found the bag of dry cat food and stooped down to spread some on the warm boards of the dock. The cat immediately began to eat, and she stayed where she was, wanting to stroke the matted gray fur but afraid that she'd scare him away and keep him from his meal. He needed to eat more than he needed to be petted. So she tucked the bag of cat food back into her purse.

When she stood again, the man was only a few yards from her, watching.

Tension coiled in her stomach as she waited for him to speak.

"What are you doing?"

"I . . . feed the cats."

"Why?"

She spread her hands. "They're hungry."

"Yeah."

"There are a lot of them on the island. And no SPCA."

"So you've taken over the job."

Her gaze flicked to his hand, then away. She wanted to touch him. No she didn't.

When she saw him swallow, she knew he was as nervous as she was.

That helped. Because she wasn't the only one fighting to act like this was a normal encounter.

Then he spoke again, and it took several seconds for the meaning to penetrate her fogged brain. "I told you my name last night."

She might have denied it. Instead, she answered with a tight nod.

"Tell me what I said."

CHAPTER
TEN

ANNA DRAGGED IN a breath and let it out before answering. "Your name is Zachary Robinson."

He shoved his hands into the pockets of his jeans. "I guess you got the message."

Before she could dredge up anything to say, he added, "So how did it happen that I got that through to you, without saying anything in front of your bodyguard?"

"He's not . . ."

"Sorry. I don't want to start off being antagonistic."

"What do you want?"

"The same thing you do," he shot back, lifting his arm and letting his hand fall back to his side.

Was that true? She wasn't sure. He wanted to touch her. She felt it all the way from her skin to the marrow of her bones.

She looked at that hand and at the tension in his body, and it was her turn to swallow.

When she didn't speak, he said, "You came here. Just as I docked."

"Coincidence," she answered, then looked around. They were standing out in the open, where anyone could hear.

And the conversation felt much too strange . . . and too personal for public consumption.

"Let's go inside."

Had he picked up that idea from her mind? The question should have felt weird. But with him it was entirely natural. Hadn't most of their communication so far been unspoken?

"Where?"

"My boat."

She looked at the open motor launch. "That's no more private than the dock."

"I don't mean the launch. My boat is down there." He pointed to a much larger craft. She'd seen it in her dream, she suddenly realized.

"And I'll be trapped there with you," she heard herself say, then wished she hadn't voiced the thought.

"I'm not planning to hold you captive. You can leave anytime you want."

Was that the truth? And did she really have a choice?

He was speaking again, and she tried to focus on his words above the roaring in her mind.

"You touch objects and capture a memory from the person. What do you think will happen when you touch me?"

That made her think again about the dream of the night before. But she wasn't going to share that with him. Instead she said, "I don't get . . . memories from the people themselves."

"You will from me."

The way he said it raised goose bumps on her arms. She would have taken a step back, but some invisible force kept her standing there.

"You and I . . . are going to mean something to each other," he said softly. "Maybe we already do."

"You have an act where you read the future?"

"No."

"Then what?"

"I just know there's something between us. Starting with that . . . fantasy yesterday."

She heard the uncertainty and the tension in his voice. Felt the intensity rolling off of him. "The fantasy," she whispered, acknowledging it out loud. She wanted him to elaborate, but he only repeated his invitation.

"Come to my boat."

She should run in the other direction. Like she had from the gallery owner. Two strange encounters in one morning were too much. But this felt different.

Still, she sensed a kind of danger she didn't understand, danger that prompted her to say, "Promise not to touch me—unless I tell you it's all right."

He slid his hands against his thighs, drawing her gaze to the motion, and pulling the fabric of his jeans tighter across his crotch. When she found herself staring at his fly, she quickly looked away.

"All right," he finally said. "I won't reach for you."

"Are you a man of your word?"

"Yes."

Could she trust him? Or perhaps the better question was, could she trust herself?

When he turned and started walking down the board-walk, she followed. He reached a pier that branched off into the water and continued down the narrower walkway until he came to a sturdy motorized craft called the *Odysseus*.

"It's beautiful."

He laughed. "Some people would call it clunky. It was a work boat—designed to take men back and forth to oil rigs."

"But you use it for diving."

His eyes met hers. "How did you know?"

She shrugged. "Maybe you told me."

"Maybe."

He pulled on the mooring rope, securing the craft against the pier. She grabbed the boat's rail, then caught her breath.

She was used to touching something small and picking up a memory—like in the dream. Now she was standing on Zach's boat, holding the railing. And a strong image came to her. Zach and another man fighting an underwater battle. The other man trying to drown Zach by pulling at his air hose.

When she swayed on her feet, he reached to catch her.

"No!"

He pulled his hand back and they stood staring at each other, the moment so intense that she could have squished the air around them into a ball and tossed it out over the harbor.

"He tried to kill you," she whispered.

"Who?"

She steadied herself against the railing. "The man who grabbed your air hose. When you were down there in the water."

He tipped his head to one side, studying her. "You're picking that up . . . by touching the boat?"

"Yes," she answered, hearing the strained sound of her own voice.

"The man in the water—his name is José. We were diving two days ago and found a wreck I'd been hired to locate. Only José got spooked by something inside the boat. And tried to come up too fast. He would have gotten the bends. Decompression sickness. I grabbed him and forced him to come up slowly."

"Pagor," she murmured. "The god of war."

He kept his gaze on her. "Yeah. He said he saw Pagor down there. I didn't get close enough to the ship to see anything. I got him back here, to the hospital. And he's repaid me by getting everyone in town spooked. Nobody will crew the *Odysseus*." He laughed. "Maybe you'll take a chance on me. Do you scuba dive?"

"Sorry. No."

"Well, that's not why you're here."

* * *

WILD Bill stood in the shadow of a building across from the dock, watching Anna talking to some guy.

He'd waited for her outside the Sugar Cane Club, and he'd followed her down the street and across to the docks. Not that he could do anything in broad daylight without the cover of the little beggars, but it would be a mistake not to keep her in sight. And now his vigilance was rewarded.

She was getting on a boat in the harbor. The boat nobody wanted to crew. Bill had heard about that. So was she a sailor? Could she help take the *Odysseus* out?

He had to hope they were staying in the harbor. Or if they went out, that they'd come back.

Wait—she had to come back. All her stuff was here. She hadn't moved it from the hotel.

Even as he reassured himself, a wave of panic gripped him. If he lost her, he was in trouble.

Could he get closer? Maybe when they went inside he could creep to the side of the craft and hear what they were saying.

"WHY am I here?" Anna shot back, struggling to keep her voice steady.

"Maybe we'll find out, if you come inside."

He crossed the deck and opened a door at the back of the ship.

She followed him into a comfortable lounge, with built-in sofas and tables.

"Luxurious for a diving boat," she said.

"I spend a lot of time on board. I want to be comfortable when I'm out at sea."

"Yes."

She hesitated a moment, then gingerly lowered herself to one of the built-in sofas.

* * *

ZACH sat next to Anna, and she moved a few inches farther away, increasing the distance between them. He wanted
to reach for her, but he'd promised to look and not touch.
The only way he could do it was to keep his palms flat on
the sofa cushions. He felt like his brain was on fire. And his
body, too. If he had to sit here like this, torturing himself,
he wanted to close his eyes and just breathe in her wonderful scent. But he knew that would look damn strange, so he
kept his eyes open—and focused on the bulkhead behind
her.

He should ask her more questions, but speech was beyond him at the moment.

Unable to help himself, he slid his hand along the cushion, willing her to press her fingers to his.

She licked her lips the way she had last night, the flick
of her tongue another small torture. He didn't understand
what was so important about touching her. Just touching.
But he knew it was.

When he started speaking, his voice was low and
strained. "After spending the day trying to scrape together
a crew, I was really frustrated. I wanted a drink. But when
I saw your picture on the poster . . ." His voice trailed off,
and he started again. "I saw you . . . and I knew that I had
to go in. Only I denied it. So I went down the street to one
of the bars. Then I came back. But before I could walk into
the Sugar Cane Club, something happened."

She was hanging on his words, which made the next
part easier to say.

"The only way I can describe it is to tell you that I
wasn't standing on the sidewalk anymore. I wasn't in
Palmiro. I was somewhere else. Somewhere that wasn't
real. A fantasy scene. And you were there. We kissed, and
it was more intense than reality. Do you understand what I
mean?"

"Yes," she whispered.

"But then you went out in front of the audience—like nothing had happened."

She swallowed. "I had to block it out, so I could do my job."

He breathed out a sigh. "Thank God. Then I'm not the only one who's crazy."

"You think that's what it was—crazy?"

"I don't have any other frame of reference."

She shrugged, and he was sure she could have said more.

All his focus had been on getting her into the boat, on making sure she didn't run away the way she had last night. But now that she was here, another question burned in his throat—a question he didn't want to ask. But he knew it was important. So he pressed her.

"In that other reality, did you think we were alone?"

He saw a shiver go through her. "No," she whispered.

"Another man was there. At least, he was watching us. And he didn't like me taking over his . . . property."

She frowned. "Don't say that."

"I'm sorry." He had said it, and it gave him no pleasure. "We have to be . . . truthful."

She answered with a small nod.

"Who was it?" he demanded.

"I don't know! I didn't want to think about it." She dragged in a breath and let it out. "The man who's been following me?"

"Following you? Who?"

"I don't know!" she said again. "That's why I came to the island. To get away from him. But I think he followed me here." She gave him a pleading look. "There was nobody I could talk about it with—until now."

"We'll deal with it."

"Okay," she answered.

When she looked relieved, he felt a guilty. *Could* they

deal with it? He didn't know. But he desperately wanted to make her safe.

"Has anything like that happened to you before? I mean like the fantasy."

She shook her head. "No!"

"Did you see the other guy?"

"No." She looked away, then brought her gaze back to his. "Is this getting us anywhere?"

When she moved to stand, panic surged inside him.

"Don't go."

"Why not?"

"We're getting off on the wrong track. We should be focusing on . . . us."

She nodded, her expression turning from fear to hope. "Okay, let's try this. The ocean's . . . big. Out in the water— when you're looking for shipwrecks—do you . . . *know* where to look?"

"Sometimes."

"And you can't explain why?"

"Yeah."

"Maybe you have . . . psychic talents. Maybe that's what drew us to each other. Somehow we sparked a reaction off each other."

"Why?"

"Maybe we can figure it out."

He swallowed hard, unable to speak. He felt like he was standing on a high-diving platform, and he was going to fly off into space if something didn't anchor him to the ground.

"Someone dragged us into the fantasy. But the dream . . . came from us," she whispered.

The way she said it sent relief flooding through him. "The dream—when you were picking up my things from the tray? Reading incidents from my life?"

"Yes," she breathed. "You had that dream last night?"

"Yeah. Tell me something you learned," he asked in a barely audible voice.

She swallowed. "Did you buy a pack of cigarettes when you were twelve and try to smoke one?"

"Jesus." She had said it in the dream. Now it was part of their reality. "You know all that about my life?"

He felt her deliberately reaching into his mind for another memory—one that he didn't recall from the night before. And she was far more practiced at the skill than he.

His face heated when he felt her pull up and examine the time that he'd thrown a sparkler at a Fourth of July party and accidentally hit Steve Gilbert in the chest and burned him.

"You didn't do it on purpose," she murmured.

"I hurt him."

"And he paid you back by leaving you stranded at the movies the next time you went to town together."

"Yeah."

When he looked down at her hand—so close to his— he saw she was watching him with an intensity that made the breath go solid in his lungs.

Then, between one heartbeat and the next, her hand darted out and she laid her palm over the top of his hand.

CHAPTER
ELEVEN

ZACH FELT A jolt, like he'd grabbed a live wire. It sent heat through his hand, up his arm and into his chest, making it suddenly hard to drag air into his lungs.

Anna gasped, and he knew she was feeling something similar. But not because of the sound she'd made.

He *knew*. *Knew* that the contact had affected her in the same way it had affected him.

In her act, she picked up objects and pulled memories from the mind of the owner. He was doing something like that right now.

His mind connected to hers on a level that he had never dared imagine.

"Anna Ridgeway. You're Anna Ridgeway."

"Yes."

"You got in trouble in school," he whispered.

School. That spanned twelve years from kindergarten through high school. But they were both focused on the same incident.

The time in seventh grade when she'd been stupid enough to tell the teacher that Clarence Myers had cheated on his history test.

As far as Mr. Ellis was concerned, there was no way for her to know about the cheating incident, since Clarence sat on the other side of the room. So she'd been under suspicion, too.

Mr. Ellis had sent them both to detention. Which hadn't improved relations with Clarence.

"After that, you kept your mouth shut," Zach said. It was difficult to talk because of the arousal buzzing below the surface of the conversation. Every one of his senses was alive and tuned to Anna.

Without even thinking about what he was doing, he pulled her into his arms, crushing her breasts against his chest, entranced by the intimate contact.

At the same time, he pulled another memory from her mind and drew in a quick breath.

"Your parents . . . left you with a bunch of debts."

"Yes," she answered.

"But you figured out how to pay them off, then support yourself."

She nodded.

He stroked his hands up and down her back.

The dream last night had been startling. This was more immediate. The flow of information back and forth made him feel like his brain was on fire, and at the same time it fueled a sensation of power that astonished him.

In the dream, she had dipped into his past. Now he was picking up facts from her.

But coherent exchange was overwhelmed by lust. Or maybe need was a more polite word.

He might have laughed at his attempt at political correctness, when now that he had Anna in his arms, he knew he would die if he didn't have her.

Or maybe he would die if he did.

She raised her head, staring at him, the mixture of intense heat and fear on her face making his throat tighten.

"We can't," she whispered.

"We have to," he answered.

"I don't . . ."

"Make love with a guy you just met?"

"Yes."

"But you know me better than anyone else in the world knows me. And now I can make it go the other way."

He dug for her memories, like a prospector digging for precious metals. The time she'd stepped into a nest of ground hornets and gotten terribly stung. The birthday cake she'd baked for her mom when she was only ten. And then her disastrous first sexual encounter with Sammy Lowen.

"Oh, Lord, don't bring that up now."

"It will be a lot different with us. Because each of us knows exactly what the other wants."

He wasn't sure why he knew that was true. But he knew he had to prove it. Tenderly, he cupped her breast, finding her nipple through the thin fabric of her blouse, loving the feel of the hard bud against his fingertips.

His breath caught. He sensed her reaction, but it was more than that. He knew how it felt for her, the heated sensation shooting downward through her body, striking at her core, creating an explosion of sexual desire.

That's how it is for a woman.

The thought darted into his mind. And he knew she had picked it up when she answered, *Yes.*

He didn't understand what was happening. All he knew was that the physical contact, the arousal, opened the gate between his mind and hers in a way he had never imagined. A way that should be impossible. Yet here they were—both so open and vulnerable that his heart squeezed.

Because he wanted her to trust him, he bared himself to her. And when she found the memory of the time he first rode a bucking bronco—and landed on his ass—she smiled inside his mind.

"Come here." He wrapped his arms around her and

leaned back on the sofa, bringing her down on top of him, loving the way the length of her body fit against his— starting with the wonderful pressure of her breasts against his chest and moving downward to the way her hips cradled his erection.

She moved against his cock, and he gasped, so hard now that he felt like he might explode.

That's how it is for a man. Focused there.

God yes.

Claiming more of her had suddenly become the only goal he could imagine. As he stroked one hand down her body, pressing her closer, he tangled his other hand in her hair, bringing her mouth to his.

He rubbed his lips against hers, marveling at their softness as he urged her to open for him. She made a small sound as she deepened the contact, and he drank in the sweet taste of her.

He had been obsessed with her since the moment he had seen the poster. Then some unseen force had transported the two of them to that high, windswept plain. It felt like that had been months ago—and he had been waiting to make love to her all this time.

Now they were alone. Not in a fantasy. Or in a dream. They were in a land they had created together, a land filled with riches beyond his imagining. And yet at the same time, he knew they were in the lounge of his boat. Docked in Palmiro.

And they were lying on a narrow sofa. Not the place where he wanted to make love to her for the first time.

He shifted their positions, helping her up, his hand locked with hers. She didn't ask where they were going as they staggered on unsteady legs down the companionway to the stateroom he used when he slept on board. Where the bed was wider and more comfortable.

She didn't question him when he fumbled with the

buttons of her blouse and threw the garment on the floor, then pulled his T-shirt over his head and tossed it after her blouse.

As he reached around her, she leaned into him, pushing down the elastic waistband of her loose-fitting white slacks while he unhooked her bra.

The tight fabric of his jeans had turned into a form of torture. And while he was thinking about that, she opened the snap at the waistband, then lowered his zipper.

Thanks.

He pushed the jeans down, along with his shorts, his cock springing free as he kicked the clothing away.

Once again, she started to tell him they were going too fast.

I know. It's fast for me, too. He gave her a questioning look. *Or maybe not. Maybe it's been building for years.*

She raised her head, staring at him. *How?*

This morning, the dream wouldn't let me go. So I went out on the water, because that's where my mind works best. And I think I realized something about us. He swallowed hard. *This is almost too weird to say. But did you have an imaginary friend when you were a kid? A boy who lived out West?*

Her breath caught. *Yes.*

I did too. A girl named Annie.

She stared at him, trying to take it in.

We knew *each other? How?*

I don't know! But maybe we're finally meeting in person.

Oh Lord. Could that be true? Or are you just saying that to get me to cooperate?

How could I lie to you now?

I guess you can't. What did I call you?

Mac. You said Zach wasn't a proper name.

She winced, because she remembered how high-handed she'd been.

He cupped her breasts, bringing her back to the intensity of the present.

BILL Cody walked down the dock like he belonged there. Maybe he was a kid delivering a message to someone on one of the boats. Or maybe he was the chicken hawk fucking one of the sailors. He didn't care what anyone thought— as long as nobody questioned his presence there.

His footsteps grew quiet as he neared the boat into which Anna Ridgeway and the man had disappeared. The *Odysseus*.

The dive boat where the crew had quit.

Creeping closer, he heard their heavy breathing. Heard the rustle of clothing, and he knew what they were doing.

Fucking.

Good.

That would keep them occupied for a while—long enough for him to get instructions from Jim Stone.

LOST in that magic that he and Anna made together, Zach gathered her close, kissing her deeply, drinking from her essence as they swayed together.

She eased her head away, looking at him with large, luminous eyes, and he saw the mixture of his own emotions echoed there.

He had always been alone. Always alone. Except for the playmate he had conjured up. Or maybe she had reached out to him. That seemed the likely scenario.

Why did you leave me?

I don't know. I lost you, and I couldn't find you again.

With those silent words came profound sadness. He remembered something then. He'd been very sick. With scarlet fever. He'd never been that sick before or since.

He'd been lying in bed with a raging fever, out of his head—having hallucinations. And when he'd gotten his mind back, his friend had been gone. He'd tried to reach her, but the connection had snapped. And finally he'd made himself forget the pain of the loss of her.

She picked all that up from him in an instant, her eyes wide.

I was in Maryland. You were in Montana. A long way away.

And now . . . ?

And now they gazed at each other, both unsteady on their feet, both coping with what must be their shared past—and their present. Tangled together in ways they didn't understand.

Before he fell over and embarrassed himself, he moved his mouth to hers while he lowered her to the bed and followed her down.

She never lifted her mouth from his as they tumbled together onto the blue duvet. The way she responded to him made his head spin. And he didn't just sense her arousal; he felt it as she felt it, his mind capturing the sensations heating her from the inside out.

He'd already discovered that it was the same for her. She was in his head, too. Sharing his physical responses as he shared hers.

He groaned, caught up in his needs—and hers.

She wanted him to touch her breast again. Easing his chest away from hers, he rolled them to their sides, then lowered his head, swirling his tongue around one of her nipples, then sucking it into his mouth as he brought his thumb and finger to its mate, pulling and squeezing, knowing just how strongly she wanted him to do it.

He felt her pleasure as he heard her breath catch, felt her arch into the caress.

He wanted more. Needed more.

More. More.

The urgency wrapped itself around them, making it hard for him to breathe. Hard to think.

Yet at the edge of the pleasure, something prickled in his brain. Danger. His mind screamed danger. Not from without. From their minds—probing at each other. Making connections. Forging new circuits—and maybe burning them out.

What's happening?

The silent question was like a gasp in his mind.

Too much! She answered her own question, her hand pressing against his shoulder.

Not enough, he countered.

To his relief, he felt her surrender to the power of the moment.

To the power of their mutual need.

Reaching down, she clasped his cock again, and he knew she was deliberately exploring what the intimate touch felt like to him.

He wanted that, too. Wanted to touch her intimately and at the same time know what she felt when he did it. His hand slid down her body, and his fingers parted her slick, swollen folds, lingering there before dipping inside her.

She gasped, moving her hips to create friction, but it wasn't enough. Not for either one of them.

I need . . .

Yes.

He circled her clit with one finger, then circled the finger just inside the sensitive opening of her vagina, sending jolts of heat through her—and through himself.

He didn't have to tell her it was time. He knew neither of them could wait a second longer for this.

She rolled to her back and opened her legs for him. He knelt between her thighs, then plunged forward. There was no need to guide him to the right place. He knew exactly where to find that delicious opening.

Yet he sensed her fear—and his. And the fear was as great as the pleasure. As he slipped inside, heat lightning flared within his head, sending sparks crackling through his senses.

And he realized in that moment of joining that he would lose his mind if he didn't finish this with her.

Or maybe it was the other way around.

She pushed at his shoulder again, trying to pull away. Mentally. Physically. Her fear came through to him, loud and clear. She wanted to stop.

No! he silently shouted. *Stay with me. For God's sake, stay with me. Not just your body, but your mind.*

When he heard her silent protest, he steadied himself—steadied her.

Trust me.

The classic male cliché. Yet he knew it was true. Knew it to the marrow of his bones.

He felt her shudder, felt her settle into the rhythm of sex—their hips moving in concert, both of them pushing toward orgasm.

As he climbed toward that peak of sensation, he felt the pain in his brain recede to a level he could push aside.

There was only room for the hot, greedy desire created by the friction of their bodies and the joining of their minds.

I need.

Yes.

He reached between them, pressing his fingers over her clit, giving her the extra jolt of stimulation that would push her over the edge.

His own orgasm was only seconds away. And he knew that she sensed that peak, felt her lifting her hips, pushing to join him.

The first spasm of release took him. Hot semen pumped through his cock and into her as climax took them both.

He shouted in satisfaction. Shouted in shock as the fury of it claimed him.

Never like this.

Never.

He cradled her against himself, absorbing new truths.

What happened?

We can talk to each other. In our minds.

How?

We must have done it when we were kids. Long ago. Somehow we connected back then. Now it happened when we made love. Well, when we got . . . aroused.

But now it's stronger . . . deeper. A connection between adults—not children.

He laughed, pressing as far as he could inside her.

She reached to stroke damp hair back from his forehead, then locked her arms around his shoulders, holding him where he was.

The feeling of closeness was incredible.

Yes.

Now we're . . .

Complete.

And nothing can separate us again.

Yet the wondrous result of their joining brought something else. In that moment of deepest intimacy, they sensed something bad, something hovering just outside their range of perception.

Someone had been following her. Now the stalker wanted to know what they'd been doing. And he would kill them if he knew that they'd been making love.

The thought was ridiculous on the surface. Who would react that way to their private liaison?

Neither one of them made a conscious decision. Yet both of them instantly joined their minds, broadcasting a lie to whoever might be listening.

We haven't done anything physical. We're just talking. We're just friends.

Because their bodies were so intimately linked, they could send out that message together. They repeated it more than once, both of them squeezing their eyes shut and linking their hands tightly in concentration.

It was hard to do. Especially when they didn't know if they were really sending a message or just fooling themselves.

When their heads began to ache, they stopped and looked at each other.

"That was weird," Zach murmured. "Why did we do that?"

"It seemed important," she whispered.

It didn't seem important now. Looking down at Anna's body glued to his, Zach laughed. "Just friends, yeah."

"Oh my." The idea was so absurd that she joined in the laughter, shaking the two of them apart. For a few moments, their focus had been turned outward. Now it snapped back to this time. This place. Them.

Something had happened between them. Something Zach couldn't describe or explain to anyone else in the world.

Soul mates, she whispered in his mind.

The concept startled him. It was too new. Too strange. But when he turned it around in his mind, it felt right. Especially since he was sure now that they had reached out to each other long ago.

Who would understand it?

Only another couple like the two of them.

Were there any others like them?

Or were they alone?

CHAPTER
TWELVE

FROM HIS HIDEOUT in West Virginia, Jordan Walker stared at the computer screen.

Dead end. Again.

After he'd lost Anna Ridgeway's trail, he'd put in a phone call to her agent and been told that her schedule was private.

He snorted. Private! What entertainer didn't want people to know where she was going to be?

Unless . . .

He stood up and paced the office, trying to hold back his frustration. But he knew it was rolling off him in waves when his wife, Lindsay, came to the door, a worried look on her face.

What's wrong?

Has Jim Swift found us?

They knew he'd changed his name, because he'd disappeared, but several deaths around the country had clued them in that he must still be hunting Dariens—their word for the other people like themselves, who were born as part of an experiment at the Remington Clinic in Darien, Connecticut.

Jordan reached for his wife and pulled her close, letting her know in every way available to him that they were safe.

It's Anna Ridgeway, Lindsay whispered in his mind, answering her own question.

Yeah. I can't find her. She's disappeared off the face of the earth.

They didn't have to speak to each other out loud to communicate. Since they'd discovered the special link they shared, they'd become very good at sending their thoughts back and forth and increasing their psychic ability.

But worry sent words tumbling from Lindsay's mouth. "You think she's dead?"

"Not dead. In trouble," he answered.

He pulled Lindsay more tightly against his body, the contact comforting them both. But it was more than comfort he felt. The closeness brought sexual awareness that sparked back and forth between them. It was part of the equation, part of what made them what they were.

But they had learned to make the sexual need work for them. It had triggered their mental powers, and it still helped fuel the psychic bond the two of them generated.

Jordan turned his head so he could stroke his lips against Lindsay's cheek, and she slid her fingers against his broad shoulders.

For the first thirty-three years of his life, Jordan had been alone. So had Lindsay. More alone than any human being should be. He'd thought he was defective in some way. Apart from the human race.

Then he'd met Lindsay, and he'd connected with her—mind to mind—in a way that was impossible for ordinary people.

The joy of finding each other had been dulled by the knowledge that they were being hunted by Kurt MacArthur, the head of a powerful Washington think tank called the Crandall Consortium.

They'd thought MacArthur and the rest of his top

lieutenants were dead. Then they'd realized that one of them, Jim Swift, had escaped and was searching for them.

Jordan and Lindsay were well hidden. Nobody in rural West Virginia where they were living had a clue about their real identities.

They'd both sold their D.C. condos and hidden the money trail, using a new last name, Jordan and Lindsay West.

Jordan had also continued his writing career, switching from nonfiction to fiction, using the real-life stories he'd investigated as a jumping-off point for creating plots that would fit into today's popular fiction market.

His agent, who was keeping his identity secret, had gotten Jordan a contract on the basis of a proposal. And they'd also contacted Lindsay's parents, who had helped them out with some cash that couldn't be traced.

But their real job was trying to save the other people like themselves. They'd thought they had a list of the other Dariens, but the data had been corrupted.

Now they were reduced to tracking their fellows down using their Web skills—and their own psychic talents.

They were sure Jim Swift had already killed several of them. But he was proceeding slowly. So they assumed he didn't have the list, either.

It was a good bet that Anna Ridgeway was one of the children from the experiment. And also that she'd tried to disappear. Because she knew Jim Swift was on her trail? Or was something else dangerous going on in her life?

In their research, they'd also discovered something very interesting about Anna—she didn't just have latent psychic talent; she was already using her mental powers. At least, she was using one ability, psychometry, since she supported herself with a nightclub act where she picked up memories from objects she touched.

She must be very strong, Lindsay whispered into Jordan's mind.

Yeah. But that won't save her if Jim Swift is after her.

Jordan closed his eyes and slipped his hand under the bulky sweater his wife was wearing, caressing her warm skin.

Do you think we can find out where she is?

I hope so.

Lindsay joined her hands behind Jordan's back, pressing against him, and he felt the link between them deepen.

After a few moments of silence, Lindsay said, *She's on a boat.*

Yeah.

And I think . . .

Jordan was the one who said it aloud. "Yeah. She's found another Darien."

Elation spiraled through them.

Who is he? Jordan asked.

I wish I could bring that into focus.

I wish we knew where they were.

Somewhere warm, I think.

So not around here, where we're stuck in the middle of a cold, nasty winter. California? Florida?

Maybe the Caribbean, Lindsay answered.

Why do you think so?

The color of the water.

We'll keep trying to get a closer fix on them.

BILL Cody stepped from the afternoon sun and into the shadow of a warehouse and pulled out the secure cell phone that Jim Stone had given him.

He wasn't supposed to make a call unless it was an emergency, but he was sure this situation qualified.

He dialed the number, then waited.

"Yes?" a grating voice answered after the first ring.

It was Jim Stone. No matter what time of day or night, he always answered his own phone, and he always sounded like a man who'd had his vocal cords burned in a fire. Bill had never seen him. He wondered what he looked like. Probably scarred.

"I have Anna Ridgeway cornered."

"Where?"

"On a boat."

"You idiot! Boats can sail away."

"Not this one. The crew quit." Quickly he explained what had happened.

"Then why isn't the woman dead?" The question was direct and to the point.

"Too many people around. And now she's with the guy who owns the boat."

"What's his name"

"A man named Zachary Robinson. He's a diver."

"Just a moment."

Stone was away from the phone for several minutes. What the hell was he doing?

When he came back, he asked, "What are they up to?"

"Talking."

"Just talking? You're sure?"

"Yes," he answered, his voice hard and positive. A little while ago when he'd been on the dock, he'd thought they were screwing. Now he blinked, trying to bring that thought into focus. It stayed blurry, wrong.

"Has she met with him before?"

"No." Bill knew *that* for certain, since he'd been following her around.

"Okay, this is what we're going to do. I'll line up some freelancers to help you. You stay down by the docks. If Ridgeway and Robinson leave the boat, let me know."

"Yes, sir."

"I'll have your reinforcements there as fast as I can."

"Okay."

"I want Ridgeway and the guy off the island. Away from other people. I'll give you further instructions later. But keep them separated. I mean, I don't want them touching each other. You got that?"

"Yes."

"It's important. No physical contact—once you scoop them up. Stay near them, and make sure nothing's going on."

"Yes, sir," he repeated, adding the honorific for effect. He didn't know why the touching part was so important, but he'd follow Stone's directions.

"I'll call when I have this set up."

"How will they find me?"

"They know what you look like."

"They do?"

"Yeah." Stone clicked off, and Bill stood by the warehouse, staring off into the afternoon sunlight reflected on the water.

He'd been sure of himself this morning. Sure of himself a little while ago. Now his brain felt fuzzy, and he welcomed the idea of reinforcements. Which was odd, because he liked to work alone.

He shook his head to clear his thoughts, then walked back to the dock.

He should check on the couple. Make sure they weren't doing anything nasty.

No, he knew they weren't. He'd just wait across the street until the freelancers came.

JIM'S mind was racing. First he took care of the immediate business—getting a line on a couple of thugs who could work with Wild Bill.

Then he went back to his computer. On the face of it, he didn't think Zachary Robinson was one of the freaks from the Remington experiment. The background was wrong. He was from Montana, not from the East. And that meant that his mother would have had to travel a considerable distance to go for treatments and follow-ups.

But what if she'd heard of Remington's work and decided he was the best?

He scanned the information he had quickly found on Robinson. The man was a diver. Had he shown any evidence of psychic abilities?

Jim dug for more material, trying to figure out if Robinson was a real threat or just some guy Anna Ridgeway had met. The Remington children tended to stick to themselves. But sometimes they did get together with members of the opposite sex.

In this case, better safe than sorry. Robinson would have to be eliminated, just to make sure he wasn't one of the gooks.

But Jim didn't want two murders on the island drawing the media down there. So they'd have to be transported somewhere else.

By boat? No, a plane was better. Faster. Unless they were both Remington's freaks and they were already bonding. In that case, the only safe course was to kill them immediately—then figure out the disposal of the bodies later.

ANNA lay curled against Zach under the duvet, enjoying the gentle slap of the waves against the side of the boat.

She felt different. Sharper. Better. Closer to reaching her potential.

"Yes," Zach murmured.

The glow of their lovemaking embraced them. And she should be relaxed and happy. But questions circled in her head. In his, too. She could feel them buzzing around, but she didn't try to read his thoughts. She was too worn out. Not just from making love. From the work of connecting with him.

"Why did that happen to us?" she murmured, unwilling to expend the energy to speak mind to mind.

"Somehow we found each other when we were kids. Then we both turned up on Grand Fernandino."

"That doesn't explain the part when we were little."

"We were lonely."

"So are a lot of other kids."

"You're a psychic. Somehow, you . . . recognized me."

She dragged in a breath and let it out. "I don't know. I thought I had one talent—picking up objects and knowing something about the owner." She went on quickly. "And you . . . have some kind of special ability that helps you find shipwrecks."

"That's nothing like what you have." He looked thoughtful. "The important point is that we have . . . more now. Together."

She moved her face against his shoulder, smiling. "It feels . . . good. I never thought this would happen to me." She didn't say what "this" was, because she was still afraid to give it a name.

She'd read a lot of articles and books about male-female relationships. They'd counseled caution and getting to know a guy before you thought about a long-term relationship. But she *had* known Zach—then had lost him.

"You can't always believe what you read," he murmured.

She knew he'd picked up her thoughts. When a flush of embarrassment warmed her cheeks, he stroked his hand there.

"You weren't prepared for something like lightning striking?" he asked softly.

"No."

"Neither was I."

"But you went after me."

"Yeah. The moment I saw you, I knew we were going to be important to each other." His breath hitched. "And for the record, it scared me. I thought about sailing away from you."

"Thank God you didn't."

They lay silent for several heartbeats, holding on to each other.

She felt a question building in his mind. A question he didn't want to ask.

Tension coiled inside her as she waited.

"Were your parents disappointed with you?" he finally asked.

"I . . ." She huffed out a breath before starting again. "Dad was always so damn busy with his get-rich schemes that I didn't know him that well. It seemed like work was more important to him than family." She unconsciously lowered her voice. "But maybe he stayed away from home so much because he didn't know what to do with a kid like me."

"Is that what you really think?" he asked sharply.

She ran her finger along his arm. "I used to think so. You know how kids are. They assume trouble in the family is their fault."

"Yeah."

"Then I guess I realized that he wasn't much for home life."

"So maybe your mother was the one who wanted a kid, and he went along with her because that got her off his back."

"Maybe." She sighed. "If so, it didn't work out the way she expected. I know Mom wished I were closer to her."

She wanted to push for answers—to find out what had made them . . . different. But because their thoughts were so close, she felt him backing away from the subject. And she wasn't going to start off the relationship by pushing him.

He combed his fingers through her hair. It felt good. And arousing. She wanted him again, and she knew he wanted her, too. But for now, she was just enjoying being close to him.

And he knew that, too.

* * *

JOSEPH Hondino stood at the window of his little yellow house, looking at the magnificent view of the harbor. It was one of the things he appreciated about the island.

He had been born and come of age in this port city. And he loved the warmth and generosity of the people who lived here.

Since he'd become a Vadiana priest forty years ago, he'd done his best to serve them. They might live in a place where tourists came to relax and enjoy the sun, but their lives were hard, and he tried to help them with their problems. To give them hope for the future.

He'd been delighted when Raoul San Donato had joined his congregation. And he'd instructed the young man in the way of the Blessed Ones. He'd thought Raoul might take over from him when he got too old to lead his flock.

But Raoul had other ideas. He wanted to push his mentor aside. And he was using the psychic powers he possessed to do it. Raoul was perverting the tenets of the religion that Joseph served. He was mixing up the results of his own psychic powers with the power of the saints.

That was bad enough. But it was worse that he pretended to be on the side of the people, when it was clear that he was working strictly for himself. He wanted to be the unofficial king of this island. Maybe even the official ruler—in the tradition of the strong men who stepped in and took over the governments of third-world countries. They made all sorts of promises to their followers. But it turned out most of the wealth and comfort was reserved for them. And that was the real tragedy of what was happening with San Donato.

He'd fooled too many people on the island—people who thought that he could lead them to a better life. Somehow the forces of Good and Evil in the universe had become unbalanced. Were the Blessed Ones really favoring Raoul San Donato?

Joseph had gone to a few of the ceremonies held by his old disciple on the other side of the island, staying well in the back. And he'd seen some weird sexual practices up on the altar that had made his jaw drop. What started at the altar spread to the congregation—so that the worship sessions ended up in a sexual orgy.

Joseph grimaced. The way San Donato was perverting their religion made him sick. Did his poisonous ceremonies find favor with the saints?

Perhaps they were intrigued. Perhaps they were waiting to see what would happen.

Although Joseph knew the balance in the universe would eventually right itself, eventually might not be soon enough, not when the negative was in the ascendance and the good had been suppressed.

One thing Joseph understood deep down at the level of his gut. The false priest would eventually destroy himself. But the people of the island were the more immediate problem. San Donato was gathering more and more of them to himself. And if he swept them into danger, Joseph would never forgive himself.

ANNA snuggled beside Zach, basking in the warmth and closeness. She'd felt like she was in danger. Now she was safe—with this man who had come back to her after years of being apart. Well, they hadn't been together in any conventional sense. And they hadn't been adults then. But she'd had a special connection with him all those years ago. And against all odds, they'd found each other again. Cosmic coincidence? Or something more?

She was turning that over in her mind when she felt a jolt of alarm.

"We have to get out of here," she whispered, climbing out of bed and picking up the clothing that she'd been wearing.

Zach didn't question her. He just stood up and began pulling on his T-shirt and jeans.

"Make the bed."

"Huh?"

"It's important to make the bed," she whispered.

"Why?"

She dragged in a breath and let it out. "I don't know." She felt frustration and a terrible urgency rising inside her. "Stop wasting time. I've got to wash. So nobody knows we were making love."

She dashed into the head adjacent to the cabin and grabbed a washcloth, wetting and soaping it, then washing quickly. After rinsing it out, she hung it in the shower, like Zach had left it. Then she dried off with the towel hanging on the rack.

When she returned to the cabin, Zach had made the bed, pulling the duvet back into place and plumping the pillows so that it didn't look like they had just climbed out of the bed—out of each other's arms.

She didn't understand why that was important. She only knew her life might depend on it. And Zach's life.

He cupped his hands over her shoulders, his fingers digging into her skin. *Life and death?*

Yes.

She dressed quickly. She had just thrust her feet into her sandals when she felt the boat sway as someone climbed aboard.

CHAPTER
THIRTEEN

ZACH HAD TO protect Anna.

That was his first thought as he whirled away from the cabin door.

"Zach, we have to . . ." Anna cried out.

"What?"

"Work together," she gasped.

"How?"

"Like we sent out that message before."

"We don't even know if it really did anything." This wasn't theoretical. It was up close and personal, and his self-protective instincts instantly went into old patterns. Without even thinking about what he was doing, he leaped toward the dresser where he kept his gun.

Before he could reach the drawer that held his Sig Sauer, two armed men burst into the cabin.

They looked tough as barnacles. And neither of them had the features of islanders. These were outsiders. Hired guns. From Terrance Sanford? Or maybe Sanford's brother? Was the whole thing with the sunken boat a setup?

The questions flashed through his mind as one of

the men rushed him, weapon drawn. The other covered Anna.

"Move a muscle, and I shoot the lady."

Zach went stock-still.

He wanted to scream as the thug closest to Anna pulled out a pair of handcuffs and handed them to her. "Put them on," he clipped out.

She held the cuffs in her hand, looking down at them, then pleadingly at Zach, and he knew she was trying to tell him something—mind to mind. Something that would save their butts. In the alley, after the two men had attacked him, he'd sent her a message. But he couldn't go the other way. Not unless they were touching.

His body rigid, he strained his mind to pick up what she was saying. But it didn't work. When he wasn't touching her, they might as well have been on opposite ends of the island.

He needed that physical contact. And he longed to lunge across the room and grab her arm to forge the connection. Hell, he should have listened to her and done it two minutes ago.

But there was no chance of that now. They'd both be dead before they could make any kind of contact.

Anna took her lower lip between her teeth. He knew she'd been playing for time. And it had just run out.

"Do it!" the man ordered.

With her lip still clenched between her teeth, she snapped the cuff around one wrist. He saw her fumbling with the other one, saw her intense concentration and knew she was still silently trying to talk to him.

He gave his head a small shake. With a defeated look, she did the other wrist.

As he stood beside the bed, he wanted to roar out his frustration, but he kept his anguish locked in his throat.

A sound in the companionway made him look up as a slim man walked into the room.

"Got them, Bill," the bigger guy said.

"No names," he snapped, giving the speaker a narrow-eyed look. Then he glanced from them to the made bed that looked like nobody had been in it.

"Keep them apart."

Anna gasped when she saw him. "You. You're the man who was following me. In Denver. And on the island."

His gaze shot to her. "You couldn't have spotted me."

When Anna opened her mouth, Zach sent her an urgent message. *Don't argue with him. Don't contradict him. Let him think he's in charge.*

She closed her mouth abruptly, and Zach relaxed a beat. It looked like she had heard him. So the communication was working—one way. She was used to picking up memories from people, and she could catch what he was saying to her. Too bad he couldn't hear her thoughts.

Not yet. Or would they ever have a chance to make it work?

Anna flicked her gaze to him, then away, and he was sure she had heard that. Almost imperceptibly she lifted one shoulder.

"Cuff him," the slim guy ordered.

The man who had come at him whipped out another set of cuffs and secured Zach's wrists—in front of him, he noted. Not the best way to restrain a prisoner, but he wasn't going to point that out to these bastards.

Bill gave him a satisfied smirk, then walked around the cabin, opening drawers and poking inside.

Zach watched him intently, but Bill didn't pocket anything, even the gun, and he didn't find the stash of U.S. bills hidden in a compartment behind one of the drawers.

Which meant that when he and Anna got out of this, they'd have some cash.

She looked at him, then away, and he gave her a quick grin, telling her that he wasn't going to give up.

He realized the reason for the search when Bill opened a cabinet and pulled out a sweatshirt.

"Hold your hands so I can drape this over the cuffs," he ordered.

With no other options, Zach obeyed.

His gaze slid to Anna. She was staring at the men with wide, terrified eyes.

Bill pulled down a jacket and laid it over Anna's cuffs, then used his own jacket to hide his gun.

"Why are you doing this?" Zach asked.

"It's how I get my kicks."

"Are you working for Sanford?"

"Who?"

The way he said it told Zach he'd never heard of the guy.

"Quit talking. We're getting out of here. Off the boat and into a car by the dock. I'd prefer not to kill you in the middle of town, but if you try anything funny, you're dead."

Zach sent Anna another mental message.

Hang tight. We'll get out of this. Do what they say—for now.

This time, her back was to him, and he didn't know if she heard him. But he repeated the words more than once, hoping that he was getting through to her. For all the good it did either one of them.

Sure, he could tell her they'd get out of this, but he didn't know how they were going to do it. Right now their only choice was to follow directions.

As he allowed the men to lead him off the boat, he silently prayed. He hadn't prayed in years. Now that he was in bad trouble, he was suddenly asking for God's help.

He looked around the dock and spotted José, the diver who had been down with him a few days ago and had been busy since then, spreading the word about their run-in with Pagor.

The man stared at him and Anna and the thugs, probably taking in the situation instantly.

Yeah, we're in trouble.

When Zach shot him a hard look, the guy turned away and pretended great interest in a nearby boat.

Well, what had he expected? Probably this was just what José had been waiting for. Bad luck—the direct result of disturbing Pagor down on that wreck.

Was there some way to make a break for it?

As the thug with Anna grasped her arm, Zach kept looking around, hoping for a car crash or something else to distract these guys for a moment.

But the port area was quiet. Nobody interfered as they walked to a black car that was pulled up along the curb.

ACROSS the street from the docks, a small, barefoot boy named Tomaso hugged the edge of a parked car, his eyes trained toward the *Odysseus*. One of the rich men in town, Raoul San Donato, was paying him big bucks to keep watch on that lady from the Sugar Cane Club. She'd gone onto the ship, and she'd been in there for a while. Long enough for her to have some fun with that diver guy. The one who was mixed up bad with Pagor.

Now more guys had come on board, and Tomaso wasn't sure what to do. Should he run to San Donato and tell him? Or should he wait to see what happened?

When the woman and the men came out, he kept his eyes trained on her. She looked scared. And her arms looked funny with a shirt draped over them.

He should get San Donato. For sure.

Or should he follow the men?

Before he could decide which way to jump, the big men pushed her and the diver guy into a car. The rest of them climbed in, and they drove away.

Tomaso swallowed. He'd lost them. Would San Donato still pay him? Or should he run away?

THEY drove out of town, with Zach in the back and Anna in the front. Were they going out in the jungle, where these guys could shoot them and bury the bodies?

After a few minutes, he was pretty sure they were headed toward one of the private airstrips on the island.

Jesus, now what?

The car stopped at the edge of a narrow ribbon of blacktop. Nobody seemed to be in the shed that served as an office. These guys had probably paid off the staff.

The men hustled Zach and Anna out of the car, then the one named Bill ran toward a small plane that was sitting at the edge of the runway.

Zach had been hoping they could get away before now. But when Bill came back, he ordered them toward the plane.

RAOUL was in his art gallery with an old guy who was staying in one of the big hotels and wanted to surprise his wife with a piece of island art. Stupid move. In his experience, the tourist guys were better off letting the women pick their own art. But he nodded and smiled and started writing up the ticket, hoping she wasn't going to return the expensive carving.

When Tomaso burst through the front door, he gave the kid a sharp look, then finished up the transaction. The boy stood there shifting his weight from one foot to the other like he had to pee.

He would have told the kid to get out of there—now—but the look on the small face told him something was up. When the customer had left, Raoul flipped the Closed sign.

"What happened?" he demanded.

"De woman leave. Wit de man who own the Pagor boat. And other men."

"She was with *him*?"

"Yeah, mon."

"Why didn't you tell me?"

"You said to stay wit her."

Raoul repressed the impulse to take the kid by the shoulders and shake him. He knew it wouldn't do him any good.

"Where they go?" he asked, hearing the raw edge of his voice.

"I don't know, mon."

"Into the city?"

"Into a car." Tomaso looked like he'd done something wrong.

Truly, Raoul wanted to throttle the boy. But what had happened wasn't Tomaso's fault. Instead Raoul took a dollar bill from the cash box and handed it over.

The kid looked wide-eyed at the money. "You want me to do sumpin' else for you?"

"Not now. Go on."

As soon as Tomaso had stepped onto the sidewalk, Raoul locked the door and headed for the shrine out back, praying that Ibena could tell him where Anna had gone. On his way to the shed, he opened the cage and plucked out a chicken, carrying it flapping and squawking to the back of the yard.

He didn't have time for refinements. He knelt before the altar, chanting his prayer and holding up the chicken so that Ibena could see. Then he broke the chicken's neck and slit the bird's throat, letting the blood drip into the bowl that sat on the altar.

"Tell me where my queen has gone," he asked. "The queen who will rule this island with me. With your help," he added, lest the goddess think that he had forgotten his place in the scheme of saints and men. "I need your help. Show me what is hidden to my own eyes. Show me where to find her."

He squeezed his eyes closed, praying that a scene would form in his mind.

At first he saw the street outside his shop's front door. But he knew that was a false image, born of his own desperation.

He banished the street scene, and opened himself to whatever image Ibena would send him.

And when he saw one of the airstrips outside the city, he gasped.

She was leaving.

No, she wouldn't leave him. Someone was taking her away.

"WHERE are we going?" Zach asked.

"To meet our boss."

The truth? Or a lie designed to keep him calm?

He thought he detected a lie, but there was no way to know for sure.

Despair threatened to swamp him. They were in a hell of a fix. And he didn't know how to get out of it.

He should have trusted Anna. He should have—

He cut off the self-accusation. There was no point in beating himself up over what he should have done. That was in the past. He had to figure out what to do now.

They hustled him onto the plane, then into a seat, where they fastened his seatbelt. Anna followed and was pushed into a seat across the aisle and also buckled in. They were in the middle of the plane. Bill and one of the big thugs were behind them. The pilot and one of the other hoods was in front.

Zach didn't know much about aircraft. Not the way he knew boats. There wasn't a chance of his flying this thing— even if he and Anna could somehow take it over.

Yeah sure. And elephants could fly.

He glanced at Anna. She looked scared. Like she'd given up. Maybe that was what she *wanted* the bad guys to think.

He hoped to hell that was true. Because if she'd given up, they were both dead.

Keep it together, he urged. *I know you can hear me. I'm with you. And we have to keep it together.* He kept saying it in his mind, trying to project the message outward. When Anna gave a little nod, he felt a surge of hope.

He heard the men conferring, but he couldn't hear what they were saying. Was Anna picking it up? Exactly what *could* she do? Together they had planted suggestions in these men's minds. Could they do it without touching?

He didn't know. But he knew their lives might depend on it.

CHAPTER
FOURTEEN

ANNA COULD HEAR Zach shouting in her mind, telling her to keep it together.

Yes, okay. They could . . .

Could what?

Before she let herself hope, she sent a message to him. *If you can hear me, raise your hands a little.*

She slid her eyes in his direction, waiting with her heart pounding to see if he got the message. Long seconds passed, but he sat staring straight ahead with his hands in his lap.

Raise your hands a little so I know we can communicate, she said again, hearing the urgency in her own silent voice. But he sat utterly still, staring straight ahead, and she knew the communication was going only one way—as it had the night before.

Although his earlier message had helped bolster her resolve, she knew she was on her own. She was the one who had to figure out what to do. And she had to do it while she let the bad guys surrounding them think they had everything under control.

As that thought lodged in her mind, one of the men came down the aisle, stopping to check that the handcuffs were still fastened. She didn't have to pretend revulsion as she shrank away from him, then sat with her head bowed and her shoulders slumped, outwardly projecting defeat.

Zach had asked their captors where they were going, and one of the thugs had told him they were going to see the boss.

But she knew that was a flat-out lie. Unless the boss was a stingray. She had heard the bitter truth in the mind of the slim guy who seemed to be in charge.

They were going to swoop low enough to push her and Zach out of the plane over the water, then fly away and leave them to drown or be eaten by sharks.

She tried to get that awful image out of her mind. Tried to keep panic from choking off her breath.

Much better to make sure she and Zach came out of this alive. She kept her eyes lowered, but she was chanting the words she used when preparing for her act.

Relax now. Relax now, she whispered to herself, calling up the self-hypnosis technique that she used before she went on stage.

The familiar mantra soothed her. The words were like a lifeline she could grab on to and use to pull herself back from quicksand onto firm ground.

However, she wasn't sitting in her dressing room. She might be able to pretend she was striving for inner peace, but when the plane began accelerating down the runway, she lost her focus entirely as reality slammed back into her.

They were taking off. Speeding toward their deaths.

She felt hysteria threatening to grab her by the throat and choke off her breath.

Stop it! Stop it! she silently ordered. If she gave in to panic, she and Zach were dead.

The harsh assessment worked. Eyes closed, she dragged in a deep breath and let it out before starting again. Her life depended on what she could accomplish in the next few

minutes, but she didn't focus on that. She focused on the
job. Like when she went on stage.

She had possessed psychic talents since she was a little
girl. She had advantages over these men. But she needed
Zach's help to do anything useful, because until today, her
only skill had been picking up objects and catching other
people's memories. Well, that and somehow making contact with Zach when they were little.

Calmly, she reached out to him, trying to link them as
they had been linked before. Today and years ago.

She could just feel the edge of his mind, because when
they'd been in bed together, she had learned to recognize
what she was looking for. But it was only the edge. Not
enough to do her any good, to do both of them any good.

The present communication between them was so new,
so fragile. If they'd only had a little more time together before the men had burst onto his boat, she was sure the connection would have been more solid—more usable.

But they'd been rudely interrupted in those first important hours together. Now she had to figure out how to increase the connection without touching him.

How much time did they have?

She didn't know. But she knew the men were restless—
and eager to get rid of their unwanted cargo.

She looked out the window and sucked in a sharp
breath. They were already over the blue Caribbean, with no
land anywhere in front of them. All she could see was water, and some boats.

*Over water. They're going to drop me and Zach over the
water. Soon.*

*Forget that. Think about what you have to do to get out
of this plane alive. You have to reach Zach. The two of you
have to work together.*

She kept her eyes closed, thinking about the connection
between her and Zach. Not the past imaginary friendship,

but the fast and furious linking in the present. She had felt it tugging at her that first night when she'd seen him in the club. During her performance, when he'd been sitting at a table in the Sugar Cane Club, she thought he might be the man from her fantasy encounter. She'd tried to ignore that insight, but ignoring him had been impossible.

Then he'd kissed her, caressed her, made love to her, and each new stage of intimacy had strengthened the bond between them.

She couldn't touch him now. Not physically. But she could bring those precious moments back—as though it were happening again.

The small plane had about eleven passenger seats. Three of them were occupied by killers. What would they think when they saw her cheeks flush? When they heard her breath quicken?

The hell with them. Maybe they'd just think she looked scared.

She thrust the thugs from her mind and focused on Zach. He was sitting close enough to touch. If either one of them could have reached out.

Zach, she silently whispered his name, trying to draw him closer as she thought about how it had been in bed with him. The wonderful feel of his hands and lips on her. The equally wonderful feel of his body under her own hands.

You cupped my breasts, then glided your fingers over the tips. They were already so hard. And you made them ache with the need for you.

As she spoke inside her head, she felt it again, his hot touch on her breasts, arousing her beyond reason. She focused on the sensations, her body heating as she got back into the scene.

Sliding her eyes sidewise, she tried to see if he was getting the message. But he was staring straight ahead, his gaze trained on the back of the neck of the bad guy in the seat in front of him.

Well, she was making herself hot. But the flames weren't crossing the aisle of the small plane.

Struggling for an analogy, she came up with—phone sex. Too bad she'd never indulged in that activity. But a few times when she'd been restless and up late at night, she'd seen commercials for phone numbers where you could call and talk to sexy women.

She'd always felt sorry for the poor guys who had to resort to that kind of activity. Now she wondered if she'd picked up any seduction tips from the girls in the commercials.

Closing her eyes, she imagined herself lying on a bed with silk sheets, leaning comfortably against a pile of silk pillows, a phone in her hand, talking seductively into the receiver while she used her other hand to cup her own breast.

The image was erotic. But when she opened her eyes and cut Zach a glance, he was still staring straight ahead, apparently unaware of her efforts on their behalf.

She dragged in a breath and let it out. At the back of her mind, she could feel her deadline looming. She pushed the time pressure away and focused on what she needed to do.

Perhaps she was being too realistic. Maybe she needed a full-blown fantasy.

So where would she like to be with Zach? She settled on a plush bedroom, maybe in Las Vegas. Details were important. What were their surroundings?

Once again, she imagined a bed with silk sheets and pillows. Only this was a king-size bed with plenty of room to play. And the sheets were a soft . . . lavender. With hot pink accents on the pillows. Velvet draperies covered the windows. But enough light drifted in from the marble bathroom so that she and Zach had a good view of each other.

She was wearing a thin gown, held up by barely-there spaghetti straps. And she knew her nipples were clearly visible through the lace-edged bodice. They were still hard

and throbbing. Begging for his touch. But she had asked
Zach to lie with his hands pressed against the mattress.

Because she wanted to be the one in charge.

He lay with his arms at his sides, with his wonderful
chest bare. But he was wearing silk pajama bottoms. She
smiled when she pictured him lying there, staring up at her
with a hungry expression on his face.

With a wicked grin, she reached to run her hand over
the front of the pajama bottoms, sliding her palm against
his erection, touching him through the thin fabric.

She could only see the vague outline of his penis through
the silky material, but she could feel the shape of him, feel
him straining against her hand.

Smiling to herself, she slid her hand up and down, playing with him, then pressed more firmly before reaching
through the opening in the front of the pajamas, finding the
swollen head, circling the ridge with her index finger, then
gliding to the top, finding a drop of moisture there and
spreading it over him.

From the seat opposite her, he made a low exclamation.

Jesus! The word echoed in her head.

I got your attention.

Oh yeah.

Good.

She didn't have to look at him to know he was grinning.
She grinned, too, then sobered immediately. She hadn't
touched him so intimately because she wanted to play
around; she had an urgent message to deliver.

*We have to get out of here. They lied to you. They're go-
ing to push us out of the plane. Over the water.*

Jesus! He said it again, but this time the tone was different.

*If we work together, we can make them change their
minds.* Even as she silently said it, she wondered if it was
really possible. But she had to believe they could do it, because it was their only chance.

From far away, she heard another silent voice. A voice in her head, chanting.

Turn the plane around. Come back to Grand Fernandino. Turn the plane around. Come back.

Zach gave her a startled look, and she knew he had heard it, too. Someone else was here. When she'd joined with Zach, someone else had connected with them. Well, maybe not with them. With *her*.

She didn't have any terms to describe what was happening. And she had only one reference point—the vision from the previous day, when she had been called to a high, windswept plain. The plain where she'd first met Zach. Only, another man had been in the shadows. Watching them and hating what he was seeing.

And she thought he was somehow here again. Chanting.

She knew Zach heard it, too. She saw him clench his fists and felt his mental shout. *Get out of here.*

No! He can help us. Let him help us.

Zach's answer was fast and furious. *He wants you! He wants to take you away from me.*

She swallowed. She understood that.

Who the hell is he?

I don't know.

The knowledge of the other man had simmered in her thoughts all along—since she had come to Grand Fernandino, if she was being honest. She had thought it was Etienne, but she had come to realize it had to be someone else.

Then she'd thought it was the guy who had followed her from Denver. But he was on the plane, so it couldn't be him.

The other man was a problem—for her and Zach. But she understood that they would have to deal with that problem later. Right now, they had to save their lives. And maybe he could help them.

Zach shot her a dark look, but he stopped protesting the

help. And when he stopped putting his energy into blocking the intrusion, she breathed out a small sigh.

Moments later, the plane swung around and headed back toward the island.

"Thank God," Anna whispered, but her relief was short-lived.

As soon as Bill felt the change in course, he stood up and charged toward the cockpit.

"Hey," he shouted. "What's happening, Hank? What are you doing?"

"We have to go back," the pilot said.

"You get a radio communication?"

"We have to go back," the pilot repeated.

"Mechanical problem?"

Again, the answer was the same. Hank only mouthed the flat statement that they had to go back to where they'd come from.

Anna hung on to the mental connection with Zach.

Yes, mechanical problems, she silently whispered. *And if the plane goes down, you don't want the cops to find two people in the plane wearing handcuffs.*

Zach picked up on the message and added his mental weight to the equation. When he did, she felt the power of the suggestion strengthen.

Together they kept broadcasting the message until two of the thugs ran toward them. One unlocked her handcuffs, while the other held a gun on her.

"Don't move," he growled.

She nodded, her mental focus still on the man, willing him to unlock Zach's cuffs, too. But he only walked away, and her throat constricted in panic.

BACK on Grand Fernandino, Raoul knelt in the shed where he'd been praying to Ibena. She had shown him where to find Anna. In a plane over the water. Flying far away from the island.

As soon as he realized what was happening, he had asked for Ibena's help again.

He had asked for a miracle. And his saint had given him one. She had done it. The pilot had turned around. He was coming back to the island.

"Thank you," Raoul intoned, his gratitude heartfelt as he gazed up at the image of his goddess that he had fixed over the wooden altar. "Thank you for answering my prayers. I will make many sacrifices to you, here and at my other altars. And when Anna is at my side, we will devote ourselves to your worship."

He rocked back on his heels, elated that Ibena had been so gracious to him.

She was fueling his power, raising him to a whole new level among men.

He should go to the airstrip outside of town where the plane had taken off.

The airstrip.

No. He had asked for a miracle. But he suddenly knew that it hadn't worked out the way he had expected.

ANNA watched Bill, the shrimp who had come into the stateroom on the boat behind the big thugs, standing in the cockpit. "You can't turn around. Not now," he shouted, grabbing at the pilot's shoulder.

"Get the hell off of me." Hank swivelled around and swatted at the intruder, then went back to his controls.

Anna looked out the window. To their right, she could see a spot of land. Grand Fernandino!

In the front, the two men were struggling now, each trying to get control. And the angle of descent was much too steep. They were going to hit the water.

* * *

FAR away, on the U.S. mainland, Jordan Walker didn't realize he had called Lindsay until she was in front of him, her arms open.

He went into them, clasping her tightly, drawing comfort from her, even as they joined their strength.

"I saw a plane," he managed to say.

He opened his mind, and she pulled the images from him. A small plane. Over water. Anna Ridgeway in one of the seats. Another man across from her. And thugs, holding guns.

He hadn't known where to find Anna, but he knew that in a moment of dire emergency he had somehow mentally tapped into the scene.

The plane was in trouble. Winging down toward the blue water at a dangerous angle.

And Jordan knew they were going to crash.

We've got to . . .

He didn't have to tell Lindsay what to do. They were far away from the scene. They didn't even know the location of the emergency. But since they had first bonded, they had increased their psychic powers—and practiced their unique talents.

Combining their mental energy, they both sent their thoughts far away—toward the doomed craft. They pulled the nose up and slowed the plane's speed, praying that they could prevent complete disaster.

CHAPTER
FIFTEEN

STRAIGHTEN OUT. STRAIGHTEN out and climb, climb, Zach silently shouted, thanking God that Bill had backed off and was letting Hank try to save their asses.

Anna joined him, frantically urging the pilot to gain altitude even as she checked to see that her seatbelt was fastened.

Again she felt an outside force joining with her and Zach.

The same man?

Or someone different? Someone far away—she sensed that much.

The source of help didn't matter. Not now.

Once, when she'd been in a plane where the landing gear was stuck, the passengers had been instructed in emergency procedures.

They'd been told to lean over and grasp their ankles.

She did that now, shouting at Zach to do the same thing.

In the long-ago emergency, the plane had made a rough but successful belly landing on a foam-covered runway.

This time, the water would have to do.

She breathed out a sigh as she felt the pilot pull the nose up so that they didn't go in head first. Instead, the plane's belly slammed into the water, throwing the thugs around the cabin. Since Anna and Zach were still strapped in and grasping their ankles, they came through the crash landing better than the others.

"Oh fuck. What the hell?" the pilot asked in a dazed voice as they floated on the waves

"You moron," one of the other men shouted.

"Shut up. We've got to get out of here."

Hank was already pulling down a life raft that was in a compartment near his head.

One of the thugs held his gun pointed at Anna and Zach as the pilot opened the door and pushed out the raft.

Uncuff Zach. You have to uncuff Zach. You don't want anyone to find him cuffed in the plane.

She sat there in terror, thinking it wasn't going to work, even with both her and Zach giving the suggestion. But finally one of the thugs turned and unlocked the cuffs, while one of his buddies still held them at gunpoint.

The guy who'd freed Zach snatched up both sets of restraints before making for the door.

The killers scrambled out, the last one still holding her and Zach at gunpoint in the plane while they climbed into the raft and began to paddle away.

Anna started toward the door. Zach held her arm. *Wait.*

"But . . . we'll drown."

"We've got a good chance in the water. We don't have any chance if they shoot us."

Conceding the point, she stayed back from the door, watching the cabin slowly fill.

"Can you swim?" Zach asked urgently.

"Yes. I was on my high school swim team."

"Thank God."

He eyed her clothing. "Better take off your slacks and shoes. You can probably keep your shirt."

He pulled off his jeans and kicked away his shoes while

she did the same. He also threw his shirt on the floor, where it sloshed in the rising flood.

When she looked up, he was scanning the cabin. "The seat cushions should float."

"Okay."

He pulled one out and handed it to her. It had straps, and she slipped her arms through, hugging the cushion to her chest as she moved toward the door.

She watched Zach move about the cabin, opening compartments and snatching out items as though he had all the time in the world to pillage.

"Can I help?"

"Stay there."

When Zach joined her again, she breathed out a sigh of relief. He was holding a sack with straps and a seal across the top.

"Waterproof. I've got some supplies," he said as she eyed the bag. He had also thrust a knife into the webbing of the pack.

He looked out the door. "When we go into the water, kick away from the plane. In a direction away from the raft."

"Okay."

She grasped the edge of the door. The water was rising fast. When the opening was filled, would the plane be sucked down? Could they get out when it was under water?

She didn't know. But she could see that the raft was still pretty close to the plane, bobbing in the afternoon sunshine. She could also see that the men were having trouble controlling the light craft. They didn't seem to know how to paddle together. Probably they were all city boys who hadn't gotten much chance to enjoy water sports.

The killers had their own problems now, which gave her and Zach a better chance to get away.

When the raft drifted behind the plane, Zach took her arm. "Now. Go."

She slipped out the door, sputtering as she went under and came up again. The water was cold at first, and a salty wave slapped her in the face, but her body quickly became accustomed to the temperature. Holding on to the cushion as she kicked away from the sinking plane, she could hear Zach right behind her.

They had gotten about thirty feet from the plane when she heard a shout.

"Over there! Get them."

A shot hit the water, then another.

The thugs frantically maneuvered the craft, trying to get a better angle. When they did, she'd be a perfect target with her flotation device keeping her bobbing on the top of the water.

She had to get rid of the cushion. But when she tried to let go, her arm was tangled in the strap, and she struggled frantically to free it, while more bullets hit the water around them.

FAR away from the scene, Jordan and Lindsay clung together, trying to view the events.

They're in the water.

Where?

I don't know!

Frustration bubbled inside them as they fought to connect with the man and woman in trouble.

Dariens. Like us.

But all that water is making it hard to tune in on them.

We need to know where they are. Jordan tipped up his wife's chin and looked deep into her eyes. They were tackling a serious problem, yet the road to success might be reached through the garden of their own pleasure.

You think? she asked, a smile in her voice.

Uh-huh. Closer contact.

Since they'd bonded, they'd been working to increase

their psychic powers. And they'd found that Tantric intimacy was sometimes the key to success.

Jordan had read that the essence of Tantra was supposed to be the merging of their sexual energy with the energy of the universe. He'd never been into mysticism—until he'd connected mind to mind with Lindsay. But since their bonding, they'd explored some strange techniques and found that a Tantric union fired both their physical and mental energy systems.

Supposedly, it created a polarity charge that connected with the primordial energy from which everything arises in the universe . . . the totality of All.

He wasn't sure what that meant. He only knew that it seemed to work—if they could focus on the problem they needed to solve and not their own pleasure.

Lindsay reached for his hand, and they walked together to the bedroom, then stood beside the bed, rubbing their lips against each other's, stroking their hands over taut flesh, working buttons and zippers.

Lindsay pulled off her shirt. Jordan did the same, then reached around to unhook her bra. When he pulled her naked breasts against his chest, they both sighed with the pleasure of the contact.

Still wearing his shorts, he rubbed his hips against hers, deliberately keeping a layer of clothing between them to slow down the pace.

He felt her arousal building along with his, felt the delicious merging of his consciousness with Lindsay's.

She slipped her hands inside his shorts, massaging his buttocks as they swayed together, like two halves of one whole.

When she eased her upper body away so that he could caress her breasts, he teased her hardened nipples with his thumbs and fingers.

The intensity built. And when standing became too difficult for both of them, she slid his shorts down his legs, and he kicked them away. He lay down on the bed, gazing up at her, treating himself to a view of her beautiful body before she climbed onto the bed and straddled his hips. Raising up, she slowly sheathed his cock, smiling down at him as they joined.

Their bodies and their minds. Fully, deeply. Like no other lovers in the history of the world.

Still sitting, she allowed them both a few slow, languid strokes before leaning forward and straightening her legs so that she was lying on top of him, her body pressed to the length of his.

He clasped his hands around her back, holding her to him as they rolled to the side, still joined together.

She let him take over then, moving his hips just enough to keep the sexual tension simmering as they locked their minds into perfect harmony, then sent their thoughts outward, looking for Anna Ridgeway and the man who had been captive with her on the doomed airplane.

His name is Zach. I can't get the last name. She just calls him Zach.

Where are they?

I still don't know.

I see the water. Endless water. No—wait. There's a raft full of . . . Oh, Lord, the bad guys are shooting at them. And she can't get her arms out of that cushion so she can dive.

Can we help her?

I . . . don't know.

ZACH swam to Anna. Before he reached her, she somehow yanked the strap away and freed her arms. She would have shouted in relief if she hadn't been filling her lungs with air.

Flipping to her stomach, she dove downward, propelling herself with strong kicks and wondering how far a bullet could effectively penetrate under the water.

Sound seemed magnified in the liquid environment. She heard a slapping noise close by.

The men in the raft!

They sounded like they were on top of her, but when she looked up frantically, she saw nothing. The water must be making them seem closer.

Would one of them take off his clothes and dive in after them? Well, he'd get his gun wet if he did. Or would that matter? She didn't even know.

Through a school of small yellow and black fish, she saw Zach swimming toward her. He moved off to the left again, then looked around to make sure she was coming with him.

She followed him through another group of colorful fish, staying below the surface the way he did.

She tried to reach his mind with hers, but she couldn't do it. Maybe they'd used up their supply of psychic powers. Or maybe this kind of physical stress simply added too much interference.

As she pulled up beside him, she felt her lungs begin to burn. He was used to diving. She wasn't. And she knew she'd need air soon.

She tugged on his arm and pointed upward.

As she held his arm, she did pick up a message from him. *Just stick your face out, then go right down again.*

Okay.

Zach held back, waiting until she was close to the top. She grabbed a breath of air. When he surfaced, he heard gunshots again and went down. *Shit!* he cursed in her mind.

She knew they had to put distance between themselves and the raft. When Zach took off to the left, she followed, then stopped short when she saw gray shapes gliding through the water just ahead of them.

Sharks. Monster sharks. They were so close that they looked like they were ten feet long. Although maybe that was an exaggeration.

Sharks! she silently screamed. But Zach kept going—
right into danger. She hurried to catch him, reaching out
and tugging on his leg.
Stop!

CHAPTER
SIXTEEN

ZACH WHIRLED AROUND in the water, then pointed ahead of him toward the gray, circling shapes. *They won't hurt you.*

Oh, sure. She'd heard the stories of swimmers getting attacked by sharks. People losing limbs or even their lives.

She was sure he had gone crazy. Or maybe he was sending out vibes, warning the animals to stay away from them. Maybe that was one of his special powers.

He kept going, swimming into the midst of the predators before kicking toward the surface.

She supposed she was dead either way. Either the bad guys shot her, or the sharks ate her.

Wrong. Zach's voice rang in her head. *We'll be okay.*

He surfaced, grabbing a breath of air. She came up beside him, cringing as one of the sharks swam past so close that she could have reached out and slid her hand against the gray skin. But she kept her hand close to her body, just in case the monster was hungry.

She had to admit that Zach appeared to be right. Six or seven tiger-size sharks were swimming lazily around them, their beady eyes aware. But their tooth-filled mouths were closed. They seemed to propel themselves with their tails, swaying them indolently in the water.

Could the damn things smell her fear?

You're fine, Zach answered.

Looking to her right, she knew that several gray bodies partially hid her from the men in the raft as she took a quick gulp of air, then another.

Zach came up beside her. "The sharks were a lucky break for us."

She huffed out a breath. "I'll concede the point."

"Keep going," he whispered. "I'm betting those guys won't come near here."

Betting your life.

If you want to put it that way.

They dove again, this time not so deeply, and they kept swimming.

When Zach tugged on her arm and pointed upward, she surfaced again.

He looked back toward the raft. It was fifty yards away.

He raised his head, scanning the watery scene, then pointed toward his right. "I see the land we spotted from the plane."

"Can we swim there?"

"We have to. Unless somebody comes along and picks us up."

Not likely, she thought.

"Is it Grand Fernandino?"

"I don't know."

He stopped swimming and treaded water. She did the same.

"Will you be all right if I leave you?" he asked.

"What?" She hoped she hadn't shouted so loudly that she'd told the thugs where they were.

"I want to cut a hole in their raft."

Fear tightened her throat and she closed her fingers around Zach's arm. "You can't."

"Unless I do, they can follow us when the sharks swim away."

She wanted to protest. But she knew he was right. When the sharks left, the men in the raft might start paddling toward them.

"I'm going to circle around the back of the raft. You keep the thugs focused on the sharks. Try to make them keep scanning in this direction."

"What if they don't get the message?"

"Do your best."

Before she could protest, he dove, and she saw him stroking back in the direction from which they'd come. She wanted to scream at him to stop, but she kept her lips pressed together and floated near the surface, holding her head down and only coming up for breaths of air.

Keep looking for sharks. You're in danger from sharks, she broadcast. *Probably the man and the woman drowned. Probably the man and the woman drowned.*

It didn't help her to say that part. It only increased her worries about Zach. And another fear gripped her. How was he going to find her again?

She waited there for centuries, scanning the water for blood, for signs of him or for anything she hadn't seen before. But she could see only the endless turquoise water, the sharks, and the raft.

Zach. Zach. I'm over here. Zach.

Was she getting through? She had no way of knowing.

Time dragged by, and when he finally surfaced beside her, she clasped him to her.

"Did you hear me?" she gasped.

"Faintly. And I knew you were between me and that land mass we spotted."

Looking back the way he'd come, she could see the raft still bobbing in the water. "What did you do?"

"I came up under them and cut a couple of slits in the bottom. If they don't sink, bailing out will keep them busy."

"Yes."

They started off again, stroking toward land. Behind them, she heard a loud curse ring out across the open water.

"I guess they found out they're going down," Zach muttered.

"Will they drown?"

"Do you care?" he asked.

She was horrified to think that she really didn't. Those men had tried to kill her and Zach. And they deserved whatever happened to them.

"They're afraid of the sharks," Zach said, a sneer in his voice. "A lucky break for us. Sharks don't go after swimmers."

She huffed out a breath. "What about all those people who lose an arm or a leg?"

"The shark made a mistake."

She sputtered a reply. "Oh, sure."

"I mean, sharks don't intend to attack people. But if they mistake an arm or a leg for something else, they might bite."

She shook her hair back. "That's kind of inconvenient."

"Yeah. But you're more likely to get killed by lightning than to get attacked by a shark. In California, there were twenty-eight fatal lightning strikes between 1959 and 2005. And during the same period, there were five fatal shark attacks."

She tipped her head to the side. "You've got those statistics at your fingertips?"

"Yeah. Because I take people out diving all the time. People who are worried about sharks. So I know about them. And I know how to avoid getting attacked. Swimming at twilight when the creatures can't see well is one of the most dangerous times for attacks."

He lifted his head and looked toward the receding raft. "We can't stay here having a shark safety lecture."

"Right."

"Where are we?"

"Closer to land."

She stared toward the dark bulk in the distance. It was still awfully far away. "I don't know if I can make it."

"I thought you were a swimming champion."

"It's been a long time."

"It's like riding a bike."

"You can't drown on a bike."

"You're not going to drown. Come on." He struck off toward the land. Grand Fernandino, she hoped.

She tried to keep pace with him, but he was a strong swimmer, and she felt herself falling behind.

He turned around and came back to her, watching her breathe hard. "Relax."

She rested in the water, and he gathered her in his arms. She let her head drop to his shoulder, feeling peaceful—and so close to him that it made her heart squeeze.

Like two halves of one whole, he whispered in her mind.

Yes.

How did I survive during the years without you? he asked, his inner voice soft.

With difficulty, she answered, because she knew it was the truth. For both of them.

Lie on your back and rest.

Okay.

She turned over and lay staring up at the tropical blue sky, watching small clouds drift by. They were moving fast—faster than she could swim.

"I was thinking . . . about how we met. I mean before."

"And?"

"I was in Montana once . . ."

"Oh yeah?"

"A long time ago. When I was five, I think. Dad was going to see a copper mine he wanted to invest in, and he took me and Mom along . . ."

Zach moved to touch her shoulder, and she continued without speaking.

I was really bored. And then I started talking to . . . a boy. I asked him if he wanted to play Sesame Street, and he said yes.

She felt him drag in a quick breath.

Sesame Street. I remember! I was being punished for leaving my bike in the driveway . . . only Craig had done it! I was in my room . . . and a girl asked me if I wanted to play. I thought I made her up. But it was you!

Yes! I think that's right.

And we didn't lose the connection until I got sick.

They marveled at the shared memory.

We played Batman and Catwoman.

And . . . Bonanza.

She wanted to drift there, remembering, but Zach broke the spell.

"We have to get to land—before twilight."

She felt a shiver go through her, remembering the information about sharks that he'd told her a little while ago. So she flipped over and started moving through the water again. But she soon became winded.

Zach treaded water beside her. "You're worn out." His voice was tender as he reached for her.

For a moment, he simply held on to her, and she clung to him. She could feel the bond between them like a warm background buzz.

I'll take care of you.

I'm used to being independent.

We both are.

Alone for a long time—until we found each other again.

Her heart squeezed. *Too bad we didn't both end up on Grand Fernandino before this.*

He hooked his arm over her chest in a hold that she recognized from long-ago lifesaving training. With her firmly in tow, he started swimming again.

"This is too hard for you. You can't get yourself to land and tow me, too."

His voice turned gritty. "What do you think I'm going to do? Leave you here?"

"No," she whispered, looking toward the bag he'd tied around his waist. "But maybe you should get rid of the other stuff you're dragging."

"No. We may need it."

"Okay." She closed her eyes and let him pull her through the water, wondering how much longer he could keep it up.

Who's Sanford? she asked him.

The guy who hired me to find his brother's boat, the Blue Heron. *From the way Bill answered, I'm sure they're not connected.*

Wild Bill, that's what he calls himself. I picked that up from him. He was the man following me in Denver, but I sensed it's nothing personal with him.

Then what?

Somebody hired him to . . . follow me. Then close in . . . for the kill. She heard his mental curse. *And you got dragged into it.*

No! We're in this together. Whatever it is.

IT was like drifting on the water with Anna and Zach. On a wide blue ocean. Jordan moved his hips, maintaining his erection and the arousal simmering between himself and Lindsay.

Not the ocean, I think. What I said before—the Caribbean.

He's a good swimmer, Lindsay replied. *Wait. Something's changed. They've made it to land.*

Where?

He felt Lindsay mentally shake her head.

I don't know.

At least they're safe.

I wish we knew for sure.

We should stay with them.

But Jordan knew that he had reached the end of his ability to drift on the currents of arousal. They were new at this type of sexual encounter, and the pressure for release had finally built to a level he could no longer ignore.

Don't, Lindsay warned, then gave up the protest as his hips began to move more urgently.

Soon they were focused only on one another, the need for climax so intense that they gave themselves up to the pleasure of each other—body, mind, and soul.

WHEN Zach let go of Anna, she put her feet down in sand, then followed him onto a brilliant white beach. He moved from the sand to the vegetation beyond and sat down heavily, breathing hard.

"Thank you," she whispered, joining him on the grass and rolling toward him, pressing her body against his in the most basic of gestures.

Heat flared, fired by the connection between them—and the knowledge that they'd made it to dry land after their ordeal.

They rocked together, and she felt arousal swamp her. They were alive and safe. And together.

His arms slackened around her. Questioningly, she raised her head and saw the fatigue etched on his face.

I'm too tired to be any good to you, he murmured into her mind.

Of course. I wasn't thinking. You'd be too tired for sex. I mean . . .

Damn, every thought that popped into her head winged its way straight to him. They didn't just have to be careful what they said around each other, they had to start with their thoughts.

He managed a laugh. "No insult taken. I know what you meant."

"I'm rested. You're not, because you've been doing all the work."

"I'll recover."

He lay back, closing his eyes, breathing evenly.

And she relaxed beside him, knowing they would make love soon. For now, she was glad the cool wind helped dampen some of the fire playing over her skin.

RAOUL knelt before the altar, asking for Ibena's help. She had been with him like a soul mate on this journey. And he thanked her for that. Or was he being too full of himself when he needed her help now—more desperately than ever? Was that the problem?

"The plane went down, and I've lost her. But I can feel her spirit. I know she's not dead. Help me find her again, and I will honor you all my days. I promise on my life."

He had already dedicated another chicken to the ceremony. A lot of chickens. He'd have to replenish his supply.

Then he brought his mind back to his urgent need. For information. For more than information.

Anna—his Anna—was with another man.

Blood fire!

He must sever that connection and bring her body and soul into his own keeping.

"Help me find her. Help me kill him," he murmured.

WHEN Zach sat up again, Anna asked, "Where are we?"

"I don't know. But I'll find out."

He untied the bag from around his waist and set it on the grass at the edge of the beach, then looked up at the palm trees around him. He picked one that was leaning over more than the others, then started toward the top, using his hands and bare feet to propel himself upward.

Apparently he'd done it before, because he went up the tree almost as fast as a monkey. And that was after a long swim through the Caribbean.

She might have laughed at his performance, but the situation was much too serious.

At the top of the tree, he found a secure position, then held on with one hand, shading his eyes with the other as he looked in all directions.

Anna watched him anxiously. "What do you see?"

"Just a minute."

When he came down, his expression was grim.

"What?"

"As far as I can tell, this isn't Grand Fernandino. It's a small island in the middle of nowhere."

CHAPTER
SEVENTEEN

THE MOMENT ZACH spoke, he wished he'd thought of a better way to put it. *Way to go, telling her we're stranded in the middle of nowhere.*

"It's the truth," she answered. "I need to know the truth."

"Shit."

This time, you're the one who's upset about too much togetherness?

He couldn't deny it, not when she could read his thoughts. "I'll learn to deal with that," he muttered. "So will you."

She switched back to the previous topic. "If we're stranded in the middle of the Caribbean, what are we going to do?"

He looked toward the horizon. They still had a few hours of daylight left. But not many.

"Find shelter."

"Like where?

"Somebody lives here. Or they used to. From the tree-top, I saw a house back that way." He pointed toward a spot that was hidden by vegetation.

She eyed the jungle. "How are we going to find it?"

"I think we can walk along the beach. Most people don't build too far from the water."

He picked up the bag of stuff he'd managed to liberate from the plane, glad that he hadn't abandoned the supplies in the water. The long swim had made him hungry. Reaching inside the bag, he sorted through the contents and pulled out two protein bars.

"We should eat something."

She accepted a bar from him, and they munched the food slowly as they walked along the hard-packed sand.

When he slung the bag over his right shoulder, Anna came up on the left and clasped his hand so that he felt the undercurrent of communication between them. But they were both tired, and it was easier to speak in words.

"First we find shelter. Then we can make love." It felt good to say the words. Then he laughed.

"What?"

"I was thinking—be careful what you wish for. I wanted to be alone with you. And here we are."

"We'll worry about . . . the details later. Maybe we can lash together a raft and get off the island."

"Sure."

Anna let her shoulder rub against his, the skin-to-skin contact making his shoulder tingle.

"Don't distract me," he murmured.

"From what?"

"Checking out the area."

She moved away a little, and they kept walking up the beach, staying on the hard-packed sand where it was easier to walk.

Beyond the beach was a stretch of wild grass, then a tangle of vegetation.

They came to a place where water tumbled down rocks, forming a small waterfall before it flowed across the sand and into the sea.

"That's a relief," he said.

"What?"

"Fresh water."

She hadn't even thought about the fact that they might not have anything to drink.

"On a lot of islands, people have to collect rainwater," he added.

"I guess I've always taken civilization for granted."

He eyed the stream, then pulled at his shorts. "We're still wet. We might as well wash the salt water off."

"Okay."

He put down his bag of booty and pulled off his remaining clothing—his shorts.

He was naked and magnificent, and she angled slightly away, determined not to let herself get turned on again until they were somewhere where they could do something about it.

When he stepped under the water, he grimaced.

"Cold?" she called out.

"Yeah. But it feels good."

The waterfall was small, and she let him finish washing. When he got out, she took off her shirt, bra, and panties, then stepped under, wincing at the cold. But he was right. It did feel good to wash the salt out of her hair and off her body.

When she climbed out, Zach offered her a thin towel. "From the emergency pack. See, it's coming in handy already."

She used the towel, then pulled on her damp clothing again. "Have you been stranded before?"

"Once my engines cut out, and I spent a few days on an uninhabited island. But I had a radio, and I could call for help."

Ahead of them was a dock with gray, aging boards jutting out into the water. Looking beyond it, she saw a house in the distance.

"If someone's home, they're not expecting visitors. And they could be armed," he warned.

"Right."

They walked beside the dock, heading into the jungle. The closer they got to the house, the more it looked like the place had been abandoned. At one time the grounds had been landscaped with ornamental trees and shrubs and flowering plants. Now the tropical vegetation was hugging the foundation—and in some cases growing close to the second story.

They stepped onto a wide patio, where weeds grew between decorative tiles.

"This is quite a place."

"Well, it was."

Sliding glass doors ran along the side of the house, and one of them was broken by a tree limb that had fallen through it. But there was no glass on the ground.

Zach peered at the patio and inside to the tile floor. "It looks like somebody cleaned up."

She shaded her eyes with her hand as she looked upward. The rest of the tree was leaning against the house and looked like it had broken through the roof.

"Probably hurricane damage," Zach said as he drew his knife.

"Are you expecting trouble?" she whispered.

"I'm trying to be prepared. Stay behind me."

FOR Raoul, the energy to stay with Anna was a terrible drain on his system. But he forced himself to do it.

As he knelt with his eyes closed, an image formed behind his closed lids. He saw a large white house, stark and modern, with the jungle closing in around it.

Was it real? Or was he making it up?

He squeezed his hands into fists, focusing his mind on

the scene, and he saw Anna and the man with sun-streaked hair standing on a weedy patio.

His image of Anna was clear, because his main connection was to her. The man's features were still blurry.

Anna looked bedraggled. But, thank the saints, she seemed to be all right otherwise.

The man stepped up to a sliding door, a door with the glass missing. Then he disappeared from the scene.

ANNA followed Zach into a large, empty room with a sizeable fireplace and a few pieces of furniture pushed forlornly against the walls. The pieces were hefty. A dining table. A buffet. An entertainment unit.

Big sheets of fabric covered something at one side of the room. When she pulled up a corner of the covering, she saw a wide sectional sofa.

"Why did they leave this stuff?" Anna asked.

"They probably needed a bigger boat to remove the oversized pieces."

Down the hall was a spacious kitchen with granite countertops and a large eating area.

Behind a set of double doors was a pantry, where rows of cans still sat on the shelves.

"We do have some food."

"If you want soup," she answered.

"Better than sea cucumber."

She grimaced. "That's supposed to be disgusting. You've eaten it?"

"Don't ask."

He stepped into a utility room and gestured toward some cases of bottled water, then began opening drawers.

"Look at this."

She hurried to join him and found what amounted to a

treasure. Someone had stuffed a bunch of shirts and shorts inside. Another drawer held tablecloths.

He pulled one of the shirts out, held it up, and sniffed the fabric. It smelled clean.

"Nice of someone to leave these for us."

"Yes."

He handed Anna some navy shorts and a long-sleeved shirt of white fabric, made for the tropical climate. She stripped off her wet shirt, bra, and panties and quickly pulled on the dry garment, looking around as she did.

"What?"

"I feel like someone's watching us."

He followed her gaze. "You're just nervous."

"I guess," she said, still sensing an unwanted gaze on her. The tails of the shirt hung almost to her knees, and the sleeves were much too long, so she rolled them up.

Zach pulled out another shirt and buttoned it up. Then he climbed into shorts that were a size too big for him.

"It's nice to be wearing something that isn't damp," he commented.

"Yes."

He dumped out the emergency pack onto the kitchen counter. "We've got soap, toothpaste and toothbrushes, toilet paper, a flashlight—all the comforts of home."

They went back to the large, open room in the center of the house, and he stared up at the long stairway and the balcony that overlooked the first level. The ceiling was extra high, making the second floor a story and a half above the first floor.

●

RAOUL was still in the shed behind his art gallery, kneeling before the altar, and his knees were red and sore. But he held the position on the wooden platform because he was thinking that the pain would be another offering to Ibena.

He'd watched with pleasure as Anna had stripped off

her clothing. Her breasts were lovely. Her hips a little narrow for child bearing. But if she needed a cesarean to bear his children, that would be no problem in the island hospital. Or did he want to share her with a child? He'd have to think about that.

Maybe she felt his presence, because she'd quickly pulled on the shirt and a pair of shorts.

Then she and the man continued looking around the abandoned house.

He was hoping that their exploration would give him an opportunity. He didn't know what it was yet, but he was open to any possibility Ibena offered.

Where was the house? Somewhere on Grand Fernandino? If so, it wasn't anywhere near Palmiro, or near the area where he'd grown up, because he would surely recognize it.

It could be on a smaller island. Nearby, he hoped.

Maybe if he described the place, someone would recognize the property.

He followed Anna and the devil man as they walked around the empty building. It looked forlorn.

Was it haunted?

Raoul shivered. He didn't like to think of Anna in a haunted house.

When the man stopped at the bottom of the stairs, Raoul felt a sudden bolt of awareness—knowing this was the sign from the goddess that he had been waiting for.

From far away, he sent his consciousness upward, to the second story, where the roof had leaked onto the wooden floor. And he knew then that Ibena was going to give him a chance to change the balance of power in his struggle with his rival.

ZACH stepped back and looked toward the balcony. Then he walked to the stairs again. "Wait here."

Anna looked around, then scuffed her foot against the floor. "I feel . . . something."

"What?"

"I don't know." She shivered. "Something watching us."

"Again."

"Yes."

"There's someone on the island?"

"I don't think so." She swallowed hard. "I think whoever it is can see from a long distance away."

He stared at her brow creased with worry, wishing he could reassure her. But what could he say?

"Right. What can you say? I'm just nervous."

He didn't like the way she'd given in to him. Maybe she was right. Maybe he should listen. But he was sure nobody was here. And if the watcher was far away, what could he do?

When he spoke, he kept his voice low and calm. "I want to see what's upstairs."

He drew the knife and climbed to the second level, holding tight to the railing and testing the steps as he went, then he paused at the top, looking over the railing at Anna. She had her hands clasped together so tightly that he could see her knuckles had whitened.

"So far so good."

He turned back toward the hall and took a couple of steps forward, just as a cyclone erupted in one of the bedrooms. He slammed back against the wall, raising his hand to shield his face. The whirring in the air resolved itself into a loud, flapping sound that made him press against the wall as a white apparition dived at him.

"What the hell?"

Seconds passed before his brain caught up with his eyes and he saw that the flapping things were egrets. Another one flew directly toward him. Two more shot past, one squawking and dropping white feathers as it hit the banister. Two more headed for a hole in the roof.

From below, he heard Anna gasp as the birds circled madly around the open area, still squawking, frightened and determined to get out of the house—if they could figure out where to find the window.

"Watch out," he shouted.

When he looked over the railing, he saw she had already ducked and covered her head with her arms.

She peered out, watching the egrets wheel in the small space. One found the broken sliding glass door and sailed into the open air. A second followed. But the third was apparently too stupid to live.

It kept flapping around the room, protesting loudly as it clipped walls and windows.

Finally, by some miracle, it found the broken door and zoomed through

"Jesus!" Zach stared after the retreating shape. "That was certainly exciting. Is that what you were worried about?"

"I don't know."

"Are you okay?"

"Yes."

Turning, he looked up at the ceiling, seeing the sky showing through a massive break in the roof where some of the birds had escaped.

"I wonder what else is in here," Anna called.

He nodded, skirting the hole in the ceiling as he started down the hallway. "We'd better check."

He was still walking cautiously. But not cautiously enough. He had covered only a few yards when he heard a tremendous cracking sound as the floorboards gave way beneath his feet.

CHAPTER
EIGHTEEN

ZACH'S KNIFE CLATTERED to the floor as he grabbed frantically for the solid edge of the hallway.

The surface crumbled away under his fingers, turning to powder in his grasp.

Then, finally, he found solid purchase.

Below him, in his head and in his ears, he heard someone screaming. It was Anna.

"I'm okay," he shouted, with his legs dangling through the hole that had opened up under his weight.

He couldn't look down, but he judged that his heels were still twelve feet above the tile floor below. A long enough drop to break a leg or sprain an ankle, if he was unlucky.

Under the circumstances, a break would be a disaster. And he had the eerie feeling that, if he *did* fall, the worst would happen.

Struggling to breathe slowly and evenly, he considered his options. Maybe he could pull himself up. Or if not, maybe he could swing his body enough to contact the flooring that was still solid.

He swung his legs, trying to lever himself up and out of the hole. As soon as he shifted his weight, more of the floor gave way.

"Shit!"

"Zach!"

He stopped moving, hoping that if he held still, the rest of the floor would stop breaking away.

With difficulty, he repressed another curse so as not to alarm Anna. But he suspected she heard him inside her head.

He should have listened to her. She'd been using her psychic talent for years, and in this situation, she'd picked up on something bad. But he'd charged up the stairs anyway, and now he was in trouble.

Her voice shot up from below. "What can I do?"

Not sure, he answered in his head, because he could feel the floor subtly shifting, and he didn't want to take the chance of doing anything—even talking—that would send him hurtling downward. *Move out of the way so I don't fall on you.*

"You won't fall!" she said, but he knew that was wishful thinking.

Her next words made his gut twist with fear.

"If I come up there, do you think I can pull you up?"

"Stay downstairs!"

As he bellowed the order, the floor vibrated.

More calmly, he added, *We don't want to add any weight on the floor up here.*

"You're right." Had she spoken aloud or in his head? He wasn't sure. Maybe both.

He might have examined the odd sensation if more of the floor hadn't crumbled. Trying to keep his motions smooth, he reached out to shore himself up, wondering how long he could hang there. His arms were strong from working on the boat, but he couldn't keep this up all day. Especially after his long swim.

Below him, he could hear Anna's footsteps clattering across the floor.

"Hold on. Just hold on."

Easier said than done.

Too bad his psychic talents didn't extend to controlling the physical world. Then he could float himself down from the second floor without risking injury.

It seemed like Anna was gone for years, and he felt his fingers starting to go numb. In a few minutes, he wouldn't have a choice about dropping to the level below.

He heard something heavy scraping across the floor, but he couldn't look around to see what it was. Along with the scraping came the sound of Anna's heavy breathing, as though she were working at some task far beyond her physical strength.

What are you doing?

"Pushing the dining room table under you."

He remembered it. A solid slab of wood that would surely hold his weight.

Another piece of the floor broke loose, and he shifted his hold again, but this time the surface gave way under the fingers of his left hand. He found himself dangling by his right hand.

The second side of the hole broke off, and he hurtled downward. But he fell only a few feet before landing on a hard surface.

The table.

The extra three feet made all the difference. He bent his knees, landing on his feet first, then dropping to his butt, breathing hard.

Anna rushed around the table and reached for him.

"Are you all right?" she asked, her voice urgent.

He flexed his limbs. "Yeah. Thanks to you."

"I was afraid you were going to break your leg."

"Me, too," he answered as he moved to the edge of the table, spreading his thighs so he could pull her close. She

walked into his embrace, clinging to him, and he stroked
her back, whispering reassurances.

He cupped her head to his shoulder, and he turned his
face so he could slide his lips against the tender line where
her cheek met her hair.

Thank God you're okay.

I'm fine, he repeated, then angled his head and brought
his lips to hers.

She sank into the caress as his mouth ravaged hers, and
she returned the kiss with equal fervor.

Her body fit against his so perfectly. And the pressure of
her breasts against his chest was heavenly.

He longed to make love with her. But it was getting dark,
and they had be sure they were secure in the house before
they could focus on each other.

Still, he couldn't deny himself a little more closeness.
And as her mouth opened and he stroked his tongue against
hers, he felt desperation welling inside her.

"What?"

*He's trying to . . . get into my head. Trying to pull me
away from you.*

Jesus!

"But I belong to you. Only to you," she gasped.

"Yes." Even as he answered, he felt a little worm of
doubt trying to work its way into the encounter.

"Who is he?"

I don't know! Her denial rang inside his mind as she
brought her mouth back to his, greedy and anxious at the
same time.

I can't lose you. You're too important to me.

Thank God. Her breath hitched.

You won't lose me.

She clung to him, her body plastered to his as he stroked
his hands up and down her back.

Then, from one moment to the next, the whole context
changed. His head spun. And the room around him seemed

to blur, replaced by another scene. It was almost like the first time he'd met her—not in person, but on that windswept plain outside the real world.

Only he sensed this wasn't outside the world. It was real. And very strange.

He saw a room that was decorated like a shrine, but like no shrine he had ever seen. The main colors were gold, coral, and red, with a strange collection of objects set around the walls and in front of a wooden altar.

He saw fans, peacock feathers, and a fountain where a stream of water shot from a turtle's mouth into a shell-shaped basin. The animal's head looked a lot like a penis.

All that registered only at the corners of his vision, because he was still focused on Anna.

Behind her he saw a high wooden altar, dedicated to a goddess called Ibena. Somehow he knew that. And knew she was one of the Blessed Ones. Like Pagor. But different. Not the god of war. The goddess of love and sensuality.

God, no! Anna screamed the protest inside his head.

As she cried out in denial, the gold, coral, and red colors faded. The strange room vanished, and Zach was left with Anna, in the abandoned house. The two of them alone.

Or were they?

He looked wildly around, seeing no one else.

"Zach, Zach."

"What happened?"

I don't know! I don't know, she sobbed out. *But he dragged me to a shrine where he was worshipping Ibena.*

Yes. I saw it, too.

Oh, God. She whimpered, and he held her to him, knowing that they were both in danger. More danger than he had thought possible.

Everything had changed when they first made love. Not just inside his head. The world around him was brighter, a kind of supercharged reality. All his senses were sharper.

Yet at the same time, he knew it wasn't happening fast

enough. The understanding between them was still new. Unless the connection went deeper, he could still lose her. Lose her to another man desperate to take her away.

As he contemplated that horrible possibility, he knew she had followed his thoughts.

"No," she sobbed out. "We belong together. Us. Anna and Zach. Not *him*."

ANNA hitched in a breath and let it out slowly, clinging to Zach.

He was with her in a way that nobody had ever been with her. Well, not since her imaginary friend, long ago. But she hadn't known that he was real then. And she had never met him. Never seen him in person.

Yet nobody else had ever been so close to her. Not her parents, or anyone who had ever been her friend. This was unique. And so real that it made her insides ache.

She simply wanted to be left alone with Zach to savor the experience. But almost as soon as she'd found him, outside forces had leaped in, struggling to tear them apart.

Not just the guy who worshipped Ibena.

The man who had hired Wild Bill to follow her—and kill her.

She closed her eyes for a moment, then opened them so she could meet Zach's eyes.

We got away from the thugs. Now we have to fight the psychic guy.

She could have said it aloud. Instead she deliberately chose to communicate mind to mind—to emphasize what they had found together. She still didn't know how or why it had happened between them, but now the connection was as much a part of her as the need to breathe.

She looked around the room.

"Whatever happened, we're alone here. I mean physically."

"Yeah. And we'd better get ready for the night."

Looking toward the window wall, she saw that the sun had been sinking, and the room was dark and shadowy.

She longed to stay in Zach's comforting embrace. Instead she forced herself to take a step away. Glancing toward the sofa, she made her voice brisk. "I guess this is as good a place as any to camp out. I can turn the cushions over, in case they're dusty. And get some of those tablecloths for sheets."

"Good idea. And I saw some dead wood outside. I'm going to get some so we can build a fire. That will give us light. And we can cook some of the soup."

He eased off the table, testing his legs to make sure they were steady.

As she watched him, she made an effort to guard her thoughts. She didn't want Zach to go out and leave her alone in the darkening house, but she didn't want him to know she was a chicken.

He picked that up, anyway.

"It's okay to be . . . jittery," he told her, stroking his hand over her arm.

"Am I that open to you?"

"When your emotions are involved," he answered.

He retrieved the flashlight from the kitchen, then walked to the sliding glass door and disappeared into the vegetation. And she knew he wanted to be alone with his own thoughts. Or as alone as he could be, under the circumstances.

Wishing she had a broom to clean up, she detoured around the debris on the floor and carefully pulled the cover from one of the sofas. At least there didn't seem to be much dust, she thought as she folded the covering and did the same for the other section of the sofa, which was backless. By turning it around and pushing it against the first one, she was able to make a wide bed. Very palatial for a couple camping out.

When she had finished, the room was almost dark, and she could hear the sounds of the night starting up. Insects, and other noises she couldn't identify.

A sudden thought struck her. *Good Lord!* She was supposed to be at the Sugar Cane Club right now, getting ready for her act.

She struggled to repress a hysterical laugh as she pictured Bertrand's panic. This morning he'd asked her to do an extra show. Now she wasn't going to be doing *any* shows.

A loud crack made her jump, but then she realized it was probably Zach out in the jungle breaking up wood for the fireplace.

Reaching for him with her mind, she came up blank.

The absolute silence brought a dart of panic—until she ordered herself to calm down. When they weren't touching, or near each other, she had trouble contacting him. His mind was closed to her now. But they'd fix that soon.

And being alone now was an opportunity. It gave her a private moment to think about what had happened after he'd fallen onto the table.

If she were honest, she'd admit that she wanted the episode to just go away. She didn't want to be dragged against her will into some weird looking shrine. But that wasn't an option, because denial was foolhardy.

She and Zach had been sucked into another place. Twice now. And she was pretty sure the same man had done it both times.

The first time had been an accident. He'd been looking for her and had found her and Zach, because they were already connected to each other—from that long-ago experience as children. She and Zach were the ones who *belonged* together.

But the man wanted to split them apart. That was dangerous to her. And even more dangerous for Zach.

CHAPTER
NINETEEN

ANNA FORCED DOWN a swell of panic.

The man wasn't here on this island. She thought he was probably on Grand Fernandino.

The distance was reassuring. Until she realized that if he had reached out to her from the larger island, then his mental powers were strong.

Wrapping her arms around her shoulders, she strained to see into the darkness beyond the window. She couldn't even see the flashlight beam. And as she stared into the shadows, she had to press her lips together to keep from calling Zach back into the house. He had things to do out there, and he would come back when he could.

Briskly she strode down the hall to the utility room and pulled out the tablecloths Zach had found. Then she got several cans from the pantry, trying to read the labels.

Of course, no matter what they contained, she had no idea how to open the cans—or how they were going to cook anything without pots and pans.

She was getting two bottles of water when a sound in the doorway made her whirl.

"Oh!"

"Sorry," Zach answered as he stepped into the darkened kitchen and brushed off his hands on his shirttails.

"I'm a little jumpy."

"We both are." He picked up one of the cans and shined the light on it.

"Lentil soup."

"That's a strange thing to have on a tropical island."

"I guess you can bring anything you want here."

He opened a drawer, fumbled inside, and pulled out a Swiss Army knife. "I saw this earlier. We can use it to open the can."

Taking it from her hand, he used the opener blade to puncture the top, then saw partway around the flat surface. After doing the same with a can of beef and vegetable soup, he folded back the sharp edges to make a smooth surface.

"What about pots?"

"That's a luxury we don't have. But I think we can work around it."

He inspected the opened cans to make sure he'd provided a safe edge that wouldn't cut their mouths. "Not very aesthetic, but it will do."

"I get the feeling I'm dealing with an expert."

"I've been stranded in the mountains at home. In a snowstorm. Me and Patrick, one of the guys who'd been on the ranch since before I was born. He'd been snowed in more than once, and he taught me some important survival skills."

"Lucky you were with him."

"Yeah."

"How long were you there?"

"Almost a week."

"Ouch."

"My dad kept the line cabins well supplied."

"How did you get out?"

"Some of the hands came in on snowshoes."

She knew he was deliberately keeping the conversation

on the surface. She followed his lead, because they both needed a little time to deal with their emotions. And she was also thinking about something that had happened in town—trying to figure out if it was connected to what was happening to them. She'd been too busy to focus on it. But now it tugged at her.

Zach stripped the labels off the cans, then offered her one. She was careful not to touch him as she strove to keep her thoughts to herself.

He led her back to the great room, where a fire was burning cheerfully.

"I was thinking we'd have to heat the cans, so I have some improvised cooking implements here. Green wood." Picking up a bent branch, he fitted the can he was holding into the rounded crook, then squeezed the supple wood around the can. "We can warm it a little. But not too much, or the metal will be too hot to drink out of."

"And we don't need it very hot—not in this climate."

"Right." He looked down into his soup. "I see I've got the lentil and you've got the beef and vegetable. We can trade them back and forth, unless you have a strong preference."

"Trading is good."

He sat down on the raised hearth and held his can over the fire, just above the flames, and she did the same.

After a few minutes, he pulled the can out and tested the edge with his finger, then took a sip.

"How is it?"

"Not bad. And warm enough."

She did as he had, sipping at her soup right from the can, as she thought about what she wanted to say. Glancing up at him, she wondered if he was picking up her mood.

"Hard to believe we started out the morning in Grand Fernandino," he remarked.

She nodded, then took a drink of water before asking one of the questions that had been chasing around in her mind. "Do you have any idea how far away we are?"

"Sorry. I've never worked a job out of G.F. before, so I don't know a lot about this corner of the Caribbean."

"You said you were out looking for a shipwreck. Did you see any islands on the way?"

"No."

"How far did you get from shore?"

"About fifty miles, but we could be in an entirely different direction."

"Can't you tell where we are—by using the stars or something?"

He laughed. "Approximately. But not within such a small area. And I went out diving during the day. I didn't get a look at the stars."

"Right."

He was silent for several moments, drinking from his water bottle, then said, "Want to trade soups?"

"Okay."

This time, when they exchanged cans, he brushed his finger against hers, and she felt a small tingle of sensation. "What did you want to tell me?" he asked.

"It's obvious?"

"There's something spinning around in your mind. I can't tell what it is. But I know it's something you don't like."

"Yeah." She swallowed and kept her gaze locked on him. "You and I . . . were compelled to touch each other."

His voice turned sharp. "Compelled? You mean by some outside force?"

"No!" she answered quickly, resisting the urge to lay her hand on his so he'd know exactly what was in her mind. Already, she was changing her way of thinking. There would be no misunderstanding if they spoke mind to mind, but she wanted to do it the old-fashioned way because that gave her some feeling of contol.

"It's something we wanted," she said, making an effort to speak more calmly. "Because we recognized each other. From before. Or maybe not. Maybe it would have happened

if we'd never heard of each other. Because there's a link between us."

"Why?"

"That's the part I can't figure out. But what if someone
knows that if people like us link up, we develop special
powers? And he doesn't want it to happen. So he's sending
agents looking for us and trying to make sure we . . . don't
get together."

"That's a pretty gigantic leap."

"I know. But it fits. If you throw Wild Bill into the mix.
I mean what did I do to him? I don't think he was stalking
me because it was anything personal. Otherwise, he would
have killed you right away and hustled me off."

"Or you could have pissed off someone with your act."

"I never do that. If it's something bad, I don't say it."

"But someone could be afraid you *know* something."

"Then why did he wait so long?"

He shrugged. "Okay. Let's work with your theory."

"I know it sounds far-fetched. But I must have . . .
tapped into it on a subconscious level. That's why I thought
it was so important that Bill not know we'd made love."

Zach sat with his hands clasped around the can of soup.
He looked like he wanted to put the can down and move to
her side, but he stayed where he was.

"We got away," she whispered.

"But not by ourselves. Somebody helped us."

She nodded.

"Who?"

"Well, the Vadiana guy. But not just him. A man and a
woman. And that bolsters my theory. I think they're like us.
And they're using . . . extrasensory abilities to look for the
others."

"You assume there are others?"

"If you go back to the theory that Bill is supposed to kill
people like us."

He nodded. "What about the man and the woman?"

"They have more power than we do—because they strengthened the bond between them. Which means they met . . . some time earlier."

"Or they started out with more power," he said. "We don't know which."

She conceded the point with a small nod before adding, "*They* want to help. The Vadiana guy wants to push you out of the scene and take over."

Zach made an angry sound. "He's poking his nose in where it doesn't belong."

She kept her hand cupped around the can of soup. "We have to get him out of our lives," she said.

"How?"

"By fortifying the bond between us. If we can get stronger, we can . . ."

He leaned forward. "What?"

She made a frustrated gesture. "Defeat him. But I won't know exactly what that means until we're stronger. Unfortunately, he's got an advantage. He's been practicing his psi talents for years."

"You've been doing your nightclub act for years!" He set down his soup and leaned back, grasping his knee with his hands. "You have more experience with psychic phenomena than I do."

"Unless you count the imaginary friend part of the equation."

"That probably came from you—not me."

"Don't sell yourself short. Maybe you were the one who reached out."

He shrugged. "Were you always able to touch objects that belonged to someone else and pick up their memories?"

"I think so. But not all psychic phenomena involve touch," she answered quickly. "There's stuff like . . . I don't know." She scrambled for the name of a talent and came up with, "Talking to the dead."

"Do you believe in that?"

"It's as likely as anything else. Or what about people who can see the future?"

"You never see the future?"

"Only the past." She paused. "There are also people who dream about something and it turns out to be real." She swallowed. "Or moving objects with your mind."

"That would be a neat trick." He gave her a long look. "Then there's seeing a scene when you're not there. That's what the guy who watches us does. And he's made us see his environment."

She shivered. "I guess so."

"And I think he figured out the floor upstairs was rotten—and helped weaken it."

Her head jerked up. "You think he can do that?"

He shrugged. "Maybe."

She winced.

When he was silent, she went on quickly, before she lost her nerve. "I think I know who he is. The guy who tried to kill you—or break your legs when you fell."

CHAPTER
TWENTY

IN THE FLICKERING firelight, she watched Zach's face take on a terrible urgency. "You *know* him?"

"That's not what I meant! I don't *know* him. But I think I've met him."

His voice turned gritty. "Who? When?"

"A man from Palmiro. A man who touched me—out on the street."

As she spoke, Anna struggled to bring the morning into focus. It seemed like a million years ago, yet she knew it was actually the same endless day.

After she had met Zach, everything else had blurred and faded into the background. But she had been ignoring something important that had happened in town.

"I was going to the club to meet Etienne. I usually give the kids coins if they ask, but this morning, a bunch of them surrounded me. They pressed in around me, begging, and I was scared. Then a man came up and shooed them away." She thought back over the incident.

"And?"

"I think he's the man who keeps trying to interfere . . . with us."

Zach stared at her. "Kind of a big coincidence."

She shifted in her seat. "I don't think it's a coincidence. I think it was a setup."

"Okay."

Because he still sounded doubtful, she rushed ahead, reconstructing the morning, seeing it in a new light and giving Zach more details. "I was having breakfast in the hotel courtyard, and Etienne sent a message that he wanted to see me at the club. That was unusual, because he'd never done it before. And after the . . . fight in the alley, he'd told me I needed some vacation time. He told me to sleep late, too. But then he changed his mind. I got dressed and went out. Only, when I was about halfway to the club, the kids pushed in around me. Usually they're polite when they ask for money. This morning they scared me. They were pulling at my clothing and my purse, acting like they wouldn't take no for an answer—until this guy came out of nowhere and told them to go away. He gave them some money and they left me alone."

She thought about the scene. About the man. "He said his name was Raoul San Donato. And he owns an art gallery in town. He talked to the kids in island patois. But he talked to me in very cultivated English. As soon as the kids left, I started thinking that he wanted something from me."

"Like what?"

"He offered to take me on a tour of the island. Up into the hills where I could get a wonderful view of the ocean. I told him I had to meet Etienne." She dragged in a breath and let it out. "The San Donato guy knew my name."

"Christ!"

"Well, he had a plausible explanation. He said he'd seen my picture on the poster."

"Like me."

"Yes. Only . . . he said he'd discussed hiring me with Etienne."

"I see."

"He acted like he owned the town, and I was worried about what he wanted."

"You were worried about what *I* wanted, too."

"But I made love with *you. Not him.*"

Zach pressed his palms against the stone hearth, and she went on. "I excused myself and went straight to the club to talk to Etienne. When I got to his office, I got the feeling that he hadn't really expected me to show up."

That made Zach sit forward. "Oh, yeah?"

"Looking back, I think the whole scenario was something they cooked up together. Etienne asked me to the club so I could get into trouble on the street and San Donato could rescue me."

"That sounds like a plot for a spy movie."

"But I think it's true." She stopped and huffed out a breath. "Maybe it even goes back further than that. What if Etienne hired me so . . ." What she was thinking was so monstrous that she could barely say it, but she forced the words out of her mouth. "What if San Donato read about me—about my act—and decided he wanted me, so he got Etienne to offer me a lot of money to perform at his club?"

"Wanted you for what?"

Her mouth was so dry she could hardly speak. But she managed to say, "He has psychic abilities. What if he thinks we can . . . join our powers and get even more from the combination?"

Zach made a sharp sound. "Jesus!"

"If you look at it objectively, it's not so different from what we're trying to do," she said softly, because she had to keep the conversation honest.

Zach swore again, then gave her a direct look. "And from his point of view, if he wants you . . . then I'm right smack in the way."

She reached for his hand, holding tight. *It sounds like our best course is to make sure we don't go back to Grand Fernandino.*

"Sorry, I don't think we have that luxury. If a boat from the island comes by, we'll have to take a chance on returning. Otherwise, we could be here for . . . weeks."

She winced. "Weeks?"

He brushed back his hair in frustration. "Hell, I don't know. I'm just mouthing off because I'm . . . upset."

"Should I have kept my theories to myself?"

"No!" He lowered his voice. "And there's not much point in your trying. I'd find out about it soon enough."

She nodded.

He reached out and stroked his hand lightly on her arm. "Sorry. That came out wrong."

"But it's true. Keeping secrets from each other is going to be difficult."

"Does that bother you?"

"Everybody has stuff they don't want to talk about."

"Yeah." He was silent for several moments, then he changed the subject. "Well, one thing we *do* know. If we're going back, we need to be able to fight San Donato—then get off the island and see if we can make contact with those other people, the ones who were trying to help us when the plane went down. If your theory is correct, they probably know about the guy who hired Wild Bill."

"There's a lot to deal with. But maybe we're lucky. I mean, because we're isolated here, we can take it one step at a time." He squeezed her hand. "Let's start with us."

He pulled her into his arms. She sighed deeply, snuggling close, comforted by the physical contact.

We need to make ourselves strong, he said directly into her mind. *Make the connection between us as solid as forged steel.*

How?

The way we did before. Lucky for us, it's the fun way. To make clear what he was talking about, he turned his head, stroking his lips against the tender place where her neck met her jaw.

The intimate gesture instantly raised her temperature, and she lifted her head, giving him better access. He kissed his way along her jawline, found her ear and traced the tender curves, then stiffened his tongue so that he could stroke the sensitive, hidden canal.

She had longed to make love to him earlier. Now she gave herself over to the arousal curling in her middle, and she knew he felt her reaction. It bounced back to him, generating more heat and reflecting the fire back to her.

He gathered her close, and she knew what was in his mind. Slipping his arm under her knees, he stood. At the same time, she anchored her arms around his neck and felt him carry her across the short space to the bed she'd made out of the couches. He laid her on the cushions and stood looking down at her as he took off his shirt.

But not his shorts.

"I want you naked."

"Not yet. I'm trying to see if we can take our communication skills to a new level."

"With half your clothes on?"

He laughed. "Don't probe too far. Just enjoy what we're doing."

"Don't probe. I thought the point of this was to get closer to each other."

"Wiseguy! Right now, just let me give you pleasure."

He sat beside her, reaching down to slowly unbutton her shirt. When she reached for him, he shook his head.

Let me take charge of this.

Okay.

She had never felt closer to another human being, never felt more confident in a man's ability to please her.

I should hope so.

When she tried to peer inside his head and see what he had in mind, he gave her a little invisible push, and she mentally jumped back.

No peeking.

How did you do that?

I don't know. Maybe this will help you pick it up.

As he spoke inside her head, he pushed aside the front sides of her shirt, baring her breasts.

Then he reached down and tugged at her shorts, pulling them down her legs and over her feet before tossing the garment onto the floor. She lay on the wide couch, almost totally exposed to him except for the open shirt she wore. And somehow that one garment made her feel more naked than if she had been totally without clothing.

He projected his intentions to her—at least what he wanted her to know. And just his sensual thoughts were enough to heat her blood.

He sat beside her, stroking the inner curves of her breasts, then delicately drawing circles around them, his fingers barely skimming her skin.

Please. I need . . .

This?

The circles contracted, coming closer and closer to her nipples but not quite touching them.

Oh, Lord, Zach, don't torture me.

He smiled down at her. And when she was almost ready to surge off the couch, he finally dragged his fingers against the raised edges of her nipples, the relief of his touch making her cry out with the pleasure of it. She knew he felt it, too, the same need, the same intensity that grabbed hold of her.

You look so sexy, lying there with the firelight flickering over you. I have to taste you. Taste all of you. He leaned over, replacing one hand with his tongue, stroking her nipple wetly before sucking the hardened bud into his mouth.

Pleasure swirled through her—through him, because her arousal was also his.

With his mouth still on her breast, he stroked one hand down the center of her body, stopping to circle her navel and dip into it before reaching lower, combing his fingers through the triangle of dark hair at the top of her legs, then stiffening two fingers. He reached the lower edge of those dark curls, playing along the edge, and she held back, ordering herself not to beg him to dip lower.

He knew exactly what she wanted, but he waited before sliding his fingers into the folds of her most intimate flesh, pressing against her clit before circling within the entrance to her vagina.

"Oh!" she cried out, moving her hips to increase the contact with his fingers.

Deeper?

God, yes.

Slowly, slowly, he slid his fingers into her, deepening the caress before pulling back.

When he did, her hips followed him, rising off the couch as her need built toward explosive proportions.

She could feel the smile in his mind as he opened her legs and climbed between them onto the couch. He bent her knees, placing her feet flat on the cushions, then brought his mouth to her sex, already slick and swollen from his attentions.

His tongue was firm as he flicked it at her clit, while at the same time slipping his fingers back inside her, caressing her hot channel as he used his mouth and tongue to play with her clit.

Her total focus was on the pleasure he was giving her. He brought her toward climax, then pulled back, and she knew he was judging her reactions, dragging her to the edge but not allowing her to slip over.

"Please," she cried out, the word bursting from her throat as the need for orgasm pulsed through her blood. "You know what I want."

In that moment, she sensed his intentions and tried to grab his hand. But instead of doing what she desperately craved, he moved quickly back, then climbed off the sofa, completely breaking the physical contact.

"Zach?"

When he took a couple of steps away, she made a moaning sound. She was too needy to reach for mind-to-mind communication. "Zach, what are you doing?"

"Seeing how far I can move away from you and still feel what you're feeling."

"Are you trying to drive me crazy?"

"I'm trying to strengthen the connection between us."

"I need . . ."

I know. I know.

His voice soothed her and at the same time inflamed her.

Can't we just do this the regular way?

He laughed softly. *It's tempting. But we're not doing this just for fun. See if you can feel what I'm feeling.*

Because he gave her no other option, she reached out to him, catching the waves of heat coming off his body, and she knew that he was as hot as she, that his need was as great as her own.

That was small compensation when he stood a few feet away, staring down at her with an intensity that would have burned her skin if he'd developed laser vision.

Maybe that's next.

Oh sure.

She lay there on the couch, silently calling to him, willing him to come back and finish what he'd started.

I will, he whispered inside his head, but he didn't move any closer to her.

Still, she felt . . . the whisper pressure of his fingers against her nipples.

"Zach?" she gasped.

He didn't speak, either in her mind or aloud, but his face was a study in concentration as she felt his touch. It wasn't as strong as when he'd been on the couch with her.

More. I need more.

I'm working on it.

* * *

FAR away, Jordan and Lindsay Walker lay in bed, their hands clasped together. Drifting. Drifting. Together they reached out toward the man and woman who needed their help.

Where are they?

I still don't know.

What about the man Jim Swift sent to kill them?

I'm not sure.

What can we do?

Nothing—unless we can find out where they are.

They're getting stronger. I can feel it.

Maybe we can communicate directly with them.

Not now. I think they're busy.

Jordan laughed. *Yeah. I think you're right. We should give them some privacy.*

Lindsay rolled toward him, and they clasped each other more tightly.

When I thought we were the only joined Dariens, I felt alone.

Yes.

But what's it going to be like when we meet them?

We'll find out.

Yes—I hope we get a chance to know them.

Fear leaped inside her. *They're in danger. And we have to find them.* She hitched in a breath.

Jordan could feel her sending her mind outward—trying to pick up clues. An image leaped into her mind.

Magic Anna. Now Appearing.

Where?

She struggled to expand the vision. *I see a sign. Grand Fernandino Dock.*

BY slow degrees, the phantom touch of Zach's hands on Anna's body became firmer.

She closed her eyes, focusing on the sensations of his fingers on her—when there was no actual physical contact between them. And she knew in some part of her mind that her response was strengthening his ability to please her.

Cooperation, he murmured. He was standing five feet away, yet now it felt like he was right beside her.

Even as the sensations became more intense, questions swirled in her head.

"How?" she whispered as she stared across the space that separated them. "How are you doing that?"

"Don't ask how. Just enjoy it. Does it feel good?"

"You know it does," she murmured.

"Yeah."

He was standing with his body rigid, his arms at his sides, his fists clenched. In the firelight, his features were tense. When her gaze swept over him, she could clearly see the massive bulge behind the fly of his shorts.

He was as hot as she was, but she didn't have to see his body to know that. She could feel the heat coursing through his veins, pooling in his cock.

I thought guys couldn't wait.

You've been watching too many porn flicks.

I never watch porn flicks.

She thought he might come to her. Instead, he took a step back and the contact wavered, then snapped.

CHAPTER
TWENTY-ONE

RAOUL KNELT IN front of the altar in the shed behind his shop. He'd been there for hours, his hands clasped in front of him as he asked Ibena for help. He had never offered her more sacrifices in such a short period of time. Half a dozen chickens, none of which he had donated to the poor. They were all in the garbage can. But he couldn't go out distributing food. He needed to stay focused on Ibena. He had never needed her help more than he had today. Yet it felt like his goddess had forsaken him.

She'd teased him. Given him just enough information to send him into a tailspin.

What had he done? How had he displeased the Blessed Ones—displeased his special saint?

He knew that Anna was out there somewhere. With the man who had determined to steal her away. Once again, he had lost track of them. It was like a curtain had dropped in front of his eyes, blinding him. And he didn't have the strength to lift it over such a long distance.

"Help me," he pleaded, his voice stiff and formal. "Ibena, I gonna dedicate my life to your worship if you help me."

Perhaps that was the incentive she needed. Because he felt the curtain waver, then begin to thin.

He saw flickering firelight. And Anna lying on a couch. naked except for a shirt that was folded back to reveal her breasts.

Her head was turned to the side, her eyes pleading. She looked aroused. Yet the man wasn't on the couch with her.

Blood fire! What was this? What in the hell were they doing. And why?

"Anna! Where are you?" he called out.

Her body jerked, and she made a sound that was something between a sob and a moan.

Go away, she shouted in her head. *Leave me alone.*

You belong with me.

No! I belong with Zach.

Zach. That his name?

Go away, she shouted again, and the picture before his eyes rippled. He cursed, trying to hold on to the scene.

"Wait! Don't run out on me."

But she was gone, and he was left on his aching knees, shouting out his frustration and his rage.

He would kill the bastard. Kill him!

"NO!" Anna cried out.

"What? What were you saying? I couldn't hear you."

"I wasn't talking to you. He was here, trying to get between us."

"Jesus." Zach took a step toward her, but she shouted inside his head.

No. We have to do this. He made me understand how important this is.

Her need to solidify the connection with Zach made her reach out desperately to him again.

She knew without doubt that she had to make the link

between them as strong as it could be. Like iron, he had said.

At the same time, her physical need surged again. And with that need, she felt his response. His phantom touch reached her once more, and she gasped as heat shot through her.

He tipped his head to the side. *Thanks for the help.*

I had to.

I was hoping I could push you to reach for me.

I need . . .

I know. Less talk. More action.

He stopped the conversation and focused on arousing her.

His hands were pressed against his hips now, his fingers spread so she could see each one clearly.

As she stared at his hands, his phantom touch on her breasts grew stronger, more arousing. And suddenly, at the same time, she felt the sensation of his two stiffened fingers slipping inside her again.

They stroked in and out of her vagina as he caressed her breasts with his other hand. It was good. But it wasn't enough. She needed more.

He was still standing a few yards away.

"Come here," she pleaded.

He gave a small shake of his head. When he stayed where he was, desperation rose inside her. If he wasn't going to put her out of her misery, then she would have to do it herself.

No. Don't touch yourself.

You've made me so hot, I can't stand it. I need to come.

I know. Let me do it.

Oh, Lord, Zach.

Need surged through her. She pressed her hands against the cushions as her hips surged off the couch, then settled back again.

"Please . . ." she cried out.

He kept his invisible fingers inside her, then reached with his thumb to circle her clit.

"Oh!"

She knew he didn't have to ask what she needed from him. He could feel it. And he kept up the intimate touch, in just the way she wanted him to do it. His fingers were inside her, on her clit, on her breasts—touching her in more places than he could have done if he had been beside her.

And as he caressed her in all those spots, sensation built to explosive proportions.

Finally, finally, they burst through her in a rocketing climax that shook her body and mind.

She called out his name as her hips surged off the cushions again and again while wave after wave of pleasure swept over her. When she settled back to earth, her breath was coming in great gasps.

Completely spent, she lay on the couch, panting, stroking her hands against the cushions, then tipped her head back, looking up at Zach. He was standing over her, breathing hard, grinning down at her.

She grinned back. *You're pretty pleased with yourself, aren't you?*

Aren't you? he asked inside her head.

Yes.

She felt his mood turn serious. *In the middle of that, you said he was here.*

I'm sorry.

Not your fault.

I hope not. She made a small sound. *It happened when you stepped away, and I couldn't feel you. He tried to get between us then.*

And that made you reach for me.

Yes!

That's good.

You don't think I want anything to do with him—do you?

Of course not, he answered, but she felt the edge of doubt in his mind.

You're the only man I want inside my head, or anywhere inside my body, she added, just to make her feelings clear. As she made the proclamation, she switched her focus from herself to him.

He'd brought her to climax, but need still surged through him.

"I think you should lie down," she murmured.

"You mean before I fall over?" he asked, and she breathed out a small sigh, knowing he was focusing on the two of them again.

"Yes."

Scooting over, she made room for him on the couch. He flopped down beside her, and she wanted to roll to her side and pull him to her.

Don't, he whispered.

You want me to . . . do what you did to me?

Yeah.

What if I can't?

Then I'm in for a pretty rough time.

To avoid further physical contact, she moved to the end of the couch and climbed off, then stood on shaky legs, steadying herself against one of the backrests, getting accustomed to being vertical after such an erotic experience.

His silent voice drifted toward her.

Don't wait too long.

She couldn't stop herself from teasing him. *I might wait hours. It would serve you right.*

Don't punish me! You said I made you hot. Well, I feel like I could fly apart into a thousand pieces.

The plea was so heartfelt that she felt her chest tighten.

Sorry.

Maybe I deserve it. I didn't tell you what I was going to do.

If you had, I might have strangled you.

Despite his tension, he laughed.

*How did you figure out how to . . . touch me without . . .
being right beside me?*

I don't know?

Thanks!

Just see if you can do it, he said in a strained voice.
*Didn't you do something like that on the plane? When you
were trying to get my attention?*

That was different. I made up a fantasy.

Make up another one!

DESPITE the heat of the island evening, a shiver traveled
over Nadine's skin as she stood outside the shed in the
backyard of the art gallery. She had tried to call Raoul on
the phone to ask if he'd be home for dinner, but he hadn't
answered. So she'd come down to the gallery looking for
him, and she'd found the shop closed.

Really, the question about dinner had been an excuse.
He'd been acting strange lately, and she wanted to keep
tabs on him. So she'd gone down the alley to the backyard.
And she'd heard Raoul inside the shed where he had a
shrine like the one at home.

He was cursing. Shouting a man's name. Asking his
goddess to kill the fucker.

She had heard him angry before. She had heard him
drunk on island rum. But she had never heard him like this,
and she shrank back—away from the front of the shed and
into the shadows, lest he burst out and see her. And direct
his wrath toward her.

He sounded desperate and dangerous. Out of control.

Footsteps came along the alley. A man, walking fast.
And now she was trapped. She'd done it to herself by
sneaking down here.

Praying that she wouldn't be discovered, she pressed

back into the greenery at the side of the yard. If Raoul found her here, would he kill her?

She hated to think he'd turn on her, but she'd given up any illusions she possessed about the man.

ZACH had already stripped to the waist.

Anna dragged in a breath and let it out. *I need to see what I'm doing. Take off your shorts.*

He turned his head toward her, giving her a long look. A flurry of heartbeats passed, and she knew that he was reluctant to comply.

I need to see you, she repeated.

He answered with a tight nod, then he reached for the snap at the top of his shorts. She saw his hands weren't quite steady as he opened the snap, then pulled down his zipper. Once he had started, he moved quickly, awkwardly pulling down the shorts, lifting his hips so he could drag the garment down his legs and toss it onto the floor.

In seconds, he lay against the cushions, naked and vulnerable. He was fully aroused, his penis hard and firm and sticking straight up in the air.

She caught her breath and couldn't stop herself from saying, *Now you know how I felt.*

Yeah. Needy.

His aroused body and the look on his face made her want to reach him. And suddenly, without understanding how she had accomplished it, she knew she had made contact.

Her hands were pressed against the fabric of the sofa, yet at the same time, she felt her fingers press against Zach's flat stomach.

And she knew it was no illusion generated by wishful thinking. Under her hand, she felt the muscles jump. And she heard him call out to her.

"Anna!"

"Right here," she whispered. Sensing power gather inside her, she slid her phantom hand lower, combing her fingers through the thatch of dark hair below his belly, then working her way toward the base of his penis.

He made a strangled exclamation as she reached her goal, then stroked one finger up the length of the hardened flesh, following the ridge of a vein.

She felt a spurt of heat inside her own body, heat coming from him.

His exclamation of gratitude rang in the darkened room and echoed in her mind.

With a sense of wonder, she trailed her invisible fingers up and down his length, hearing his breath accelerate.

She knew it felt good, but she knew it wasn't enough. Again she focused on what she needed to do, and somehow she was able to close her hand around his cock and squeeze him.

He felt full and so hard that it was like grasping tempered steel covered with velvet.

He didn't speak again. He didn't move. Yet she sensed the tension radiating from him.

It was wonderful to touch him like that. Wonderful to feel him harden even further under her phantom touch.

She clasped him more tightly, playing with him, experimenting to see what he liked best. As she moved her hand up and down, faster and faster, she felt his whole body go rigid.

Letting his reactions guide her, she increased the speed and pressure.

His hips surged upward off the sofa cushions, punctuated by groans and gasps.

The sight of him, the feel of his penis in her fist, brought heat blasting through her. Her breathing came hard and fast—from arousal and from the effort she was expending.

But she pushed her own needs to the background and kept her focus on him, driving him toward orgasm.

His eyes focused on her face. And she clenched her teeth, awed by her view of him and the pleasure she saw on his features.

She ached to go to him. But she knew she had to see this through, in the way that he had showed her.

Then, from where she stood, she felt his body jerk, heard him call her name as climax rocked him.

His breath sawed in and out, and so did hers.

"I can't . . . stand here anymore."

He held out his arm, and she crossed the space between them, flinging her body onto the couch as he cradled her against his length.

"I did it," she whispered.

"Oh yeah."

He grinned at her, and she grinned back.

"So, do I get to have you make love with me? I mean, the real way."

They settled down together on the couch, and he stroked his fingers over her arm.

"I think we can honor your request—if you give me a few minutes," he answered, turning his head to nuzzle his lips against her neck.

But she had picked up some disturbing stray thoughts from his mind, and she turned to look at him.

"You're planning to put me through hell again," she murmured.

He laughed softly. "I prefer to think of it as training, but not until we both have some fun."

A shout from outside the shrine made Raoul start.

Someone was calling his name.

He stood up and flexed his legs. His knees ached from kneeling before the altar. And all for nothing. He'd been able to see Anna and the man, at least in some fashion. He knew what the hell they were doing.

Making each other hot. Playing sex games.

Damn the man for thinking up something so inventive!

Raoul ached to break the connection between Anna and the man, but he couldn't do it. Not from here. They were too far away, and he needed to figure out where they were.

"Raoul!"

"Just a moment." He stepped out of the shed and carefully closed the door behind him.

Etienne was standing in the courtyard between the shed and the back of the shop, his eyes wild.

"Where is she?"

"Anna?"

"Of course Anna. Who else? She was late for work, and I sent around to her hotel. But she wasn't there. What have you done with her?"

Raoul's anger flared. "I haven't done nothin'."

"She's supposed to be at the club. But she's gone. What the hell am I gonna do?"

"Some men took her."

"Son of a bitch! And you didn't tell me?"

"Calm down. I've been trying to locate her."

Etienne looked like he wanted to punch someone out. "The club is full. The audience is waiting for her first show. She's a big hit."

"Tell them she's sick."

Etienne swore again. "I already did that—to stall them."

"We'll she's not coming back tonight," Raoul said.

"Blood fire! People will think I don't deliver what I promise."

"It's not your fault."

"It don't matter why she's not there. They'll blame me. Did you hide her away?"

"Not me. Like I said, some other men took her. If I can find her, I will."

"With your . . . powers?"

Raoul kept his face from reflecting his inner doubts. "Yes. But she's not on the island."

"Where is she? What did they want with her?"

Raoul heaved in a breath and let it out. "They wanted to kill her."

"No shit?"

"No shit," Raoul repeated. "But she got away from them. She and the guy with her."

"Who?"

"A man who has a boat in the harbor."

"You know him?"

"Not face to face. I saw him in a vision."

Etienne waited a beat before saying, "So they left by boat?"

Raoul waved an impatient hand. "No. By plane. But it went down in the water."

Etienne sucked in a strangled breath.

"The hot steppas who had them were in a raft. The other guy—Zach—swam over and knifed the bottom. Anna's okay," Raoul went on quickly. "She and the stateside guy swam to shore."

"This is true?"

"You think I could make it up?"

Etienne scowled. "You shoulda told me soon as you knew."

Raoul didn't explain that he'd forgotten all about the club owner's problems. Instead, he said smoothly, "I was praying to Ibena. And trying to find them." He omitted any mention of what else he'd been trying to do. "You seen the guy—Zach?"

"I think I know who he is. He got in trouble wit Pagor."

"Good. Maybe that will help us."

"Help us! How?" Etienne looked like he wanted to lunge across the space between them. But he knew his place, and he wisely stayed where he was.

"Maybe Pagor will fuck him up." He closed his eyes. "I

can see where they are, but I don't know the place. It's a grand white house—with some storm damage."

"Abandoned?"

"Yeah. I tell you more about the house." He paused and collected his thoughts. "It's very modern—a rich guy's pad. Maybe on a private island. It's got sliding glass doors leading onto a patio. One of them is broke. The ground level has tile floors and a big fireplace. It's got a two story ceiling in the big room. The floor in the hall upstairs is broke. The garden's a mess."

Etienne waited impatiently. "What am I supposed to do with all that information?"

"Go aroun' town. To the brothers who work for rich foreigners. See if you can find someone who knows the place."

"That's not enough to tell them."

Raoul gave him a fierce look. "There's a pier. And a waterfall."

Etienne sighed.

"Give it a shot," Raoul growled, "because I think Anna and the guy are stuck there. We can rescue them and get her back."

"But maybe not for days."

"It's better than nothing."

Etienne grunted in protest, but he didn't really have any options.

"Someone in town surely worked there. Or carried stuff from the island to the house. If we can find out who, we can go there, kill him, and pick her up."

Etienne blinked. "Kill him?"

"He think she belong to him. But she's mine!"

Etienne's face paled. "I didn't sign up for murder."

"I didn't mean you personally."

Raoul walked around his friend and into the back of the shop. "I've been praying since I found out she was gone, and I've got blood on my shirt—from the chickens. I have to change before I go out."

He strode to the closet where he kept several of the shirts that Nadine had ironed for him and brought over from the house. She hadn't been much good at ironing or cooking when she'd first come to live with him, but she'd responded to his gentle suggestions.

Now she would make some guy a good wife. But not him. He knew the wife he wanted.

"For a good cause, murder isn't much different from sacrificing a chicken," he said in a soft voice.

CHAPTER
TWENTY-TWO

NADINE COWERED IN the bushes with her heart pounding, afraid to move until Raoul and his friend had walked through the yard and into the art gallery.

When the door closed, she let out the breath she was holding, then rushed back into the alley and headed for home.

Home.

That was a house owned by Raoul.

Now what the hell was she supposed to do? Go back there and pretend she hadn't been here? Or maybe she should make a break for it. Because she wasn't that good an actress. When Raoul saw her face, he'd know something was wrong. Because she'd heard him talking about murder.

Not just of chickens. The murder of a man.

If he could kill some guy he'd never met, what would he do to her when he got angry?

It sounded like she'd better start thinking about her options. Like, was there a quick way to get the hell out of Dodge?

She had more than enough bread for a plane ticket, but Raoul had spies at the airport. If she tried to buy a ticket, he'd know about it. And nobody on the island would hide her from him. She was stuck.

As she stood in the dark, trying to figure out what to do, an idea came sneaking into her mind.

That priest—Joseph Hondino. He'd said he would help her. Maybe in exchange for some information, he'd help her get away.

Or was it better to go down to the docks and see if any new boats had come in? Maybe she could pay someone to take her to Jamaica. Even that was risky. But she was thinking that she'd better chance it.

She clenched her hands into fists, trying to decide which way to jump.

ZACH woke with a feeling of well-being, which he understood was strange, since he knew the instant he opened his eyes that he and Anna were stranded on a deserted island somewhere in the Caribbean.

But her presence next to him on the makeshift bed made all the difference. She was warm and totally relaxed, her posture telling him of her utter trust in him.

That gave him a small twinge. She trusted him. But he couldn't let go of the nagging doubt about the other guy who kept barging into their relationship.

If she didn't want him there, would he really be able to interfere?

He hated himself for asking the question. But he'd learned not to trust easily. Not after his own brother had made his life hell for years. Craig had been jealous of him from the time he was born. At least the way his mother told it. And maybe he'd even caused some dangerous accidents when Zach had been just a toddler.

Zach couldn't prove the early incidents. But he sure recalled being pushed off an outcropping of rocks.

And he remembered his father's reaction. Dad had called him clumsy. And Craig had walked away with a smirk.

Shoving the past from his mind, he turned his head just enough so that he could see Anna's face. She was still sleeping, with her lips slightly parted and her lashes very dark against her pale skin.

They'd been through a terrible ordeal the day before—then celebrated with hours of lovemaking. He knew she needed to rest, and he lay very still, trying not to wake her.

After they'd made love, they'd talked—not out loud, but in their minds. He now knew more about her than about any living human being. And she knew as much about him.

Maybe to prove how much she trusted him not to make fun of her, she'd shared some of her worst memories.

Like the terrible embarrassment when she'd gotten her first period in the middle of gym class.

And he'd let her see the awkward scene when he'd seduced a girl in his college class because he was embarrassed to still be a virgin.

Then she'd told him how much she hated riding the school bus, wondering who would sit next to her.

As he kept his gaze on her, he saw that her eyes were moving back and forth under her lids.

Rapid eye movements. He knew what that meant. She was dreaming.

About what?

And could he join her in that dream? A couple of days ago, the thought would have been incomprehensible. But the first time he'd met her was in a kind of waking dream. And after he'd made contact with her, they'd reached toward each other in ways that a normal person would never have thought of—or even believed possible.

Still, there were avenues they hadn't explored. And

things they hadn't done to strengthen the connection between them.

What if he joined her in her dream? Would that cement their relationship more tightly?

Or was he looking for excuses to spy on her?

He didn't like the image of himself as a man who had to control his lover's actions and her thoughts. But at the same time, he wanted to know about the other man. The man she said was named Raoul San Donato.

Would San Donato try to reach her in her dreams? Or would Anna's subconscious reach out to him?

Or maybe she couldn't control what she was dreaming. She could be having a nightmare. And if so, he could change the equation.

Once again he questioned his own motives. But that wasn't going to stop him. He wanted to know where her subconscious had taken her. And he was going to find out—if he could.

Physical contact had been the door to mental intimacy between them. As they lay on the bed she'd made from the sofas, he was snuggled up against her, her hip and shoulder wedged against his—very intimate physical contact. The right kind of contact to get into her mind.

He'd done it many times now when they were both awake and she was reaching for him at the same time. He hadn't tried it while she was sleeping.

Should he close his eyes to concentrate? Or should he watch her face because that was yet another kind of bridge to her spirit?

He opted for the latter, his fingers pressing against her hip as he reached toward her sleeping thoughts, not even sure what he was doing. Or if she would stay sleeping while he tried to probe her mind.

Hoping he wouldn't wake her, he strove for contact on the very deepest level. He couldn't explain the process he

was using—even to himself. But he figured he was on the
right track when the room around him went away, much
like when he'd first been standing on the street in front of
the poster of Magic Anna.

Lord, that seemed like a long time ago.

He hadn't even met her in person then. But they had
held each other and kissed for the first time in that dream.

This time was different. He could still see her lying next
to him on the couch.

Then the image faded, leaving him in a twilight place
with no sound and no sense of touch. He knew his hand
was still pressing against her hip, but suddenly he couldn't
feel her warm skin. And then he couldn't even see her—or
anything else.

Before panic could bloom, everything changed again. In
the space of a heartbeat, he stepped through a translucent
curtain onto the sea grass at the edge of a beach. Very
much like the beach where they'd washed up yesterday.

The sun was shining in a brilliant blue sky. A gentle
breeze blew off the water. And the waves broke gently on
the wet sand, each one with a curl of foam where it re-
ceded.

He scanned the scene, then took a step forward. The
beach seemed to be deserted except for some plovers running along the edge of the waves, searching for crabs and
other sea creatures.

He looked to his right, and elation surged through him
when he saw that Anna was standing on the sand on a spot
that was formed from recent waves. In bed beside him, she
had been naked. In the dream she was wearing a South Sea
island sarong made of bright flowered material. It blew
gently in the breeze, as did her hair, which was dark and
shiny around her shoulders.

When he took a quick look behind him, he could see the
white walls of the house poking up through a tangle of vegetation.

So in the dream Anna was still on the island, but she had come down to the water's edge and dressed herself in something comfortable but simple.

He was still as naked as when he'd awakened. But this was a dream, after all. And he grinned as he thought about what he might put on.

Not just clothing, but a whole persona. He could be anything in the world. He could come to Anna as a Greek god. Or a rock star.

He decided on being himself and wearing a pair of loose-fitting trunks with a random blue and white Hawaiian pattern.

He grinned again when they appeared on his lower body. Too bad he and Anna couldn't stay here. Then they'd have everything they needed.

He thought about asking the god of dreams for a cup of coffee and a bagel slathered with cream cheese and apricot jelly. But that would only be a cruel joke when he woke up and had nothing to eat besides canned soup and protein bars.

Anna raised her hand to shade her eyes as she looked out over the ocean, apparently searching for something.

Barefoot, he walked lightly across the sand and came up quietly behind her. Before he reached her, she stiffened.

"Zach?"

"Were you expecting someone else?" he asked, unable to keep a gritty sound out of his voice.

"Of course not."

When she tried to spin around and face him, he circled her waist with his hands and held her where she was.

She settled against him, then asked in a high, breathy voice, "What are you doing here?"

"You know that this is a dream?"

She hesitated for a moment, apparently considering the situation. "Yes," she finally said. "It's my dream, isn't it?"

"Yes."

"Then how did you get here?" She tried to turn again. "Are you really Zach? Or did I invent you?"

"It's really me." He laughed. "I wanted to see if I could join you. I mean I wanted to see if we could find one more way to connect with each other."

"Always inventive."

He caught the tension in her voice. "Is that a complaint?"

As he spoke, he pulled her more tightly against his body, then bent to skim his lips against her neck. "I like your outfit."

She looked down and laughed again. "I guess it must be the right dress for a shipwreck survivor."

"Plane wreck."

"Oh, right. Maybe I don't want to remember that."

"What's wrong?"

She looked around and shivered. "Someone's watching us. I guess it's him."

Zach's head snapped up, and he looked out toward sea, then to his left and right and finally behind him.

He saw no one.

"You don't feel it?"

He didn't answer, but he couldn't stop a shiver from racing across his skin. The same shiver that had seized Anna.

YES. It's me, Raoul thought with satisfaction. *You can't hide from me. Even in your sleep.*

He and Etienne had gone out to ask questions, staying out late until almost nobody had been left on the streets. He'd gone home to bed for a few hours of sleep. Not with Nadine. He didn't want the interference of Nadine now. So he bedded down in one of his other houses.

In the morning, he'd gone back to the shrine. He'd learned that Ibena was capricious. She was teasing him. Or maybe she was testing his loyalty. But he would let her know that he hadn't lost his faith in her. And when she realized his dedication to her service, she would reward him.

He'd begun to pray again. And as he had knelt before the altar, he had stumbled into Anna's dream.

She was standing on the beach, staring out to sea. At first he'd been elated to find her alone. He'd been about to contact her when the man named Zach had stepped into the scene.

"Damn you, you fish bait!"

As soon as Raoul muttered the curse, he struggled to calm his emotions. Emotions would get him into trouble. He wanted to lash out immediately. He wanted to hurl a thunderbolt that would shatter the peace of the dream. But he held back, biding his time, thinking about what he could do.

And as he watched and waited, he saw something else.

There were more people in the dream. Not just Anna and Zach. Another man and woman.

Blood fire!

"CAN you feel him?" Anna whispered, as though keeping her voice low would prevent someone else from hearing their conversation.

"San Donato?"

"Yeah." Determined to make it clear that Anna belonged to him, Zach skimmed his hands up and down her sides, his fingertips caressing the outer curves of her breasts.

He was gratified to feel her instant response to him. Looking down and over her shoulder, he could see her nipples bead under the fabric of her sarong.

She arched against him, her bottom pressing to his erection, and he started thinking that he should throw some blankets on the grass so he could make love to her. That would show the bastard which man belonged in this dream and which man didn't.

Yes, she whispered in his mind.

But before he could lead her off the beach, a movement out in the blue water caught his attention.

Anna's mind must have been tuned to his, because she followed his gaze.

"What's that?"

At first the object was far away and indistinct. Then he saw that it was a boat—speeding toward the island.

Anna made a small sound.

"It's him! He's coming here."

CONFUSION swamped Zach.

But the thought uppermost in his mind was to protect Anna.

"Don't run." Keeping her close, he shifted her so that his body was between her and the beach.

Maybe San Donato had invaded their dream. But he didn't think the bastard was on that boat.

But if not him, then who?

The craft was speeding toward them, and Zach dragged in a startled breath as he took in the shape.

He blinked. It was *his* boat. "What the hell?"

"What?" she asked.

"It's the *Odysseus.*"

As he stared at the approaching craft, he could see a man and a woman standing at the rail, staring intently toward the island.

They both had dark hair. The woman was small and pretty. The man was taller and tougher. But they both looked determined—and also relieved. They stopped about thirty feet from shore, the boat bobbing in the waves.

Who are you? Zach challenged, deliberately asking the question in his mind—not out loud—to see if these people could communicate that way.

We've been trying to reach you, they answered together,
the words echoing in his head—and in Anna's, he knew.

You're in danger.

Yeah. We know that. Who are you? he asked again.

*Jordan and Lindsay. We helped the pilot keep the plane
from crashing.*

You! Anna exclaimed.

How do you know us? Zach asked.

*We've been casting our thoughts outward, trying to lo-
cate other people like us.*

Other people like us? Psychics?

*Not just psychics. There isn't time for a long explanation
now. But we're all the result of the experiment at Dr. Remington's fertility clinic. He was trying to create superintelli-
gent children. Instead he created telepaths whose powers
are dormant until they connect with another subject from
the experiment.*

A fertility clinic, Anna gasped.

Your parents told you about it?

Yes, she answered.

But Zach shook his head. He'd never known that part of
his personal story. Now he had a sudden insight into why
his father had been so disappointed. He'd paid through the
nose to have a child with his second wife. And he hadn't
been pleased with what he'd gotten.

*The clinic was funded by a quasi-government agency
called the Crandall Consortium. But the project went wrong.*

Anna raised her head. *Wait a minute. My powers weren't
dormant. I was using them to make a living.*

*We know about your psychometric act. We're impressed
that you could do that by yourself. But your powers have
blossomed since you bonded with Zach, haven't they?*

Yes! she answered.

*A man named Jim Swift is trying to kill as many of us
as he can find. That's why we changed our last name from*

Walker to West. He hired the thugs to get you on the plane.

They drowned, Zach said.

The woman breathed out a small sigh. *I hope so. We're trying to find out what happened to them.*

We have another problem, Zach said. *A local man who wants Anna for his wife.*

But you've bonded with her. He can't.

He's trying, Zach answered. *He'll be happy if he can get me out of the picture.*

The woman started to speak again, but her silent voice was cut off by a strange roaring noise. The ocean began receding from the shore, sweeping the boat farther from where Zach and Anna stood.

Wait. Come back, Anna cried out.

The woman shouted something, her voice drowned out by the the roaring water. Zach reached out a hand to them, but they were too far away for communication now.

"What's happening?" Anna whispered.

Your Vadiana friend's screwing around with us, Zach silently answered.

His gaze went from the receding water to Anna. She stood stock-still, staring in terrible fascination at the suddenly exposed sand and rock, where fish and other sea creatures flopped up and down on the wetly shining surface.

"How?" she breathed.

"I don't know. But this didn't come from your mind—or mine. He did it somehow." As he grasped the implications, he grabbed her hand and pulled her away from the shoreline. "Run. Run for your life."

JIM Swift—or Stone, as he called himself now—checked his e-mail again. Wild Bill should have checked in by now. But he hadn't heard anything. That was bad news.

Had the woman freak gotten away? And the guy? And where the hell was Bill?

Afraid to check in because he'd screwed up?

Jim wouldn't put that past the little bastard. But that left him in the dark and cursing.

Maybe he could find out if the plane had even taken off from Grand Fernandino—and if it had come back.

He opened an Internet window and started searching the news. A plane *had* taken off from the island and not come back.

So did that mean Anna Ridgeway and Zachary Robinson were dead? And what about Wild Bill and the freelancers?

If luck was running his way, something had happened on that plane. And the problem had taken care of itself.

But he wasn't going to count on it for sure.

CHAPTER
TWENTY-THREE

"RUN!" ZACH SHOUTED again, tugging on Anna's arm. "Run!"

She made a strangled sound, then turned and dashed back into the jungle.

He pelted along beside her, and they reached the tree line just as a roaring noise sounded behind them.

Images flashed through his mind—footage that tourists had shot of the tsunami in Thailand. They'd captured pictures of an enormous wave plowing in from the ocean, pounding resort towns along the coast, destroying everything in its path, knocking down buildings, sweeping away men, women, and children who were caught in the deluge.

He knew Anna had picked up the horrific images from him. He hated scaring her. Yet he knew the vivid pictures made her run faster.

He led her back toward the house, keeping pace with her as they plunged into the underbrush, his hand still firmly clasped in hers, willing her to speed up.

In one part of his brain, he was thinking that this was a

dream and the water gathering speed behind them couldn't really hurt them. But he knew deep down that if he went on that assumption, he was going to end up dead.

Had San Donato seen the same tsunami TV footage, or was he making this up as he went along?

Would the bastard kill Anna, too? If he couldn't have her for his own, would he make sure nobody else could?

The roaring sound was coming closer. Zach kept running, pulling Anna along, even when he knew the water moved faster than they could.

Not just a tsunami. A super tsunami.

The leading edge of the tidal wave reached them, slamming them in the back. His hold on Anna's hand snapped.

"Anna!"

He heard her call his name as he went flying into the trees. She screamed, and he thought he saw her being swept toward the house. Toward safety, he hoped. If the water didn't bash her into one of the walls.

He was pretty sure now that San Donato didn't want to kill her. He wanted to kill his rival.

As if in confirmation, the water swept Zach in the other direction—into the jungle. He banged against tree branches and hidden obstructions as the huge wave carried him inland. Desperately he struggled to grab something that would stop him, but the branches had turned slippery.

All he could do was try to stay on the surface, but the wave dragged him under, down, down into water churning with logs and fish and other debris.

From years of diving, he'd made himself into an excellent swimmer. He was as at home in the water as he was on land. And he could hold his breath longer than anyone else he knew.

Trying to keep his cool, he pushed toward the surface. He had almost reached the open air when something caught his foot and dragged him back under the surface.

It was exactly like what had happened two days ago, when he'd been at the shipwreck with José and the man had been terrified of Pagor.

Zach made a disgusted sound. He knew where the unfortunate image had come from. His own mind supplied the information to San Donato, who was happily using it against him.

Screw you, he silently shouted as he called up the rest of the remembered episode. José had wrenched himself away. He'd done it then, and Zach could do it now.

Zach pictured the earlier scene, focusing on the moment when the panicked diver had broken free. But the hold on his ankle only tightened. And he knew that he was going to drown.

Drown in a goddamned dream.

And the worst part was that he'd done it to himself. He never should have come here in the first place.

No you don't, he snarled. If San Donato could change the rules, so could he.

He pictured a long-bladed knife in his hand. As he did, he felt his fingers closing around the hard rubber handle.

His lungs were bursting, but he reminded himself that he was perfectly comfortable underwater. He could hold his breath for three minutes—if he had to.

He whipped around, seeing a hand clamped around his ankle. No body, no arm. Just a damn ghostly hand.

Lunging for the fingers, he slashed at them with his knife and had the satisfaction of hearing a bloodcurdling scream. The rest of San Donato might be invisible, but that didn't prevent him from feeling the pain of cut flesh in the dream he'd invaded.

How do you like that? Zach gibed as blood spilled from the cut fingers, turning the water red.

Zach stabbed again, and the grip around his ankle loosened, then let go entirely.

Freed from the ghostly hand, Zach shot toward the

surface. He could see the sunlight above him, but before he reached it, a log came shooting through the water right toward him like a torpedo launched from a submarine.

Before he could dodge the guided missile, it hit him in the head, and the dream turned black.

FOR a long time, he knew nothing. Maybe he was dead. Or on the way to heaven. His mind floated in blackness. And that was fine with him.

Then, from somewhere below him, he heard a woman's voice.

"Zach. Wake up. Don't you dare leave me, Zach. I can't do this by myself. Not when I've finally found you."

The words drifted by him, like fish swimming in a calm pool.

He wanted to be left alone.

But the woman kept talking.

After a long time, he realized it was Anna. Her name was Anna. And she said the same thing, over and over.

Too bad he couldn't come back. His thoughts were vague and disconnected, but one thing he knew. He wasn't supposed to return to the earth. His enemy had told him he was supposed to stay up here in blackness, detached from his body until the husk of his mortal existence withered away and died.

"No!"

Maybe Anna had caught the finality of that wayward thought floating through his mind. If she could, more power to her.

Come back, damn you.

Leave me alone.

A searing pain slashed into the hulk of his body, and from far away, he heard himself moan.

"That's it, you coward. Come back."

Coward? Where do you get off calling me a coward?

If you're not afraid, then you can damn well come back.
The pain flashed through him again, pulling him back.

"Cut that out!" he shouted.

The pain came again, and this time his eyes blinked open. To his astonishment, he was lying naked on the couch where they had gone to sleep the night before.

Anna was also naked, and she was crouching over him, her expression fierce and her hand raised to slap him in the face, and he knew she must have done it before, more than once.

"What the hell?" he gasped out.

"Thank God."

"What . . . ?" he tried again.

"What's the last thing you remember?" she asked, her voice urgent.

"Going to sleep . . ." He considered that for a moment. "No, waking up. You were still asleep. And dreaming."

He dragged in a breath as memories came flashing back at him—fast and furious as his brain began to function again.

He'd seen she was asleep. He'd decided to see if he could join her in the dream. He remembered the beach, and a man and a woman on the *Odysseus*. And then . . .

Anna had followed his thoughts. "The tsunami caught us," she supplied.

"Jesus!" The end of the dream flashed into his mind, and he made a strangled sound. "He tried to kill me. Every time I almost made it to the surface, he came up with something else."

"He washed me up onto dry ground. Into the house," Anna said, as she curved her hand around his shoulder. "I saw you go under. I was so scared."

"He dragged me down and held me under."

She gasped. "Was he really there?"

He made a gagging sound. "Just his hand. But I gave myself a knife, and I cut him."

"Good."

"He had control of the flood. He sent a log slamming into my head." As he spoke, he pulled her down so that she was lying half on top of him.

"He was trying to keep me asleep," she whispered. "I fought him. I woke myself up. It seemed to take forever. But when I finally did, we were both lying on the couch. Only you were pale as death. Your skin was clammy, and you wouldn't wake up when I shook you."

He grimaced. "Was I breathing?"

"Barely."

He pointed toward the ceiling. "I was up there. Well, not in this room. Somewhere up there in the darkness. I mean my consciousness. I heard you yelling at me, trying to wake me up."

"I was shaking you."

"But I couldn't feel it." He dragged in a breath and let it out. "When the shaking didn't work, you slapped me, right?"

She took her lower lip between her teeth. "I'm sorry. I didn't know what else to do."

"You did the right thing. You finally got my attention." He stroked his fingers over her shoulder and down her back, comforted by the contact with her soft skin.

"I thought you were going to die," she whispered.

"I thought I *was* dead. I'm sure I would have been—if you hadn't brought me back. How long was I out?" he asked.

"I'm not exactly sure. It felt like hours. It was probably only a few minutes." Her hold on his arm tightened. "Does he know where we are?" she asked.

"I don't know. But we have to be on our guard."

She winced.

He hugged her to him, wanting to make love to her, but wondering if they were safe from the San Donato guy. He was getting stronger, more able to invade their minds when they were closely bonded.

She caught his thoughts and eased away. They both stood up, and he saw that neither of them was quite steady on their feet.

"We found out something good," she murmured. "I was right about . . . Lindsay and Jordan wanting to help us."

"Yeah. If they can."

He pulled on his shorts and shirt, then walked outside to the edge of the patio, momentarily astonished that the landscape hadn't been flattened by a giant wave. That had only been a dream, he reminded himself.

Something else struck him. In the dim light of evening he hadn't noticed that whoever had lived here had planted a virtual forest of fruit trees. Not just one variety but a whole bunch of them.

Well, that certainly increased their range of food options.

After looking at the trees, he walked down to the beach, unable to face the water without cringing. But again he reminded himself that the dream had not been real.

Still, he didn't know how much power San Donato had to reach into their real lives.

If the bastard found them in a dream, could he find them in reality?

Zach shaded his eyes, scanning the sea. No boats. Which meant this place probably wasn't on anybody's regular shipping or recreational route.

They'd have to worry about that later. Right now, they needed to eat.

Returning to the vicinity of the house, he picked some ripe bananas off a bunch, then pulled off his shirt and used it to hold avocados, figs, plums, mangos, and breadfruit. At least they had some variety. With protein bars added it would be nourishing.

When he came in, he found Anna had opened two bottles of water.

Deliberately not touching her, he asked, *What are you thinking?*

She caught the question and answered immediately. *That we have to get out of here before something else happens.*

I agree.

And get away from Grand Fernandino.

They carried the food out to the patio, where they sat on another tablecloth, eating and sipping the water.

Zach picked up a plum. "All this fruit may have a bad effect on our . . . uh . . . digestion."

"The banana will help with that." She looked out toward the jungle. "Maybe you can find a bird's nest and get us some eggs."

"How about snake eggs?"

She winced.

While he ate some avocado, he thought about what they should do.

She picked up a banana, then started to move so that her shoulder would be touching his.

Don't touch me.

Okay.

I want to practice talking in our minds without physical contact.

She hitched in a breath and let it out, and he knew she was probing his thoughts. *You think there's not much chance of boats passing this way.*

I don't know how long we can hang around here. I thought it was safe, but not if he can come here so easily.

She nodded. *You think . . . Lindsay and Jordan can find us?* she asked suddenly.

I wish.

They did it in the dream.

But it might be harder in reality.

She answered with a tight nod.

He reached out and squeezed her hand, then broke the physical contact.

We're doing good!

She grinned at him. *Yes.*

I think our best bet is making a mental distress call. And at the same time, building a signal fire on the beach. That will make it look like we're ordinary stranded shipwreck survivors.

The idea had leaped into his head. And for a moment he wondered where it had come from. But he decided it was a logical approach.

Which leads to the point that we need a cover story.

Like what?

He thought for a minute. *Something that can't easily be checked on Grand Fernandino.*

Like maybe we came in from Jamaica and ran into a storm. Our boat sank, and we managed to swim here. We could say we've been stranded for almost a week.

What's the name of the boat?

Hm. Maybe—the Penelope?

A nice touch.

And we'd both act like we don't know much about boats—or navigation.

She laughed. *It wouldn't be much of an act for me.*

She moved then, stroking her fingers against his arm, and he felt an instant spark of arousal.

Do we have to be turned on to put out a distress call?

Good question. If so, that's a little inconvenient.

Maybe it's a bonus?

He turned his head and rubbed his lips against hers, and they were instantly both caught up in the power of the sexual pull that hadn't let go of them since their first meeting.

Hmm. While we're in this state, maybe we should try out another skill.

Like what?

I've been thinking about the talents that people with

psychic abilities possess. Do you think we can affect the weather?

She looked at him doubtfully. *I never tried.*

Well, let's try now. He stood up and scanned the sky, seeing some dark clouds in the distance. *Let's pull them over and see if we can make it rain.*

I thought you wanted to build a fire on the beach. We'll get the wood wet.

Umm . . . right. He shook his head, wondering what he'd been thinking. *We can call a storm, but no rain.*

They spent the next half hour bringing dry wood from the jungle and piling it on the beach.

Then they stood close together.

You be in charge, Anna murmured inside his head as she reached to knit her fingers with his.

Okay.

He looked at the clouds, imagined them turning dark and drifting closer.

He could feel Anna adding her power to his, but it seemed like nothing was happening.

Start smaller, she suggested. As she spoke inside his head, he could feel her shifting her focus. After a few moments, the wind began to blow. She built on that success, making the trees around them sway. And as the wind picked up, she used it to drag clouds closer to the island.

How are you doing that? he asked.

I don't know.

Even if she didn't understand the process, it was clear that she could use it. Soon the sky was dark. Trees thrashed in the jungle.

They kept their focus on the storm for several minutes.

I'm getting tired, Anna finally said.

Yeah.

Almost as soon as they stopped focusing on the weather, the clouds drifted away and the sun came out again.

"I'd give us a C plus," Anna murmured.

"Well, that's not bad for a first try."

"We could see if we can strengthen our abilities in that area." She slid him a seductive look. "Or you could decide to reward me for the effort."

The suggestion was tempting, but he felt like they were running out of time. And he wasn't even sure what that meant.

Hold the thoughts. We'll have a hot and heavy celebration when we get off the island.

You're going to make me wait? As she spoke, she turned her head and nibbled on his earlobe, then sucked it into her mouth and ran her tongue along the edge.

He let himself enjoy the sensation for a moment, then said, *Business first. Pleasure later.*

When he'd gotten a fire going, he said, *We should call a boat to us.*

They stood with their shoulders together, staring out to sea as they sent their thoughts outward.

He gave her a quick look. He knew they were following his suggestion, but now that he was trying to do it, he felt pretty strange.

Help us. Our boat sank, and we're stranded on this island. Help us. Somebody help us.

It was like sending a broadcast into outer space, trying to bring an alien spaceship to earth. As they stood there on the beach, it felt like nobody could hear them. And if they did, they wouldn't respond.

I think we've bitten off more than we can chew.

Don't give up so fast, Anna murmured in his brain as her hand tightened on his.

Maybe it was a dumb idea.

You want to try and make a raft out of the dining room table?

Not unless we get a whole lot more desperate.

Well, I don't have a better suggestion. So let's stick with it. For a while, at least.

* * *

ANNA glanced at the fire. It had been burning for a while, and if they wanted to keep it going, they would need more fuel soon. She looked toward the dock.

"It may be leaning to the side, but it's probably hard to pry the boards loose," Zach muttered.

"I'm going for more wood."

She was about to walk into the jungle when something tingled at the edge of her mind, and she stopped short, then shaded her eyes and looked out to sea.

All she saw was a line of five pelicans heading from east to west.

"Wait," Zach advised.

She waited, staring as far into the distance as she could manage. After a few minutes, she saw a lighter speck in the blue water.

"A boat?"

"I think so," Zach answered.

They hadn't spoken about it, but both of them had apparently decided to keep the conversation aloud now that someone was coming.

She waited, her breath shallow as the boat grew bigger. "What is it?"

He stared at the boat as it plowed toward them. "A cabin cruiser. Maybe for fishing charters. Or just for motoring around."

"Okay."

She wanted to send her mind toward the boat, but she didn't want the crew to think she was probing them.

Did that make any sense? She didn't know. But when the impulse to run leaped into her mind, she gave Zach a quick glance.

"Who are they?" she whispered,

"I wish to hell I knew," he answered, clasping her hand more tightly.

The boat was close enough that she could see a couple of men on board. Two dark-skinned guys who were probably islanders crewing the craft. The other occupant looked like a tourist who'd interrupted a fishing trip when he'd heard their distress call.

They were all wearing shorts and knit shirts. And as far as Anna could see, they had no weapons.

She relaxed a fraction, but she still wasn't totally comfortable with the situation.

The tourist guy cupped his hands around his mouth. "I saw the smoke from your fire and came to investigate. Are you in trouble over there?" he called out.

"Glad you saw the signal," Zach shouted. "We're stranded, and we'd appreciate a ride back to civilization."

"I'll come get you."

After he used a winch to lower a small motorboat into the water, he and one of the crewmen climbed in and headed for the shore.

"Lucky I was fishing in the area."

When the bow touched the sand, he stopped, with the stern still in the water. He and the other man waded through the shallow water to the beach.

The tourist looked toward the house. "This is the De-Beck place."

"How do you know?"

"I was a guest here, before the storm damage. I guess if you have to be stranded somewhere, this is a better place than most."

Anna nodded.

"Come over here. Let me show you something you might have missed." He was speaking to Zach, who hesitated, then followed him a few feet away.

She watched the crewman follow them, then come up quickly behind Zach.

In that moment, she knew something was wrong.

Zach, she cried out in her mind, desperately trying to send him a warning.

He must have heard her, because he dodged to the side just as the crewman brought his hand down in a chopping motion.

It missed Zach's neck but connected with his shoulder in a loud thump.

Zach staggered, then regained his footing, going into a fighting crouch. But it was already too late for him to come out on top in the fight.

The man playing the tourist was already behind Zach, ready to coldcock him.

He brought something down on the back of Zach's head, and Zach made a sharp exclamation and crumpled to the ground, where he lay in the sand without moving.

"Zach," she screamed as she tried to rush forward. But the tourist stepped in her way and caught her by the shoulders.

CHAPTER
TWENTY-FOUR

FOR A MOMENT, Anna was incapable of organized thought. On a scream of rage, she flailed at him—then tried to lash out with her mind. When the man ignored the mental jab, she tried something else.

Don't kill Zach. Don't kill him. Don't kill him. Don't kill Zach, she repeated over and over.

The islander slapped her across the face, and she gasped.

The man who looked like a tourist came up behind her and grabbed her arm. His partner pulled a plastic bag out of his pocket, ripped the top open, and clamped a damp cloth over her face. It smelled strong and unpleasant.

She tried to scream again, but the sound ended in a gurgle as her head began to spin. She would have dropped to the ground if the man behind her hadn't held her up.

She tried to turn her head away from the cloth pressed over her nose and mouth, tried to struggle against the pungent smell that was turning her mind to oatmeal. And then she lost the fight and sank into oblivion.

* * *

MAYBE it was a long time later. Or maybe it was only a few minutes. By slow degrees, woozy consciousness returned, and Anna found that she was lying facedown on a flat surface. Something soft and comfortable. Her eyes blinked open, and she saw a bright pattern near her face. A bedspread or maybe a comforter.

Confusion simmered in her mind. She hadn't seen anything like that in the white house on the island. So then where was she?

The bed swayed gently.

Was she on a boat?

Had Zach taken her away on the *Odysseus*? Yes. That was what she wanted. So much. Yet she wasn't sure it was true.

Someone stroked his fingers through her hair.

"Wake up," he said softly.

She tried to move, but found that her arms and legs wouldn't obey her commands.

"Zach? What's wrong with me?"

"Forget about him. He's dead."

"No!" she gasped, trying to jerk to a sitting position. It was then that she realized that her wrists and ankles were strapped to the sides of the bed.

As she struggled against the bonds, she heard a swishing sound. Then something came down sharply on her bottom. Her bare bottom.

She screamed in surprise and pain. And fear as she realized she was naked and lying spread-eagle, facedown on a bed.

In desperation, her mind tried to reach for Zach—and came up with *nothing*.

When the man pressed his hand over her shoulder, panic threatened to swallow her whole.

"The sooner you forget about your dead lover, the easier it will be for you."

He stepped back, and his advice was punctuated by the

swishing sound. This time, when the stinging pain seared her bottom, she knew that she had been struck with a whip.

Since she'd awakened, her mind had been foggy. It was instantly sharp and clear.

She took her lip between her teeth, struggling not to scream again. She knew it would get her nowhere. And she didn't want to give him the satisfaction of knowing he had caused her pain.

He struck her twice, and she braced for another bite of the lash. Instead, the man lowered himself so that he was sitting on the floor beside the bed, his face even with her eye level.

She gasped when she saw it was Raoul San Donato— the gallery owner who had saved her from the street children. The man who had invaded her mind when she and Zach had been together. The man who had struggled to take her away from Zach.

And now he had her.

She closed her eyes, willing herself to stay calm. If she went stark raving mad, it would do her no good.

"I'm sorry to hurt you," he whispered. "I can feel your pain. It's almost as bad as if I were whipping my own flesh."

His voice was low and calm and chilling, and she felt his words like the lie that they were.

Struggling for her own calm, she whispered, "I'm not very comfortable like this. Let me up."

Again he stroked her hair, then lightly caressed her face with his finger. When she cringed away from him, his features took on a look of sadness.

"You're afraid of me now." '

"You kidnapped me. And you . . ."

"Punished you?"

"Yes."

"It was necessary to adjust your thinking. You belong to me. Not that other man."

"You're wrong," she answered immediately, without considering the consequences.

He stood, and the lash came down on her bottom again, this time with enough force to make her cry out.

"The sooner you forget about him, the better."

She swallowed and said nothing. Then she jumped when she felt his fingers lightly caressing the skin he had just abused.

His touch hurt, and she struggled not to wince. He took his hand away, and when he touched her again, his fingers were sticky with a lotion that eased the pain of the lash stings. Gently he caressed her as he spoke.

"You think you bonded with him. But that's nothing to the bond you will forge with me. His powers were puny. Mine are formidable."

Somehow she managed to press her lips together and say nothing.

"We will not speak his name again," he said, as though the matter were settled. "I'll just call him your old friend. I know that you and your old friend swam to the island. But I also know you couldn't have done it by yourself. So I'll keep you on my boat until we're ready for the ceremony that will bind us together for the rest of our lives."

"We don't belong together," she said in a soft voice, then knew instantly that she should have kept the observation to herself.

The lash cut the air, then came down hard—this time striking across her back.

"Soon, you'll realize how foolish you have been. You and I have a bright future together. We both have great power granted to us by the Blessed Ones. And with that power joined, and with the help of the saints, we will rule Grand Fernandino. You and I together. It will be a great thing."

She could feel him standing above her, looking down at

her. When he sat down on the bed and stroked his hand along the length of her spine, she struggled not to cringe away from his touch.

"I have freed you from the slavery of falsehood. I could do the ceremony now."

Fear leaped inside her.

"But you have been with him in the small hours of the morning." He made an angry sound. "And I don't take sloppy seconds."

Slowly, she let the breath trickle out of her lungs. He wasn't going to . . . do anything to her right away. Thank God.

Could he read her thoughts? She guessed not, since he didn't hit her again. But she kept her gaze downward so as not to reveal anything.

"Tomorrow, in front of my most important disciples, I will cement my bond with you."

He stood staring down at her, and she felt his mind probing at hers. The sensation was like hot pokers digging into her brain. No, not pokers—heated probes that gave her a little taste of his sick and sorry mind. She struggled not to react, either with any facial expression or mentally.

He came down on the floor again and lifted her chin, staring into her eyes.

"You felt me," he whispered.

She didn't deny it, because that might bring the lash again, so she only lay there, willing him to go away and stop tormenting her.

Did her silent entreaty have any effect on him? She didn't know. But he left her strapped to the bed and walked out of the cabin.

As soon as he left the room, she pulled against the bonds, trying to free herself, but she only hurt her wrists and ankles.

Defeated, she lay still and closed her eyes, fighting panic.

He had said Zach was dead. Could that really be true?

Again, she cast her mind outward, searching for him. But, again, she found nothing.

She wanted to cry. And scream. She wanted to call out to someone who would release her from her bonds. But the only other people she had seen on the ship were the men who had hurt Zach.

And San Donato must have been hiding below deck, waiting for the men to bring her to him.

Despite her best efforts, tears leaked out of her eyes and slid onto the bedspread. She wept for herself. And for Zach.

But one thing she knew—San Donato would never have her. Not the way he wanted her. Because submitting to him would be a living hell.

She wanted to disappear inside her own head, which was the only safe place to hide. But that gave him too much of an advantage. She had to stay aware. And she had to think of a way to get herself out of this.

Fighting the sickness in her throat, she thought back over the conversation.

He had said he would join with her in front of his most faithful followers. Could he really mean that? She knew he didn't just mean a mental joining. He meant it to be physical as well.

She shuddered. Did he intend to rape her in front of a bunch of other people?

Because that was what it would be. Rape.

She would rather be dead than join her body and her psyche with a man who had the mind of a reptile.

Rather die.

She'd said it automatically, but if that was her only way to escape, she would take it. But not unless it was her only option.

"WAKE up."

The command was soft, a woman's voice. For a moment,

Zach thought he'd been caught in another dream—where a boat had come to the island and he'd ended up in a heap on the sand.

"Anna?"

"Wake up."

His eyes snapped open, and he saw a woman sitting beside him and a man standing behind her.

Zach wasn't on the beach. He was on a bunk in a cabin on a boat.

Am I dreaming?

"You're awake."

His head throbbed. Around the pain, he remembered a boat. Men had come on a boat. The woman must have been inside, hiding. Along with this man.

He would fight them. But he was weak, and he must get some strength back. So he stalled—with a question.

"What have you done with Anna?"

"Nothing," the woman answered.

You're lying!

No!

Somewhere in his bruised mind it registered that he'd asked the question silently and she'd answered in the same way. The special way he and Anna could transmit meaning mind to mind.

But he wasn't capable of making sense of that at this moment. He only knew that these people had appeared. And Anna was gone.

Unable to contain his emotions, he lunged toward the woman, grabbing her, his arm across her throat, pulling her back against his chest where he could hold her securely.

He saw the man's face go white. "Let her go."

"I'll kill her if you don't tell me what you've done with Anna."

He tightened his hold, and the woman gasped.

The man's gaze shot to her face, then to Zach and back again. It all happened in less than a heartbeat. Something struck him. Something he couldn't even see. But it hit him with the force of a lightning bolt. And in the next second, he felt as though his head were splitting open and his brains were oozing out and running down his neck in slick rivulets.

ANNA'S body jerked as pain shot through her head. She gasped and flopped against the comforter, too weak to move. Yet even as the agony overwhelmed her, she felt joy swell in her heart. She felt Zach's pain.

And that told her something important. Something precious. She knew he was alive.

In the next moment, she understood the selfishness of that thought. He was hurting, and she could only think of herself.

Yet she understood her reaction. She had felt hopeless. She had vowed to kill herself if that's what it took to get away from San Donato. Now she knew that Zach was alive.

Was he here, on this boat? She didn't think so, because that would have been close enough to reach him with the ability they now had. So was he still on the island?

Zach. Zach. She called out to him, all the time expecting San Donato to come bursting in on her and punish her effort with more lashes of the whip.

Zach. Zach. I'm on a boat. I don't know where. Please, please find me.

She tried to send her mind out to him, to tell him where she was. But the distance was too far.

She'd only gotten that one moment of awareness—joined with a burst of pain. Now she was alone again.

And afraid.

ZACH heard a scream and knew it came from his own throat. As his breath choked off, his arm dropped away from the woman's throat.

She gasped and sprang off the bed, stumbling and almost falling in her haste to put distance between them. The man caught her and pulled her to him, holding her in his arms, his expression fierce with worry as he looked down at her.

"Are you all right?" he asked.

"Yes."

He looked over her shoulder, his eyes like lasers on Zach's face, and as he felt his own throat closing up, he wondered if looks really could kill.

The woman cupped her hand over the man's shoulder. "Don't hurt him," she whispered.

"Why not? He hurt you," he ground out.

"He's already in enough pain."

He gave her a long look, and the pressure on Zach's throat eased.

She was the one who spoke.

"We came to help you. We didn't take Anna. When we got to the island, Anna was already gone."

He dropped his head into his hands. "I'm sorry I . . . grabbed you. I thought you had her . . ."

"No."

"I have to get her back."

"We will."

He looked at them, seeing them as individuals for the first time. "You were here—in the dream."

"Yes."

"Who the hell are you?"

"Jordan Walker."

"And Lindsay Walker. Those are our real names, although we don't use them in public anymore. Now we're Jordan and Lindsay West."

He studied their faces again and was sure they had meant him no harm.

"I have to find Anna," he repeated. Then a terrible sick feeling grabbed him, and he made a strangled sound. "Shit!

San Donato's got her. After he tried to kill me in the dream, he was here again—distracting me. He got me to light a fire and send out a mental distress signal, so I'd think we'd called the boat that came. And he got me fooling around with the weather—to make me focus on the wrong thing and use up my energy."

Lindsay winced. "I'm sorry."

"Not as sorry as I am." He wanted to surge up and bang his head against the wall.

Lindsay put a firm hand on his shoulder. "Don't."

"I let him sucker me."

"And now you're feeling like . . . without her you're . . . only half alive," Lindsay murmured.

"Yes."

"We'll help you find her, but not yet."

Panic welled inside him, and he tried to struggle up again, but Jordan stepped quickly forward and pressed a hand firmly against his shoulder.

"You have a concussion. We've got to heal it before you can go anywhere," the woman said. "Your head hurts, doesn't it?"

"Yes," he whispered, looking at Jordan. "From that . . . mind zap you gave me."

"Not just that," Lindsay answered. "Someone hit you on the head and left you to die. Slowly, painfully. You would have done just that—if we hadn't found you."

He winced.

"Lie back. We've started healing you. We need to finish."

He didn't want to lie back. He had to find Anna. He was sure San Donato had her. He had no real proof. But he was sure the bastard had figured out their location and come to the island.

He'd captured Anna. Next he was going to steal her mind away. And Zach was the only person who could stop him.

Lindsay pressed a hand to his shoulder.

"Let us work on you," she murmured. "Otherwise, you won't be any good to Anna—or to yourself."

He made a frustrated sound. He could feel time slipping through his fingers like grains of sand that he could never recover. Every second that San Donato had Anna brought her closer to disaster.

Still, he knew that Lindsay was speaking the truth. Even the smallest movement felt like little men with pickaxes were banging away inside his head.

With a sigh, he lay down on the bunk.

Lindsay knelt beside him. Jordan walked forward to join her. They clasped hands, and Lindsay pressed the fingers of her free hand to Zach's forehead.

"Relax. Close your eyes," she said as she stroked her fingers over his sweaty skin.

He did as she asked, knowing he was taking a chance. She had talents he had never dreamed of, and she could hurt him or heal him. She was the one who would make that decision.

He could feel power radiating from her, flowing into him like warm, honeyed syrup. It felt good. And as the healing energy enveloped him, he sensed something inside his head change for the better. He had been hurt. Now he was mending. And quickly.

"How are you doing that?" he whispered.

"We've been practicing. We can show you and Anna how to heal."

He answered with a small nod, thinking that he had to get her back first.

Or was he kidding himself? Was it already too late?

CHAPTER
TWENTY-FIVE

RAOUL STRODE UP the companionway and out onto the back deck. Two of the men he'd brought along nodded at him, and he nodded back but said nothing. They knew better than to disturb him unless he invited them to approach.

In the past few years, he'd done many services for his people—using the powers the gods had given him. And he was known on the island for his ability to curse an enemy or create a favorable outcome, like when he'd helped William Banda's son pass the test that would get him into a school on the mainland. He'd brought people back from the brink of death. And he'd caused deaths—with the help of the saints.

More than that, he'd sent money back to his village. Not just to individuals, but to the whole community. He'd built better houses for the people who lived there. He'd constructed vacation residences for rich people who wanted to get away for a week or a month—and have a ready pool of servants at their beck and call.

And he'd created an enclave where his followers could meet and worship the saints with him.

People in Palmiro and people still living up in the hills had come to rely on him to bring the favor of the gods into their lives. And when he'd needed this boat, some of his followers had borrowed it from a rich man who was not in residence now.

He'd earned the loyalty and the respect of his people. He had made himself their priest. And his power with them was more than Joe Hondino had ever commanded.

But his powers were nothing compared to what they would be when he joined his mind with Anna. She was already strong. And she would get stronger as he taught her the ways of the Blessed Ones.

He walked to the rail and stood staring toward Grand Fernandino as they motored in the direction of the island.

He had lied to Anna about being far from his base of operation, but he felt no guilt about telling her what he wanted her to believe. She had thought she could get away from him, but he had found her and brought her back. He would do anything necessary to keep her and bind her to him.

And the sooner the better. In her dream, he'd sensed another man and woman—offshore in a boat. Were they real? Or had she made them up? He couldn't be sure. But in case they were looking for Anna, he wanted her to be under his control before they found her.

Let her think that she had more time. Probably she was trying to figure out how she could escape him. But he had a little surprise he would spring on her very soon. And then there would be no more thought of escape.

One of the men came toward him, the man who had posed as a tourist earlier, and stood respectfully waiting for Raoul to acknowledge him.

He allowed half a minute to pass before saying, "Yes?"

"We'll be landing in two hours."

"I want the grounds ready for the ceremony," he said, expecting that his order had been obeyed.

"I spoke on the radio to Franco. The brothers and sisters up at the enclave are making everything ready for you now."

ZACH pushed himself to a sitting position. "I'm fine," he snapped.

Lindsay looked doubtful. "Your head isn't completely healed."

"This will have to do." He swung his gaze to Jordan. "I have to find Anna."

"I know. I know what you're feeling."

"How could you?" he shouted, somehow keeping himself from making the protest physical. His emotions were barely under control, and the calm sound of Jordan's voice grated at his nerve endings.

Lindsay gave him an understanding look. "Because we've been through it," she whispered. Closing her eyes, she clutched Jordan's hand, even as she pressed her fingers more firmly against Zach's forehead.

Panic shot through him as the bunk where he sat and the boat disappeared. He was in another time. Another place. Lindsay was in a room with cold stone walls, strapped to a chair, unable to move. A man stared down her. Casually he reached toward her and ripped her blouse open, manhandling her breasts.

Somehow, at the same time, from another vantage point, he saw Jordan, sitting in an office in the same building, facing two other men who kept their malignant gazes on him. And he understood that Jordan was struggling not to give away that he knew what they were doing to Lindsay in a basement cell. Because if they figured out Jordan and Lindsay could communicate when they weren't touching, they would kill them both.

As quickly as the images and impressions formed in his head, they snapped off, and Zach was left staring at the two people who had opened up their minds to him and let him share a few horrible and very personal moments of their life.

He gulped in a breath of air and let it out. "That happened to you?" he heard himself say.

"Yes," Lindsay answered.

"And we got away," Jordan added. "Otherwise, we wouldn't be here."

"Who did that to you?" Zach asked.

"The man sitting behind the desk was Kurt MacArthur. He was the head of the Crandall Consortium. Years ago, they funded Dr. Remington's fertility clinic in Darien, Connecticut. The one we told you about."

Jordan stopped talking, and Lindsay took up the narrative. "Jim Swift was standing behind him. When we burned down the Crandall Consortium headquarters building . . ."

Zach stared at her. "You burned down the building?"

"That was the only way we could escape. So you see, we're not afraid to take desperate measures to defend ourselves. For the record, someone else shot MacArthur and killed him. We escaped from the building, and went into hiding. We thought Jim Swift had died in the fire. But he survived, and he's going after any of the Dariens he can find."

"Why?"

"He thinks we're . . ." He stopped and shrugged. "Well, I don't know exactly what's in his warped mind. But apparently he sees us as a threat to civilization as he knows it.

"For years, he was MacArthur's chief hit man. So we're assuming he was too badly injured in the fire to keep up the wet work on his own."

Zach winced at the casually delivered assessment. Obviously, Jordan Walker's recent experiences had hardened his outlook on life. But the same was true for himself, Zach silently admitted. Until a few days ago, he hadn't been associated with any hit men.

"Well, the men who shanghaied us are dead. After we ditched in the sea, I slashed holes in the bottom of their raft. So I guess I took the same attitude as you. If I had to do it to save my life—and Anna's—I would."

Lindsay let out a sigh. "They may not be dead."

His gaze shot to her. "Why do you think so?"

"I can't be sure. But I feel . . . something." She shrugged. "Maybe I'm wrong. Maybe it's just that Jim Swift is still out there. He was focused on Anna. He could have figured out that you bonded with her."

ANNA closed her eyes, taking deep, even breaths of air, the way she did before she got ready for her act.

She had gone to pieces. San Donato had *made* her go to pieces, and she'd better be ready to fight him when he came back.

But first, maybe she could get some information.

She couldn't move her hands more than a few inches, but she pressed her fingers against the comforter, trying to pick up memories the way she picked them up on stage.

She caught an image of a man, not San Donato, lying on the bed. She studied his face. He had gray hair, a narrow mustache, and a thick gold chain around his neck. A rich tourist. Or maybe someone who lived in Grand Fernandino part of the year?

He looked contented and prosperous. Probably this was his cabin cruiser, and he had no idea that a bastard named San Donato had borrowed it. Too bad she couldn't contact the guy and tell him that a gallery owner in town had taken his boat—and was using it to kidnap a woman.

A shiver went through her, and she was immediately sorry that she'd thought about herself. She gave another tug at her bonds, then flopped on the comforter, willing herself not to cry.

Zach. Oh, Lord, Zach. San Donato thinks he can bond

with me. I won't let him, she vowed, then couldn't help adding, *but I'm afraid of what he's going to do. Don't let him . . .*

She couldn't put the next part into words. She was sure she knew what it was. But she didn't want to think about it. Not when she was lying naked and helpless on this bed.

So she struggled to pull her elbow toward the place where San Donato had been sitting. It took a long time, but finally she reached the spot.

When she did, she gasped.

ZACH stood and paced to the other side of the room, then turned to face them.

For a moment he thought . . .

"What?" Lindsay asked.

"Just for a moment . . . I . . ."

"Was that Anna? Trying to reach you?"

"Yes!"

He squeezed his eyes closed and concentrated with every fiber of his mind. But it didn't do any good. Not now.

"Maybe we should talk about the Darien children a little more," she suggested.

"Why?"

"So you'll understand better," Jordan answered. "The more you know, the more effective you can be."

Zach sighed. He didn't want to take a side trip into his own background. He wanted a direct line to Anna. But maybe Jordan was right.

"Bonding turned on our psychic powers. And yours, too," Jordan said.

"But what about Anna?" Zach shot back. "She was already a psychic."

"She was only using a tiny part of her talents. Joining with you made the difference. Together you were awakening her latent abilities—and yours," Lindsay said.

"But we met earlier. When we were children."

Lindsay blinked. "You did?"

"Not physically. I had an imaginary friend, and it was her."

Jordan whistled through his teeth, then glanced at his wife. "Maybe we need to reevaluate some of our assumptions."

"But not now!" Zach almost shouted. "Anna's gone, and we're sitting here and talking, instead of going after her."

"Where should we go? Where is she?" Jordan asked.

Zach whirled toward him, his fear and frustration bubbling over. "I don't fucking know! That's the problem. I don't know. I got a flash of . . . something. But I don't know where it was coming from."

"Maybe we can find her," Lindsay murmured.

"How?"

"When we were on the run, one of the talents we developed was viewing a remote location."

He didn't dare let hope bloom. Not yet. Still, he asked, "You mean like what San Donato did when he spied on us?"

"Yes," Jordan answered. "Lindsay is better at it than I am."

"I saw a friend of ours shot and killed," she said, the horror of it bleeding into her voice and into her mind.

Zach winced. The more these people revealed, the more he understood what they'd been through. And they'd escaped with their lives. Together. If they could do it, so could he and Anna. He had to believe that was true.

"Jordan and I did the remote viewing together," she said.

"Can you do it now?" Zach demanded.

Lindsay and Jordan looked at each other. Jordan was the one who answered. "We don't have a focus for the search. We were hoping you could direct the process."

Zach slammed his fist against the bulkhead. "In other words, you're offering me false hope."

"No!" Lindsay shouted. "But the question is, can you trust us enough to open your mind to us?"

That was certainly a big question. Jordan and Lindsay had dropped into his life, and they could be lying to him.

"No," Lindsay said, and he knew she had caught the thought. "Trust us," she whispered.

"What if I can't?"

Her face grew so sad that he felt his heart squeeze. And he knew in that moment that rescuing Anna meant more to her than he had imagined.

Before he could say anything else, she crossed the cabin and reached for his hand. Jordan seized both her hand and Zach's free hand.

At the three-way contact, Zach felt a shock go through him. Much like the sensation when he'd first touched Anna.

"We healed you. Now let us join with you," Lindsay murmured. Did she actually speak? Or did he only hear it in his mind? He didn't know. But he felt them opening to him, opening and sharing secrets that no person would willingly give up.

He saw Jordan as a boy—locked in a closet.

He saw Lindsay at a school dance, being pulled tight against a boy she couldn't stand.

He saw the two of them sitting in a restaurant, sharing the shock of touching. And then they were in a garden, wildly kissing—until an old woman yelled at them to cut it out.

It had been like what had happened between himself and Anna—that wild, out-of-control need to connect on the most basic level. And because he recognized the desperate need, a door inside his head opened.

Thank you, Lindsay murmured.

We care about you and Anna.

He knew in that moment that they had risked their lives to save him. He hadn't been thinking about that. Instead, he'd been fighting them.

I've been acting like an ungrateful lout, he said.

You're acting like a man who was alone for all of his life—then found a partner who brought him more than he ever expected from another human being.

He looked at Lindsay, knowing that the words softly spoken in his mind had come from her.

Lie back and relax.

He lay down, and she moved her hand from his and pressed it against his forehead.

Try to find Anna now, she said.

Panic surged. She was gone, and he had no idea how to search for her across the wide blue water of the Caribbean.

But he could feel Lindsay's calm strength and Jordan still with them in the background. He was there, but he was letting Lindsay do the heavy lifting.

Send your thoughts outward, she told him.

Oh sure. Easier said than done when he had no idea which direction to look. Then he remembered he had often done something like this when he searched for a shipwreck. Whatever he did then, he could do now.

Closing his eyes, he focused all his concentration on the woman he loved.

He had never used that word before. Not even in his mind. He should be embarrassed to use it now, when two other people were inside his head. But he didn't have energy to spare for embarrassment.

With every shred of concentration he could muster, he reached toward Anna. He felt Jordan helping him, and Lindsay adding an extra burst of power—something that he didn't possess himself.

But it was hopeless. It wasn't going to work.

He sagged back against the bunk. And just as he was about to give up, he found Anna. He didn't even know how it had happened. Suddenly, he could see her.

And what he saw was like a knife slashing through his chest.

She was on a boat. Lying on her stomach, naked, her wrists and ankles secured to the corners of a bed.

Across her buttocks and back, red slashes marred her beautiful skin.

He screamed in anguish, and the picture snapped off.

ZACH lay panting on the bed, the image burned into his mind. He couldn't cope with it.

"The bastard's . . . already raped her," he managed to say, although his throat was so clogged he could barely speak.

"No!" It was Jordan who spoke.

"What the hell do you know about it!"

"I caught the edge of her thoughts. She was horrified he was going to use sex to bind her to him. He hasn't done it yet. He's only . . . punished her."

"Whipped her!"

"Yes," Lindsay answered as she stroked her fingers over the hot flesh of his forehead.

"We won't let him rape her," Jordan growled.

"We don't even know where she is!"

"What did you see?"

"The cabin of a boat. An expensive boat." He stopped, thinking. "It's the boat that came to the island. The crew pretended to rescue us. Then they hit me over the head."

"So he hasn't gotten very far."

"They're going somewhere." Somehow Zach forced himself not to howl at the two other people in the cabin. This wasn't their fault. They were trying to help. "She doesn't know where San Donato is taking her."

"That's right."

"But he does. And we have to figure that he's nearby. On the same boat. If you can get into his head, you can find out."

"Into *his* head?" Zach asked, the idea making his guts twist with pain that was only partly physical.

"You have a better suggestion?" Jordan answered.

"No."

"We'll stay with you."

"But what if he knows we're there? If he knows I've found him, won't he rush ahead with what he's doing?"

"He could," Lindsay whispered.

"Can't the three of us . . . do something? Can't we cut her bonds or something?"

Jordan looked doubtful. "Did you develop a lot of skill at telekinesis?"

"No. I was hoping you had."

"Only a little. And not from this far away."

Zach lowered his head into his hands, pressing his palms against his forehead.

"Maybe we can fool San Donato," Lindsay said.

"How?"

She looked apologetic. "I picked up something from you."

"Oh yeah?"

"He worships a goddess named Ibena."

"What about it?" he snapped.

"If he figures out we're there, I can take the lead and tell him I'm Ibena—and praise him for the bold steps he's taken."

Sickness rose in Zach's throat at the very idea of praising the bastard. Yet it might work.

San Donato was so sure of himself. So convinced that he was making the right moves. Maybe that *was* the way to get him. Maybe the goddess could tell him to turn Anna loose.

He knew Lindsay had caught his desperate thought when she said, "We have to keep this in character. If we try to go that far, he'll think something's fishy. Let's leave it at praising him."

He shot her a dark look, but he knew she was probably right.

They were both gazing at him expectantly, waiting for his decision.

"Let's do it," he said, surprised that his voice sounded strong and determined. Inside, he was cringing.

CHAPTER
TWENTY-SIX

LINDSAY SAT DOWN on the bunk beside him. Jordan took the other side.

"Go for it," Jordan said.

He closed his eyes, sending his mind out again, toward that ship where San Donato was holding Anna captive.

Because he'd done it before, it was easier to get there this time. And he could go in by slow degrees. First he saw the ship below him, sailing through turquoise water. Then he came closer and saw men standing on the deck.

One of them was San Donato. He'd never met the bastard in person, but he knew it was him—just from the arrogant way he was leaning on the rail, staring at land that was rapidly approaching.

Grand Fernandino? Or somewhere close?

He felt Lindsay take the lead now, dropping down toward the man, who jerked when he felt her presence.

So there was no sneaking up on him.

"Ibena?" he whispered, awe in his voice.

Yes. I've come to tell you how proud I am of you, she answered.

The arrogant bastard didn't question that for a moment.

A goddess had dropped in on him, and he was totally sure he was worthy of her regard. Still, he kept his inner voice reverential.

I do your bidding, always.

I know. I am so happy to have you as my most powerful follower. You have gone through much to bring the woman back.

Yes.

We will talk more, after you bind her to you.

Zach could hear the surface conversation. He thought Lindsay was probing more deeply into the man's mind, but he couldn't tell exactly what she was doing.

San Donato kept flapping his silent mouth.

As soon as we get to shore, I'm heading to the ceremonial ground.

No. I want you to wait. Until midnight. It will mean more if you wait until the midnight hour.

If I can.

You dare to question me?

Pardon, goddess. But I must do this quickly—to serve you better.

You serve at my pleasure. Do not forget your place.

Zach felt the man cringe.

I am your servant, San Donato silently said.

Lindsay broke the connection, and Zach fought the sickness in his throat.

"We got a lot of information from his mind," Lindsay said.

"Like what? Why didn't you *make* him wait longer for his damn ceremony?" Zach demanded.

"Because I could feel his impatience. He wants to serve the goddess. But on his own terms."

"Oh, great."

Jordan jumped back into the conversation. "He's heading for the village where he was born. But this boat is faster than his. We made an educated guess about his destination after we picked you up, so we're already heading toward Grand Fernandino."

Zach had been so preoccupied that he hadn't realized they were already speeding toward the island.

Jordan left the room to tell the captain to aim for the far side of the island, and Lindsay looked at Zach. "He's poured a lot of money into the place—making improvements for the residents—so they'll be loyal to him. And he has a ceremonial ground halfway up the mountain."

"A ceremonial ground?"

"Where he and his followers worship the goddess."

Zach tried to take that in.

Lindsay laid a hand on his shoulder. "We'll get there."

"And then what? How many people will he have around him? All loyal to him because he's bought and paid for their loyalty, so that every one of them will be ready to stop us?"

Jordan came back into the room and fixed him with a direct look.

"You're not giving up, are you?"

"Of course not."

"On the way there, we'll talk strategy."

"Like what?"

"You'll be closer to Anna. You can contact her. Get her to help you. Maybe she can disable San Donato. Or we can provide a big distraction."

"Yeah," he answered, wondering if that was just wishful thinking.

ANNA closed her eyes, but her mind was racing. They were at sea. And probably everyone on the boat knew she was tied to the bed. So could she leap over the side before they figured out what had happened?

She knew it would do her no good to try and pull her wrists and ankles free. Instead she thought about the leather cuffs that held her. Could she make them loosen?

She'd never tried anything like that. It meant affecting the material world. But hadn't she and Zach done something similar?

Yes, she told herself. This was like making love to Zach without touching him.

She'd half thought that he'd just been wanting to play around. Now she knew that it had been a deadly serious game.

She set her mind to the task, focusing on the leather, imagining each strap getting longer, just long enough for her to slip her hands through. If she could do that, she could escape from the room and dive off the ship. It didn't matter where she was. She'd rather take her chances in the water.

Trying to get away helped hold her panic at bay. But her mental powers seemed to have no effect on her bonds. Because he'd drugged her? Not just to put her to sleep but to keep her from using her psychic abilities?

That could very well be true, because she felt a kind of deadness in her mind.

Still, she kept up the effort until she felt something different about the movement of the ship. The engines slowed, and she tried to raise her head and look out the porthole. Then the boat bumped gently against something. A pier.

They were docking. And she wondered if San Donato had lied to her. He'd said he wouldn't hold his ceremony yet. So what was happening now?

Long minutes ticked by as she lay on the bunk with her heart pounding.

When she heard a sound in the corridor outside, she cringed. She wanted to hide, but there was no place to go. Still tied to the bed, she couldn't stop her gaze from shooting to the door. It opened, and to her profound relief, it wasn't San Donato who stepped in. Instead, there were three tall, muscular-looking women, all wearing white shirts and loose white pants. The one who was a head taller than the other two stayed in the doorway.

A bronze-skinned woman with a thin angular face and short-cropped hair strode to the bunk and stood looking down at Anna with an awed expression on her face.

"You are very pretty," she murmured in a soft island voice. "And our priest has said you have powers that will match his own. You will be a good mate for the blessed man."

Anna cringed. "I don't want to be his mate. Let me go and I'll . . . I'll reward you."

The woman's reverent look changed immediately. "Quiet," she advised. "We are here to prepare you and take you to the ceremonial ground."

When Anna opened her mouth to speak, the woman raised her hand in warning. "We do not want to hurt you, but you will be punished if you step beyond the bounds. Nod if you understand." It sounded strange to hear those words in the woman's softly accented voice.

Anna gave a small nod.

"I am Evelyn," the woman said. "My assistants are Maria and Wilhelmina." She gestured toward the other two. "We do not want to hurt you," she repeated. Then, in a softer voice she added, "Among all the women of the island, you have been granted a great honor, and we only wish to serve you."

"Then why can't I speak?" Anna dared to ask.

Evelyn gave her a kind smile—like the smile a teacher might have given a slow student. "You are blessed among all women, but you are not ready to address us yet, because you are ignorant of the ways of the saints. After the ceremony, we will be pleased to hear your words of wisdom."

So what did that mean? After the ceremony, her mind would belong to San Donato?

A shudder went through her. She would fight him with everything she had. Before the ceremony. During the ceremony. And afterward.

ZACH came up on deck and inspected the boat. Then he stepped to the helm.

They'd hired a captain from Palmiro—a man who wasn't afraid of San Donato.

But as the most experienced seaman aboard, Zach took over the job of piloting the craft, getting as much speed out of the twin 225HP Mercury Optimax engines as possible.

Jordan and Lindsay stood on either side of him, correcting his course because they knew the destination. But they couldn't give it to him as GPS coordinates. All they could do was tell him when he was going wrong and when he was on the correct heading.

It was a strange way to travel, but he didn't question their ability. They had proved what they could do.

As they plowed through the water, he sent his mind out toward Anna. He had made contact with her briefly. But he couldn't find her now, and he struggled not to panic. He had to trust that they were getting closer to her.

It was dark, but he didn't turn on the running lights. They sped through the black water, and he began to see some lights winking on the shore.

"We're getting close," Jordan whispered.

Zach clamped his hands on the wheel and mentally urged the boat forward.

ANNA figured she might as well save her breath—for her escape. She hadn't gotten away while they were at sea, but she could still do it.

"We are chosen among women, too. We have been trusted to serve you."

Oh, sure.

We will release you from the bed," Evelyn said. "Then we will take you to get ready for the ceremony."

Anna lay very still, staring at them, trying to get inside their minds. If she could just plant suggestions in their consciousness that they should let her go, maybe they would do it.

Breathing shallowly, she tried to send her thoughts outward. She met what felt like a wall of resistance.

Either these women had been chosen because their minds were difficult to contact, or they had been given some kind of training or treatment by San Donato that made them less susceptible to her psychic powers.

Working quickly, Evelyn unbuckled the cuffs that held Anna's wrist and ankle on one side of the bed. Maria unbuckled the bonds on the other side. And Wilhelmina, the one who looked like she'd inherited football player genes, stayed blocking the doorway, presumably ready to swat their prisoner to the ground if she tried anything funny.

When Anna was free, Evelyn and Maria helped her to her feet—a naked woman among three other women who were fully dressed. She might have hunched her shoulders and bowed her head. Instead, she kept her chin and shoulders up. She had been lying down for so long that her legs were unsteady, and she would have fallen if they hadn't been on either side of her, holding her up.

She moved one leg and then the other, trying to restore her muscle tone after having had her movements restricted.

"You'll feel better soon," Evelyn whispered.

"I hope so," she answered, sliding her gaze to the porthole. She could see that night had fallen. Well, that gave her some idea of how long she'd been here.

From what she could see, she thought they were in a small harbor, with the outlines of a few buildings visible on the shore. And jungle-covered mountains rising behind them.

A harbor in a sparsely populated area? It didn't matter; wherever she was, she was going to make a break for it—and take her chances in the water or the jungle.

Too bad she was so sluggish, she thought as she urged her body back to life, secretly clenching and unclenching the muscles in her arms and legs. But she continued to pretend she was very weak, hoping the deception would give her an advantage.

Wilhelmina bent down and picked up a bag that she'd set on the floor. With one eye on Anna, she pulled out a white terry cloth bathrobe, like the kind that hotels sometimes provided for guests.

She handed it to Evelyn, who helped Anna put it on. Then she tied the belt at the waist.

"Do you feel better now?"

"Yes."

Her nakedness was covered, but the robe was heavy, weighing her down. And her feet were bare. Not the best getup for an escape attempt. That was probably the point of the outfit.

When she was dressed in the robe, Wilhelmina knocked on the door. It opened, and two men stepped in.

Her heart sank as she saw they were large and well-muscled. Apparently San Donato had only wanted women to see her naked. But he'd provided a couple of burly male guards to make sure she didn't get away.

The newcomers eyed her appraisingly, and she felt her stomach clench. Hating the expectant look on their faces, she turned her head away quickly, glad of the robe.

"Let's go." Evelyn gestured toward the door. When Anna hung back, Wilhelmina grabbed her arm and marched her through. The men took up the front and rear of the procession, and the little parade made its way up the companionway and onto the deck.

As she walked, Anna silently appealed to the men and women guarding her.

This is kidnapping. Don't you know you can get into bad trouble for this? What do you owe San Donato? He just wants to use you, the way he wants to use me.

Anna repeated that mantra and more choice words. The message didn't seem to be getting through to anyone around her.

She fought the sick feeling rising inside her. When she stopped walking, the woman behind her pressed against her back.

"Come."

She started forward again, feeling like a farm animal being led to a slaughterhouse.

Her gaze darted from side to side, and at least she saw no sign of San Donato.

They climbed a short flight of stairs to the back deck of the boat, which was about fifteen feet wide and twenty feet long.

Evelyn held her right arm as she stood there on the teak boards. Raising her head, Anna surveyed the scene around her. She saw houses with lighted windows. Beyond them was dense darkness, maybe the jungle. It looked like the boat was docked at the end of a pier that jutted about twenty yards into the water. She could see a light at the end.

The man at the front of the line spoke to someone, and the group halted.

For a moment, no one seemed to be looking at her. Wrenching herself away, she dashed to the rail, dragging in air, and jumped over the side. The white robe dragged her down as soon as she hit the water, but as she sank, she fumbled with the belt and pulled it free, then wiggled out of the robe and let it float away.

Above her she heard shouting, the voices distorted by the water.

"Hellfire!"

"She got away."

"Over the side."

"Get her."

The sharp order came from San Donato, and she knew he had been at the end of the dock waiting to gloat over her arrival.

She swam under the dock, came up on the other side, and took a breath before going down again.

Should she head into the sea? Or was her best chance on land?

Too bad she didn't know more about this damn place. Or about the island.

But she figured that she'd be in more danger on land. So she struck out in the water, angling away from the shore, hoping the darkness would hide her.

For a few minutes, it seemed to work. Then she saw a light skimming over the water.

When it focused on her, she dived again, going deeper, changing the angle of her strokes, thinking that she would go farther out in the water, then head back to the shore. If they'd found her in the water, she'd take her chances on land.

"Come back," a loud voice boomed, probably augmented by a bullhorn.

She had no intention of obeying.

And now she had another goal. She'd lost contact with Zach, and that had been part of the reason for her despair. But once she'd gotten free of San Donato's prison, she sensed Zach—speeding toward her.

She was sure he was out there. In a boat. In her mind, she could see him standing at the wheel, urging the craft forward.

Or was she making that up because she wanted so desperately for it to be true?

As she swam away from captivity, she plowed some of her energy into contacting him.

Zach? Zach? Can you hear me?

At first, there was no answer. She wanted to cry out in

frustration, but she didn't waste the energy. Instead, she tried again, and this time she was rewarded with the sound of his voice inside her head.

Yes! Thank God. Did you get away?

Yes. I'm coming. I'm coming to you.

Are you all right?

Yes.

When she heard splashes above her, she began swimming faster. Behind her, lights flashed on the waves.

More people were coming into the water, looking for her. But did they know where she'd gone?

She was praying they didn't—and that the light wouldn't find her.

Her only option was to keep swimming, and hope that Zach could get to her before San Donato's followers caught her. But after being tied down to the bunk for so long, her muscles felt flabby, and she could already feel her energy flagging.

"SHE got away. She's swimming toward us. Thank God," Zach called to the other people on the boat.

He felt a tremendous sense of relief. Still, he couldn't relax until Anna was with him. Leaning forward, he stared into the darkness, straining his eyes, trying to see her—even when he knew she was still too far away for visual contact.

"Maybe I can spot her."

When Zach reached for the lights, Jordan grabbed his hand. "Don't."

"I need her to see us, so she'll know where she's going."

"If you shine a light on her, you'll give away her location."

"Christ! You're right."

"The two of you are telepathic. Focus your thoughts on her. Don't turn on the light until she's closer," Jordan suggested.

"And another thing," Lindsay added. "You don't want them to know you're here."

"What does it matter?" he asked, triumph welling up inside him. Anna had done it. She had gotten away from the bastard who'd kidnapped her, and she was swimming away as fast as she could. Toward Zach. The man she belonged with.

"Come on. You can do it. Come on," he shouted across the water.

He was starting to breathe easy—until she screamed, and his heart leaped into his throat, choking off his breath.

CHAPTER
TWENTY-SEVEN

A BLOODCURDLING SCREAM ripped from Anna's mouth as a hand caught her leg. Kicking out, she tried to dislodge the fingers that closed around her ankle and pulled her under.

She tried to gasp in a breath of air, but she went below the surface too quickly.

The water churned around her. The hand that had yanked her down pulled her up, and someone threw a cloth over her head. It smothered her senses, smothered her brain. All at once, she couldn't put two coherent thoughts together.

Strong hands grabbed her under the arms and hauled her up into the small boat. She was naked and dripping except for the cloth over her head.

She lay there sprawled across something hard—a seat. Someone threw a blanket over her naked body, covering her face.

Then a harsh voice spoke. "Take her back. Make her ready for the ceremony. Now."

She cringed away. It was San Donato. And he was sitting right beside her.

The cloth over her head felt like it was choking off her breath, choking off coherent thoughts. San Donato pulled the fabric up, exposing her face, leaving the top of her head covered as he took her chin in his hand and turned her toward him.

"Did you really think you could get away from me?"

Her lungs burned. Her pulse thundered in her throat. When her lips moved, no sound came out.

She had tried to escape. And this is where it had gotten her—closer to doom.

The boat jerked, then leaped through the water, cutting a wide circle, and she knew they were heading back to the shore. Away from Zach and toward the end of her life as she knew it.

I tried. I'm sorry. I tried.

She had no idea if her silent words had reached Zach. The only thing she knew was that it took too much energy to say more, when the covering was smothering her mind. She closed her eyes and sagged back against the seat. She had thought she would kill herself if it came to this. The fabric over her head suffocated her determination. It felt like the clinging material was an extension of the man who loomed over her, like he'd infused an inanimate object with his will.

He made a rough sound and moved, making the boat rock dangerously. But he didn't seem to care.

He spoke into a radio or something, and she could hear him giving orders to people on the land.

"I don't want to go up to the village. It want this finished as soon as possible. We'll use the walled enclosure down here. Set up an altar there. Make sure it's ready for the marriage ceremony."

As he spoke, the boat lunged forward. Soon they were bumping up against a solid barrier.

The dock? The shore?

San Donato stood and climbed out of the boat. She could hear him berating someone.

Good, she hoped they got in big trouble. At least that gave her some satisfaction.

"You fool! You should have been guarding her."

A man answered, his voice high and scared. "We thought . . ."

The lash bit through the air, and the underling screamed. San Donato slashed at him over and over, and Anna cringed. The man had been calm, but he was losing control of himself.

Then San Donato bellowed an order, and someone scurried forward.

Strong hands lifted Anna up and hauled her onto the deck, and the cloth fell back, partly exposing her face to the night air. She saw San Donato talking to someone, and when he stepped aside, she gasped. It was Etienne Bertrand.

She blinked, trying to focus on his face. "You . . . did . . . this . . . to . . . me," she managed.

His expression was stony.

"Why? What did I do to you?"

"You were perfect for my master."

"Your master! What are you, a slave?"

"No," he answered, his voice low and hard.

"You're fooling yourself."

Two strong men grabbed her arms and marched her along the boards.

Neither of them let go of her until she had been hustled into a house and down a darkened hall, where they pushed her through a door into a brightly lit room.

The ceremony?

She shuddered, made an effort to focus on her surroundings, and found she was in a large, well-appointed bathroom. The walls were marble. The counter was black granite, with white double sink bowls. And there was a separate Jacuzzi tub and a stall shower large enough to wash a small automobile.

The three women who had come to her cabin in the boat were waiting for her, their eyes narrowed as they stared at her. They wore the same white uniforms, only now they had thin rubber gloves on their hands.

"You betrayed us," Evelyn said, her voice sharp. "He was angry with us."

Anna shrugged, and the cloth that had half fallen off her head hit the floor. Desperately, she tried to clear her thoughts. As soon as the cloth was gone, she felt some of her intellect come back. Raising her chin, she said, "I'm in love with another man."

"That is very foolish, when our priest wants you for his bride."

The word "bride" made her cringe. "I don't want him."

"You will," Evelyn said in a strangely calm voice. She flicked her hand, and Maria stepped to the shower and turned on the water. It came pouring out of a rounded fixture like rain.

While Maria adjusted the water, Evelyn pulled the blanket away and tossed it across the counter.

Evelyn and Wilhelmina each took one of her arms and led her into the shower.

"What are you doing?"

"Cleaning you up and making you look nice."

"For what?"

Nobody answered.

Fear leaped inside Anna's breast. But despite her roiling emotions, the water pouring down on her felt good. Still wearing her white uniform, Maria stepped into the shower, poured lemon-scented shampoo into her hands, and began to wash Anna's hair.

She washed it quickly, rinsed it off, and finished with an application of conditioner and another rinse.

As Anna stood under the water, a pungent smell made her head jerk up. She saw Evelyn pour a thick white liquid from a small bottle and lather her gloved hands.

"What's that?"

"Fire soap."

"What?"

"You'll like it." When her hands were sudsy, she stepped into the shower and stroked her hand over Anna's shoulder. The moment the lather touched her skin, she felt as though she'd been touched by a handful of itching powder.

When she tried to jump away, Maria held her in place.

"Don't fight it."

"Please, no. What are you doing to me?"

"Making you ready for our priest," Evelyn answered, working the lather down Anna's back, making her skin burn, then switching to the front, lathering her chest, her breasts, her abdomen.

At first it burned. Then it settled down to a sizzling, erotic heat that caught her in its grip.

Evelyn reached lower, sliding the soap through Anna's pubic hair and between her legs.

"Don't."

"Relax. It feels good, doesn't it?"

"No."

"Liar!"

"Don't . . . do . . . this to me." Panic clogged her throat as she tried to twist away, but Maria held her in place.

Evelyn slid her hand over the curve of Anna's ass, then stroked up and down the crack between her cheeks.

"We want you all nice and clean for the priest," she murmured. "And all nice and hot, so you'll be pleased by his attentions."

"Please. No."

"It's too late. The fire soap sinks through your skin, into your blood."

Anna looked down, seeing that her nipples had tightened. Maria followed her gaze and laughed.

"You look all sexy."

"Let me go!"

"And what will you do? You need a man now. Don't lie about it."

"No."

"Oh yes. You need our priest, to satisfy the heat in your blood."

Anna made a whimpering sound. Maria was right. She was aroused. Not because she wanted to be, but because the soap was laced with some damn aphrodisiac drug.

She reached down, rubbing at her skin, trying to rub it away, but her fingers only inflamed her further. Her body was on fire and her brain had started to fog again. When she slumped back against the wall of the shower, Wilhelmina caught her.

"You'll be better soon. After he makes love to you at the ceremony. He'll make you come again and again."

"God, no."

Maria turned off the water. Wilhelmina brought a large towel and wrapped her in it, drying her body while Maria used another towel and then a handheld dryer.

Wilhelmina dried her arms and back, then swished the towel over her nipples. Need shot through her. And when the towel stroked between her legs, she felt her knees buckle.

"Enough," Evelyn ordered. "We don't want to make her come. Not yet."

God, yes. Please do that. She couldn't stop the plea from shooting through her mind. She had never felt her body clamoring more urgently for release. And there was nothing she could do about it.

ZACH cut the engine, and they drifted toward the pier. The moment the boat bumped against the dock, he jumped out and secured the line.

Jordan and Lindsay followed, leaving the captain they'd hired. The man was nervous. Even if he'd agreed to go along, it was obvious he didn't want to anger San Donato. But they were paying him a fortune, and he wouldn't get the rest of the money until they returned to Palmiro.

Jordan wanted to leave his wife behind. But they needed her powers.

They had landed in a small village—not of native huts but of grand houses. This must be a rich man's enclave. Maybe even property that San Donato owned. The compound seemed empty, but there were probably guards on duty.

"They've taken her up to the real village," Zach whispered. He wanted to switch on the flashlight he was carrying, but unlike when he'd been out in the water, he knew that was a bad idea.

So they stood for a few moments letting their eyes grow accustomed to the darkness. Then they started toward the enclave.

There must be a road, Zach said, glad that he didn't have to actually speak the words. He'd spent enough time linked with Jordan and Lindsay that he could silently communicate with them.

They looked around, then saw a path winding upward through the trees. When they started in that direction, a figure detached itself from the shadows. A man holding a gun.

THE women picked Anna up and laid her naked on a flat surface, a stretcher. And when she tried to press her legs together and give herself some relief, they moved them apart, fastening her ankles to the sides the way she'd been fastened to the bed on the boat, only the stretcher was more narrow than the bed on the boat.

When she tried to slip her hand down her body, they snatched it away, securing her wrists to the sides so that she couldn't touch herself.

Maria quickly used a dryer and brush on her hair, then brought a bouquet of small orchids and studded them around the top of her head.

"You look very pretty," she murmured.

Evelyn brought a gauzy piece of fabric and laid it over her body. Even that light touch made her nerve endings twitch.

"He'll give you release soon," she promised, then turned away and stripped off her wet clothing. The other two women did the same. When they were dressed in dry white gowns, Evelyn opened the door.

More women were waiting outside. They looked excited as they lifted the stretcher and carried Anna down the hallway, then outside, where the cool evening air hit her skin. It felt good. But it wasn't enough to quench the flaming inferno that had become her body.

She could see the moon and the stars above her, see the light of torches flickering around her, as though she were the star attraction in some pagan ceremony.

No, not *as though*.

It was real. All too real.

The women carried her behind one of the houses to a fenced-in area. She sensed people around her, men and women, some dressed in white like the attendants who carried the stretcher and some wearing colorful clothing. And she smelled the scent of sweaty skin and arousal filling the enclosure. Not just her own arousal.

These people were turned on. And they were going to do something about it. But not yet. Not until after they watched the damn ceremony where San Donato inflicted himself on her.

* * *

ZACH faced the guard, wondering if he was going to take a bullet in the chest. Had San Donato told these guys to shoot first and ask questions later? Or what?

Get ready to grab the gun.

Jordan's voice echoed in his mind. He wasn't aware that the other telepath had disappeared until Jordan stepped from the trees directly behind of the man.

"Don't move." As he spoke, Jordan clamped a hand on the guard's shoulder.

Hoping to hell that Jordan was controlling the man with his mind, Zach rushed forward, grabbed the gun hand, and pointed the weapon toward the ground.

The guy made a strangled sound. Quickly, they moved him back into the shadows.

"Stop. You don't understand," he gasped.

"Oh yeah?"

"I'm here to save your . . . lover."

"What the hell do you know about it? And why did you hold a gun on us?"

"I wasn't sure who you were—not at first. Then I felt your desperation. Are you Zachary Robinson?"

"Jesus. He knows we're coming."

"No! He doesn't expect you. He doesn't even know I'm here. I asked the saints to send you to this place. And they have honored my request. They are on my side, not the side of San Donato."

"What the hell does all that mean? Who are you?"

The man drew himself up straighter. "I am Joseph Hondino. I am a priest of the Vadiana religion. The people used to follow me. Now they are following the false priest, San Donato. Because he promises them things that are impossible." He looked at Lindsay, who was at Jordan's side now. "You have powers—like San Donato. All three of you have powers. But you are the strongest. Go into my mind and see if I am telling the truth."

Lindsay stared at him, then stepped forward and put her

hands on his head. After several moments, she looked at
Zach. "He came prepared to die, if that's what it took to
stop San Donato from joining with Anna. San Donato's
lover warned him about what was happening. He arranged
for her to get off the island, then came here."

Zach sucked in a sharp breath, wondering what the hell
he was doing, standing here talking.

"You don't have to sacrifice yourself. I'll save her."

When he started to push past the priest and run up the
hill, the man grabbed his arm.

"You're going the wrong way."

He whirled around, his pulse pounding

"She's not up there. Raoul's in too much of a hurry now.
He's moved the ceremony down here—so he can get it
over with as fast as possible."

Zach's gaze shot to Lindsay, who still had a hand on the
priest's head. "Is he telling the truth?"

"Yes. Anna's . . ." She pointed toward one of the houses.
"She's behind there.

Zach saw a high fence. From beyond it, lights flickered.

"San Donato uses his gifts to do evil. And you do not.
Use your powers to save her. Quickly. Before it's too late."

Zach started running again, praying he was in time.

THE women carried Anna to one side of the enclosure. In
the flickering torchlight, she saw an altar looming above
her. Like the one she had seen before in a vision. Only this
was no dream. This was reality. A horrible reality. Where
her life as she knew it ended.

They laid the stretcher down on a table in front of the
altar. Quickly the women unfastened her wrists and ankles.
They pulled her hands up and refastened them above her
head.

The stretcher was removed, and her hips were posi-

tioned at the edge of the table with her legs pulled open
and secured with ankle straps. She wanted to pretend that
it was happening to someone else, but the flames leaping
inside her body anchored her to the table.

They slipped a pillow under her head so she could see
the crowd around her. She would have been horribly exposed, but one of the women had pulled the cloth down so
that it dangled between her open legs.

It was all happening in a blur of unreality. Then a stir
at the back of the enclosure made her go rigid.

The crowd parted, and San Donato stepped forward. He
was naked to the waist, with a kind of long white skirt knotted around his hips. She could see his erection under it, and
she cringed away.

A horrible tattoo fanned across his chest. It seemed to
be a montage of faces spread across the front of him and
onto one arm. And she thought it must be a living symbol
of the horror that festered in his mind.

Tall men stood on either side of him. One of them was
Bertrand.

Oh, Lord, Bertrand must be one of his most trusted
men. And he had brought her to the island—for this twisted
ceremony.

The throng went absolutely silent as San Donato and the
other men walked toward her.

She shuddered. Were they all going to rape her? What?

San Donato had a look of satisfaction and anticipation
on his face.

Even the faces on his damn tattoo looked satisfied.

No. Oh, God, no.

Bertrand and the other men moved to the sides of the
table, standing at her shoulders.

San Donato knelt before the altar, speaking in a strong,
confident voice.

"Ibena, I thank you for all the power you have granted

me in the past. And I thank you for bringing my bride to this place. We will join together and we will be stronger than any who have come before us."

This was it. Her last chance to get away. She focused on the thongs that bound her wrists, trying with every ounce of concentration to free her hands.

Nothing happened, and she held back a sob. But she kept trying, desperate to free herself, and all at once she felt something change.

Zach?

Yes.

He was here. Or was she just grabbing at a fantasy because it was her only hope of comfort?

But it felt like he was lending her his strength.

Still, what could the two of them do against San Donato and his mob?

Her mind zinged back to her surroundings as a hum of approval rose from the crowd when San Donato stood again and walked to her, his hand brushing her erect nipples through the thin fabric, sending a surge of arousal through her.

As he did, hatred shot through her. And energy. He thought he could join his mind with hers with this sick ceremony. But he was wrong. She would fight him with every shred of determination in her mind.

Zach. Please, Zach.

I'm coming. Hold on. Just hold on.

Help me.

The voice inside her head seemed louder. Yet maybe it was already too late.

San Donato reached for the cloth.

She raised up as far as she could, looking from San Donato to his followers and back again.

"I curse you, you disgusting animal," she shouted, aloud and in her mind. She knew he felt the words as well as heard them because she saw pain flicker in his eyes. He gave her a murderous look and yanked the cloth away, the touch of the fabric like fire against her flesh.

The cloth fell to the ground just as someone in the crowd let out a shriek. Seconds later, cries of fear spread all over the enclosure.

"Fire!"

"Fire!"

Anna's head jerked to the side as she saw the stockade fence erupt in flames.

CHAPTER
TWENTY-EIGHT

THE BURNING TORCHES were suddenly dwarfed by the tongues of fire shooting up from the walls of the enclosure—flames that reached for the sky and turned the arena into an inferno.

People who had been waiting for the show in happy anticipation made a mad dash for the exit, screaming and crying and trampling each other in their haste to get away.

Some of them screamed in pain. But she spared them no sympathy. They had come here to see her ravaged and humiliated, and they were paying a high price—and getting a performance they hadn't anticipated.

In some part of her mind, Anna knew it wasn't real. Couldn't be real. Someone had turned the ceremonial ground into a nightmare inferno.

Not Zach. Someone else.

The man and woman who had contacted them before? Yes, they must be here, too.

With a new surge of hope, she struggled against her bonds. Triumph welled inside her as she pulled her hands free and struggled to a sitting position, bending to free her ankles. Then Zach was beside her, and she sobbed out his name.

"He didn't . . . he didn't . . ." She wanted him to know that right away, even if she still felt like she was going to jump out of her skin.

"Thank God."

Zach had found her. And everything was all right. She was just about to sob out her relief when a new fear leaped inside her. One man hadn't made a run for the doorway of the flaming enclosure. It was San Donato, and she saw his shadow towering against the wall as he loomed behind Zach, a wicked-looking knife in his hand.

"Watch out!" she screamed.

Zach dodged to the side as San Donato lunged. The knife came down on the table, inches from her thigh.

"You bastard!" Zach would have sprung at the man, but Anna's silent shout held him back. *Don't . . . I want him to know he should never have gone after me. Help me.*

The need to free herself from San Donato—finally and completely—gave her purpose. And for the moment, she was able to ignore the horrible heat that still held her body in its grip. She flexed her fingers, and Zach reached for her hand. The moment her body connected with his, she felt energy surge through her.

Zach!

Right here.

He let her do what she wanted, and she wanted justice. Or maybe it was revenge. For leaving Zach lying lifeless on the beach. For the whipping. For the horrible way he'd displayed her to his followers. And for the fate he'd tried to inflict on her.

As Zach opened his mind to hers, she gathered power from the flicker light of the fire—the fire she knew had no basis in reality—and turned it against the man who had wanted to enslave her.

Flames engulfed him.

"You bitch," he shouted, his anger surging up to meet hers. He came rushing toward her, looking like his body had been doused with gasoline.

When Zach started to step in the way, Anna warned him with a mental shout to stop, then turned her attention back to San Donato.

But he must know the fire had never been real. That was why he had stayed in the enclosure when all of his followers had run.

She had turned his body into what looked like a flaming torch, but she was new at this, and she hadn't made him feel the pain of the fire. Realizing her mistake, she struggled to add that sensation—using the power that Zach lent her and the power of the man and woman who had come here with Zach.

They were there—in the back of her mind. They had conjured up the fire in the first place, and now they helped her make it as deadly as it looked.

And someone else was here, too. A man she didn't know. But he wanted to help them.

She knew she had succeeded in her goal when San Donato screamed and staggered back, dropping the knife and rolling across the ground as he beat at his body with his hands.

His anguished shrieks rose into the night as he rolled over and over, trying to put out the fire. But there was no way he could do it, because the flames had come from her mind.

He stopped rolling. His body jerked and twitched.

Finally, he lay still and lifeless. His body untouched but his chest no longer rising and falling.

As quickly as the inferno had engulfed him, it faded away.

Zach folded her into his arms.

"Thank God," he breathed.

She clung to him, relieved yet hardly calm. With her

focus off of San Donato, she felt the full force of the terrible arousal that she had banked.

"I need . . . oh, Lord, Zach . . . I need."

"I know, love. I know," he murmured. And he did know, because his mind was tuned to hers now, and he felt the terrible heat burning her from the inside out.

They were still out in the open, and he bent over her, shielding her body with his own as his hand pressed between her legs.

She should feel abashed at the intimacy. Yet she was incapable of stopping him. Incapable of doing anything besides responding.

She needed his touch. Burned for it.

As he rubbed his fingers against her clit, her hips surged upward, rocking frantically against him. It didn't take much to send her over the edge.

She climaxed in a great welling burst of sensation, pressing her mouth against his shoulder to keep from screaming as aftershocks zinged through her.

Thank you, Zach. Oh, Lord, thank you for rescuing me. Thank you for being the one to do that.

Do you feel better?

I . . .

She did feel a little better. But she knew the terrible wave of arousal wasn't over. Even as relief left her weak, she felt strong needs gathering again.

He caught all of that in her mind. Reaching down, he picked up the cloth and wrapped it around her, then lifted her into his arms. "We're getting out of here," he muttered.

The embarrassment broke through when she sensed two other people beside them. She had just reached orgasm, and the thought of sharing such a private moment with anyone besides Zach made her cringe.

Of course, in the back of her mind she knew that San Donato had wanted to share it with scores of his followers.

A voice spoke softly in her head—the woman who had

contacted them earlier. On the island. The woman who had been with them when the plane went down.

Lindsay . . . West. The name came to her as the silent voice began to offer reassurances.

It's okay. It's not your fault. I know this is horrible for you. But can you hang on a little while longer?

I guess I have to.

We're going to get you out of here.

Okay.

The flames licking at the walls of the enclosure had died down. But their remnants remained, still bathing the area in an eerie light.

As they turned toward the entrance, a figure stepped out of the shadows.

Zach stopped short, but the man rushed past him and knelt beside San Donato.

Who is that? Anna asked.

The priest who came here to stop San Donato. But we did it for him.

"He's dead," the man whispered.

"Then you're free to get your people back."

"I hope I can." He swept his hand around the enclosure. "I can't offer them anything like this."

"You can take over this place. And make it into something a lot better," Zach said.

Anna couldn't focus on the conversation, because one phrase kept running through her head. *I killed him.*

With our help, Zach, Lindsay and Jordan instantly answered. *It's no more on you than on us.*

She knew they were trying to comfort her. But in reality she didn't have any regrets about killing San Donato. He had planned to take over her mind, and his death had been the only way to free herself from him.

Zach spoke again to the priest, who was standing again and looking around the empty compound.

"I guess the ceremony was too much for him. But maybe you'd better get out of here, before they blame you."

"I stayed here to bear witness." He turned and walked away, with his shoulders straight and his head held high.

Silently, Zach carried Anna toward the dock.

Outside the enclosure, the night was dark. Around them she sensed people watching. But nobody approached, and she thought that perhaps Jordan and Lindsay had put up some kind of shield around them. Or maybe the people understood their power and were afraid to mess with them.

She didn't know. And she was losing her focus on anything external. Her body had heated up again.

I can feel it inside me. So hot. Too hot.

Soon. We'll be alone soon. Just hold on. I'm right here. I'll take care of you soon.

The crunch of gravel under his feet changed to the sound of his shoes crossing wooden boards.

Where are we?

On the dock.

Zach was walking quickly now—practically running.

The stars above her swayed. And the solid surface seemed to sway below her.

No, that was a boat rocking. They were on a boat.

And Zach was climbing down the stairs, still holding her in his arms as he stepped into a cabin and slammed the door closed with his foot.

"Please," she moaned.

He came down beside her on the bed.

"What the hell did he do to you?"

"The women washed me with something called . . . called fire soap." She gulped. "As soon as it touched my skin, I started getting hot. And it must have sunk into me."

"I'll kill him!"

She managed a laugh. "I think he's already dead."

"Already rotting in hell."

She lifted her head, hardly able to focus on her surroundings. Her body was clamoring for release again. But she needed to know that it was okay to let herself go. "Where are we? Are we safe?"

"Jordan and Lindsay rescued me after that guy hit me over the head. They saved my life."

"Thank God."

"We're in a cabin on the boat they chartered in Grand Fernandino. They paid a captain to get me and then come here."

"Wasn't he afraid of San Donato?"

"Not everybody loved him. Maybe the guy was hoping they'd get rid of him."

As he spoke, she felt the engines surge to life, and the boat headed out to sea.

"Thank God," she whispered again. They were safe.

But she was still on the verge of madness.

Zach eased the covering off of her.

"I . . . need . . ."

"Anything. Just tell me."

I've got to come again. Now.

With shaky fingers, she grabbed his hand, pressed it between her legs, rocking frantically against the pressure of his palm. He bent his head, closing his lips around one nipple, sucking strongly while he slipped two fingers inside her, stroking in and out as he used the other hand on her clit.

She couldn't hold back a scream as she came, lifted up on wave after wave of release that slammed through her system like a hit of some exotic drug.

For long moments she gave herself over to the roiling climax. When the sharp sensations ebbed, she lifted her hand and touched Zach's face.

It's you. Thank God it's you.

Thank God, he echoed.

He's gone. I can feel he's really gone. I mean, he's not trying to horn in on . . . us.

He nodded against her hand.

"But it's hard to have you see me like this," she whispered.

"It's okay. You're okay," he murmured, easing down beside her on the mattress.

"No . . . I'm still out of control . . ." she sobbed out. "I can feel it coming back. I'm going to need to come again."

"I'm here. I'll take care of you."

"I need . . ."

She didn't have to tell him. He could read it in her mind. More than read it. He felt it as keenly as she did.

Standing, he stripped off his shirt and pants, taking his briefs along with them so that she could see his erection jutting toward her.

He came down beside her again. Gathering her to him, he stroked her tenderly but firmly, his fingers tightening on her swollen nipples. She found his mouth with hers, drawing on him for a long, greedy kiss as she reached down and clasped her hand around his erection.

In me. I need this in me.

Oh, yeah.

He rolled her to her back, and when he had buried himself inside her, she sobbed out her relief and joy.

She knew it was the same relief and joy he felt. Knew without his having to say a word.

He began to move, his strokes coordinated with her rising need—and his own. She wanted it to last. Wanted to wrap herself in this time together. But she was still too far gone for the luxury of long, leisurely lovemaking.

Next time. We'll make it last longer next time, he whispered in her mind.

Before the words faded, orgasm took her, sending her spinning out of control and into an altered state of consciousness where release became the center of the universe.

When it was over, she lay panting on the bunk, her skin slick with perspiration.

He eased off of her, then cradled her against him, stroking her hair. When his fingers encountered the orchids, he plucked one out. "What the hell is this?"

"They wanted me to look pretty for the ceremony."

"Christ."

"They were going to have an orgy after they watched him . . . rape me. I could feel their arousal. Smell it."

He made an angry sound. "Too bad they can't burn in hell with San Donato."

"They're poor, and he offered them hope."

"Don't make excuses for them."

"I understand how it happened."

"You're too . . . tender. They're not stray cats. They can think for themselves."

"Let's not argue about it."

"Right. We have more important things to do."

She curled her body against his, her breath still jerky. "Thank you for being here."

He knit his fingers with hers and held on tight.

"I'm a little better. But I know it's coming back soon. That terrible need. How many times am I going to need to come?"

I don't know. But I'll be right here with you. His lips stroked against her cheek, slid to her mouth. *Maybe this time, we'll take control.*

How?

We'll ride the wave up, not get caught in the undertow.

He kissed her deeply, bringing his lips and teeth and tongue into the discussion.

What a good idea.

And when she was still vibrating from the kiss, he slid his mouth to her throat.

She arched against his lips, barely catching her breath before he slipped lower, rubbing his face against the inside curve of her breasts, then nibbling and licking his way to one nipple.

And as she caught the sensations swirling in his mind, she knew he was as aroused as she.

He had already brought the heat back to her body, and she cried out as he sucked her nipple into his mouth while teasing its mate with his thumb and finger.

My turn, she breathed, reversing their positions so that she could play with his broad chest.

Her teeth on his nipple wrung a cry from him, and she smiled. It was good to feel like she was the one in control again, and she meant to make the most of it.

But she was in no shape to hide her intentions. As she slid down his body, she could feel him tense in anticipation.

Without using her hands, she maneuvered her mouth to the head of his cock, circling it with her tongue, then sucking him partway into her mouth, sliding lower, then withdrawing, gratified by the response she felt.

You don't have to do that.

I want to. I need to feel like I'm taking charge.

By turning me into a basket case?

Uh-huh.

She punctuated the observation by sucking on him as though he were a delicious lollipop, then switching to the ice cream cone method—little licks, working her way around so that no side melted before the others.

"Jesus!"

She knew he liked it. Not just from his exclamation. She could feel what he felt, the exquisite sensation of her mouth on his penis. What she did to him was making her hot, and this time it felt like it was really her, not the damn fire soap.

Good!

She knew he was commenting on the thought—and the sensations.

And she knew he was close to climax. She could hear it inside his head and in the sound of his harsh breathing.

Come up here.

As she read his mind, she knew what he wanted most. And she straddled his body, coming down on his cock with an exclamation of triumph.

She had made herself hot. And him, too. And now she rode him like the magnificent being he was. Her man. Her lover. Her soul mate.

She grinned when she felt his control slipping. Grinned again when he climaxed.

After she followed him, they collapsed in a tangle of arms and legs. When she could move, she shifted off of him and slid onto the mattress.

He cradled her close. "I love you."

She nodded against his sweat-slick chest. "Loving you was the only thing that kept me alive when he had me."

"Anna!"

"The idea of his . . . invading me was terrible."

"For me, too."

She tightened her hand on his. "I know."

By mutual agreement, they stopped talking aloud.

I feel . . .

So close to you . . .

Yes . . .

What does it mean for us?

I guess we can talk to Jordan and Lindsay.

She felt her face go hot. *I didn't exactly meet them under ideal circumstances.*

Neither did I. I thought Lindsay had something to do with kidnapping you. And I tried to strangle her.

Anna gripped his hand.

He gave her a mental summary of the past few hours, and she winced.

You had a bad time.

Not as bad as you.

Then, swiftly, as only they could through mind-to-mind communication, he relayed what Jordan and Lindsay had told him about the Remington Clinic, about Jim Swift, about the couple who had discovered their powers a few months earlier.

They can help us figure out where we go from here. And they can help us figure out what powers we have—and how to develop them.

Yes.

Did we really loosen my bonds?

Yes.

She dragged in a breath and let it out.

Will we have to hide from Jim Swift—or whatever he calls himself—now?

I'm afraid so—until we figure out where he is and . . . get rid of him.

Is that what we've turned into? Killers?

CHAPTER
TWENTY-NINE

NOT IF WE'RE left alone to live our lives, Zach answered. *That's all I'm asking.*

Her life. And his. They had found each other, after years of being apart. But she hated the direction fate had swept them in. It was so sudden. So unexpected. So frightening.

Including the part with me? Zach silently asked, the question like a flame burning in her mind.

No. You're my touchstone.

The look on his face told her he wasn't sure she was telling the truth.

You don't think I'm lying, do you?

Before he could answer, she opened her mind and her heart, making herself totally vulnerable to him, letting him know everything inside her.

He didn't have to speak for her to know he'd understood her heart and her mind.

Anna!

I love you. I'd be in hell by now without you.

I was in hell when he had you.

He reached for her, and they held each other tightly for long minutes.

It's hard for me to trust, he whispered in her mind.

I know. But I wouldn't be here in your arms if we didn't have something extraordinary together. She felt him absorb that truth, and felt him settle into the miracle of their bond.

They were warm and close for a long time. Finally, he moved his hands to her shoulders.

We need to talk to Jordan and Lindsay.

I know.

We can't hide down here forever.

You weren't naked and spread-eagle on an altar when they first saw you.

No, I was lying on the ground, almost dead. Then I attacked them. He gripped her shoulders more tightly. *They're good people. They understand what you've been through.*

It's still hard to face them.

I'll be right beside you. And I'll punch Jordan out if he's stupid enough to . . . think . . . anything you don't want to hear.

She laughed, feeling a little better. But she was still hesitant, and she knew Zach had caught her thoughts when he said, "Want to take a shower before you go up?"

"Yes. Thanks."

She disappeared into the head attached to the cabin. And when she came out, she found that Zach had ducked down the companionway and taken a quick shower in another head. He was dressed in the jeans and T-shirt he'd been wearing. And he'd laid out clothing for her—a man's long-sleeved shirt and a pair of sweatpants—which she donned.

Finally, she couldn't stall any longer. With her insides jumping, she walked hand-in-hand with Zach to the main deck.

Jordan and Lindsay were standing at the rail, looking toward land. But Anna could tell from the way they stood that they were very aware that she and Zach had arrived.

When Zach cleared his throat, they both turned. Lindsay's

eyes went to Anna. Then she crossed to her and gave her a long, warm hug.

"I'm so glad we found you," she murmured. "How are you feeling?"

"A lot better," she answered.

"You and Zach are lucky to have each other . . . like me and Jordan."

"And lucky for us you got here in time," Zach said, his voice thick with emotion.

He and Jordan shook hands.

"We were so alone," Lindsay said. "You don't know what it means to us—finding you. When we first bonded with each other, we were . . . afraid of what was happening."

"Maybe I had an advantage because I already had the mind-reading act," Anna answered.

"You've been in hiding since you escaped from the Crandall Consortium?" Zach asked.

"Yes," Jordan answered. "And we've been looking for other Dariens."

"I guessed that!" Anna said. "Did you find any?"

His expression turned grim. "We were on the track of several others. Jim Swift found them first. They didn't make it."

She felt her stomach clench.

"I hope you'll join us," Lindsay said. "We could use some help locating other people like us and saving their lives. And getting Jim Swift off our backs."

Anna took that in. "You mean kill him," she whispered.

"Yeah. Before he kills us," Jordan answered.

She swallowed hard.

"It's hard to get used to the idea," Lindsay murmured. "That somebody hates you so much that he wants you dead."

"Yes."

"If we can get Swift out of the picture, we can save a lot of lives—not just our own."

She nodded, then scuffed her foot against the deck. "I

Zach and I need to hide and can't pursue our professions, how do we make a living?"

"We'd like to establish a self-supporting community."

"Where?"

"We haven't figured that out yet."

Zach looked uncertain. "I'd hate to give up my salvage business."

"If we can eliminate Swift, you can go back to work. If we can't, it's not safe for you to be out there under your own name doing the same kind of job. And if you take another identity, he might be able to find you anyway, by studying the probabilities."

Zach made a rough sound.

"He'd be more cautious now, because he knows that the two of you have bonded," Jordan said. "That means you are more than the equal of anyone he sends. So he'd want to figure out a way to take you by surprise."

Zach nodded tightly, digesting the information.

"And what about the police? San Donato is dead. Are they going to come after us?" Anna asked.

"Did any of us touch him?" Zach asked.

"No," Anna answered. "So what can they prove?"

"Nothing."

Lindsay spread her hands. "Let's assume nobody can figure out *what* happened at his ceremonial ground. Or if they come up with theories, they will involve the Vadiana gods; he tried to take too much power, and they smacked him down. For all we know, maybe that's what *did* happen. Maybe that's why our plans worked out."

Anna's eyes widened. "You're joking, right?"

Lindsay shrugged. "Who knows who they really are. Maybe they're spirits who have been on his island for thousands of years. Maybe they're space travelers stranded here, meddling in the lives of the islanders."

They were all silent for several moments. Then Jordan turned toward his wife, and they exchanged a long look.

Moving to Lindsay's side, he addressed Zach, "I think we can't solve the big questions in one conversation. For now, we should let the two of you settle down a bit. So why don't we dock this baby? Then you and Anna can stay on board and hide out, and we can go to a hotel in town."

Anna heard the words, but she caught the edge of something more in Jordan's mind. Jordan wanted to leave them alone, but he also wanted to be alone with Lindsay.

She and Zach had felt a strong sexual pull from the first time they'd wanted to touch each other. Was it the same for Jordan and Lindsay? And had it continued?

Yeah. The ghost of an answer flickered in Anna's mind, and her gaze shot to Jordan.

When he grinned at her, she struggled to hold her gaze steady.

"Sorry. I picked that up. And I couldn't help answering. Probably I should have kept my mouth shut."

"The four of us can communicate . . . silently?" Anna asked.

To some degree, Lindsay answered. *We can get better at it if we practice,* she added.

Later, Jordan urged.

He wasn't saying so, but probably they'd gotten caught by the undertow of the intense encounter between her and Zach. Probably that had worked on them, and Jordan really did want to spend some quality time alone with his wife. They deserved it. They'd come down here to help her and Zach, and they'd saved his life—and helped save her sanity.

The captain piloted the rented boat to the slip where it had come from.

After they'd tied up, Lindsay hugged Anna again, and also Zach. "Let's plan to get together tomorrow morning," she said.

"Where can we find you—if we need to get in touch?"

"We dropped our stuff at the Eden Hotel before we rented this boat."

"Okay. In old town. I know where it is," Anna answered.

They stood on the deck, watching the other two Dariens and the captain leave. He was going with them to get the payment they'd promised him.

Dariens, Zach murmured in her mind. *That's what we are.*

Yes.

I like having a name for our strange condition.

She smiled at him, then sobered. *There must be a lot of people around here who were at San Donato's ceremony. Like Bertrand. Do you think they'll look for us?*

Zach's face turned fierce.

I think he's got sense enough not to tangle with us, she said quickly. *After what we did to his master.*

His master?

That's what he called San Donato.

Zach made a disgusted sound. *Just to be safe, maybe you'd better go below. There are probably a lot of kids around the docks who'd like to earn some money by picking up a carryout dinner for—*

He stopped short.

She looked around in alarm. *What?*

I just saw Claude, the guy who was with me when José tried to kill me on the dive.

Anna sucked in a sharp breath, trying to rearrange her thoughts. "You think he's after us?"

"No. I think he doesn't even know we're here."

He gestured down the dock, and she saw a muscular man chatting casually with a boat owner about twenty yards down the pier.

"I'd like to try and use our powers on him."

"How?"

"Somebody set me up—let's see if we can find out who."

"You think he can tell us?"

He gave her a steady look. "I'd like to see."

"What do you want to do?"

He switched to silent communication. *Call him down here—if we can. Not out loud. Then when he gets here, we'll ask some questions.*

She could read how important it was to him, so she whispered, "Okay."

They held hands and he led her back into the shadows. Then she lent him her power, helping him send out a call to the man twenty yards down the pier.

Claude, come down here. Let's have a little talk. I don't blame you for anything. I just want to know what happened.

She watched the man's head jerk, but he stayed where he was.

Claude, come on down here. Let's talk.

Claude straightened up, said something to the man he'd been chatting with, then looked up and down the dock.

Over here. Come chat with me.

Finally, Claude turned in their direction and started walking down the dock, his stride a bit jerky.

When he reached the boat where she and Zach lurked in the shadows, he stopped.

Come on board.

When the man hesitated, Zach repeated the invitation.

Claude gripped the rail, pulled the boat against the dock, and stepped aboard.

"Anybody here?" he called out.

"Yeah." Zach stepped from hiding, and Claude gasped.

"You! What you want, mon?"

"Nothing much," he said out loud. But his silent message was different. *How did you and José happen to set me up?*

Claude's lips moved, but no sound came out.

Come on. You can tell me.

"Git away from me."

Anna stepped forward, and he stared at her. "Who are you?"

"I'm Zach's friend."

As she delivered the bland line, she heard Zach's silent laugh in her mind. *How about fiancée? And we'll change that to wife as soon as you'll agree.*

What a time to bring that up! She wanted to talk about the two of them, but Claude was standing in front of her, looking terrified.

"Don't be afraid," she said, then reached to lay a gentle hand on his arm. "Just tell me who hired you to go out with Zach and look for that wreck."

As she spoke aloud, she sent the question directly to his mind, urging him to level with her.

"I don't know," he whispered. "I just got . . . a letter with instructions and money."

She sensed that he was speaking the truth. He didn't know who had hired him. But as she touched his sleeve, her old talent surged up. She saw a letter, with a return address—a post office box in Winslow, Montana.

Zach gasped. *It came from Winslow. It must be from my brother.*

Claude was standing stock-still. Anna moved her fingers to his hand.

"The letter asked you to look for Zach?"

"To be there when he was looking for crew. That's all."

You don't know anything else?

"No."

He seemed to be speaking the truth again. "Thanks for stopping by," Anna said.

"See you around," Zach added.

Claude blinked, turned, and hurried to the rail, then climbed back onto the dock. He strode down the dock, and Anna moved closer to Zach as they watched him go.

She reached for Zach's hand. "Your brother wanted you dead?" she whispered. "So he arranged for you to go down with a guy who would freak out? That's kind of a risky way to set up a murder."

"Maybe he was thinking it wouldn't really be murder. If it happens, it happens."

"You think there are really two guys named Sanford? Terrance and his brother?"

Zach shrugged. "At least Terrance has an e-mail address." But it was obvious he was still thinking about his brother. "I knew how badly he wanted me off the ranch. I never dreamed he wanted to make sure I wasn't coming back."

She turned and wrapped her arms around him. "Your own brother. He must be a monster."

"He always acted like I didn't belong in the family. His whole life changed when my father married my mother. Then I came along, and from his point of view, things got a lot worse. We never got along. I left because I couldn't stand it anymore."

"I'm so sorry."

"But we don't even know if the letter Claude got still exists. Or if we can prove where the money came from," he muttered.

"And trying to investigate is going to be a problem if we've got to stay hidden."

"Yes. Did you get any more from Claude?"

"Well, I know what happened to your crew from the States!"

His head shot toward her. "What?"

"Apparently they arrived yesterday. And when they got down to the docks, someone told them you'd left and you weren't coming back."

"Shit. I guess it was someone working for San Donato who thought I was already dead. Or I was going to be dead soon." His face turned grim. "Did the crew leave again?"

"Yes."

"So I left them in the lurch."

"It's not your fault. And maybe it's better this way. You don't have to face them and make up some story about why you're going out of business."

"Yeah. And they're good—they'll find other work."

She cleared her throat. "You're sure this came from your brother, not San Donato?"

"I can't be *sure*. But we hadn't had that daydream where we met. Not yet."

She nodded. "This island has a long tradition in the Vadiana religion. San Donato didn't have to be the only one using it for less-than-savory purposes."

He nodded. Suddenly his body jerked and she felt a shock wave coming off of him.

"What?"

He didn't answer, but he had turned to stare down the dock toward the street.

She had been expecting him to make a further comment about Pagor, but when she caught what was in his mind, she followed his gaze, then went stock-still.

Claude had paused under a streetlight, and Anna gasped as she saw that he was talking to a ghost.

CHAPTER
THIRTY

THE MAN STANDING under the streetlight turned toward the dock.

"Wild Bill," Anna gasped. "I knew you cut a slit in their raft; I thought he drowned."

"I guess somebody picked them up," Zach growled. "Lindsay kept saying she didn't think he was dead. I didn't want to believe her, but I guess she was right."

Bill was huddled at the end of the dock with two other men. Not the guys who had been with him before. Probably they were too smart to get involved with the fugitives again. But these new thugs didn't know anything about what had happened.

"So much for Jordan's assumption that Swift wouldn't come after us until he figured out how to do it more safely." She made a strangled sound.

"It's not Swift. I mean, I'm picking up that Wild Bill knows him as Jim Stone."

"Yeah."

"But Wild Bill also has a private score to settle with us."

"You mean, like we tried to kill him and now he's back to get revenge?"

"Yeah. And he doesn't know about our special talents. Because his boss didn't tell him. So he thinks he can take us."

"Maybe he can," she whispered.

"No," Zach answered, his voice hard and sure.

As they watched, the man started down the dock, flanked by his hired hands. They were all wearing untucked flowered shirts and she saw a bulge on each man's hip. Handguns.

Feeling trapped, Anna looked around wildly. "What are we going to do?"

He gripped her hand, and the scene he'd conjured in his mind made her gasp.

"Can we do it?" she asked.

"We have to," he answered, watching the men stroll down the dock like they owned it.

As they drew closer to the boat, Zach hurried to the controls and started the engine. With her heart hammering in her chest, Anna started to cast off, making it look like they were trying to make a hasty getaway.

She didn't have to pretend to look scared; she was.

Wild Bill and his friends leaped onto the boat.

As soon as they were on board, they pulled out the guns that had previously been tucked in their belts.

"Hold it right there," Bill ordered, his voice sharp and his eyes flat as a smear of mud.

Figuring Bill wasn't going to start shooting in the dock area, Anna whipped the line free. The boat leaped forward as Zach gunned the engine.

"What the hell?" Bill shouted.

There was no time for real preparation. No time to practice what Zach had in mind. And no margin for error, if they wanted to come out of this alive.

She knew Zach planned to jam the throttle in the high position, using his mind to keep it there. But when he gave the mechanism a jolt, the engine sputtered.

Anna gasped, sure the boat was going to leave them sitting in the dock area with Bill and his friends.

Desperately, she funneled mental energy to Zach as he focused on the throttle. When the engine settled down to a steady hum, she breathed out a sigh.

The boat was already moving. Suddenly it leaped forward.

Bill and the other two thugs whirled toward the controls. "What the hell?"

Jump.

Without question, Anna obeyed the order, jumping off the side and hitting the water as the gunmen lost their balance and toppled backward, grabbing frantically at the rail to keep from splatting onto the deck.

Anna went down, then kicked to the surface in time to see the boat bounding across the harbor like a killer whale zooming after prey.

On the deck, Zach lurched to the rail and launched himself into the the water.

If the thugs had been smart, they would have followed. Instead, as Anna looked back, she saw two of them leap toward the the throttle.

"Stop this thing!" Wild Bill screamed.

"I'm fucking trying."

"You idiot. Just turn the key."

"It doesn't work!"

As Bill wove his way toward his colleague, Anna switched her attention to the water, frantically searching the harbor. When she didn't find Zach, her heart leaped into her throat.

Zach.

He swam to her and came up beside her, treading water. "Are you all right?" he asked anxiously.

"Yes. Are you?"

"A scrape on my arm. That's all."

From the water, she saw the craft speed across the harbor and almost hit a fishing boat. When she realized where it was heading, she made a strangled sound. Zach hadn't told her that part.

If there had been boats over there, I would have aimed differently.

Seconds later, the cabin cruiser plowed into the fueling station at the harbor mouth, slid up onto the dock like a hippo clambering out of the water, and hit one of the gas pumps—where it burst into flames.

"Oh, Lord."

"I think that's the end of Wild Bill and his friends."

"Yes. Why didn't they jump?"

"They thought they could cut the engine. If we hadn't jammed it with our minds, they could have."

She looked around the harbor. Other boats were in the water, but at this hour, none of them were close enough to be in danger. Thank God.

A crowd had gathered on the dock and along the street that bordered the harbor.

As she and Zach swam toward the pier, Anna heard a silent voice from the street.

Anna? Zach? Are you all right?

Yes, they both answered.

The mental conversation was punctuated by the sound of fire engines racing along the street toward the conflagration.

What in the name of God happened? Jordan asked.

You were right, Swift's guy was still out there. Only the man's changed his name to Stone.

Good catch!

His hired killer and two thugs were waiting for us.

And you sent them across the harbor in the boat, Jordan said.

Yeah. Zach looked toward the flaming craft. *Sorry. I guess your names are on the rental agreement.*

Jordan shook his head. *And I guess some guys stole it and crashed it into the fueling station.*

Yeah.

Since you're obviously not on board, Anna added, then she thought of something. *But Claude saw us here. Can you find him and make him think we were on the* Odysseus *all the time?*

Which one is he?

Still in the water, Anna scanned the crowd. *He's standing at the edge of the harbor. Coffee-with-cream skin. Curly hair. About five ten. Wearing a Miami Dolphins T-shirt.*

Got it! After we take care of him, we'll talk to the police.

Anna and Zach reached the dock. She climbed up and Zach followed. With everybody's attention focused on the fire, she and Zach were able to hurry down the narrow walkway and climb onto the deck of the *Odysseus*. As far as anybody knew, they'd been on board his craft all along.

Once inside, they went down to the master cabin, where he pulled out dry clothes. Anna was towel drying her hair when Lindsay and Jordan climbed on board.

"You decent?" Jordan called.

"We'll be up in a minute."

They all gathered in the main cabin.

"Before the action started tonight, I found out something disturbing," Zach began, then told about the encounter with Claude.

Jordan whistled. "Your brother was the one who set you up on that diving expedition?"

"I may not be able to prove it."

"But now you know to watch out for him."

Zach sighed. "Yeah."

"Right after Claude left us, he bumped into Bill. Then Bill and his guys came after us, and we sent them to hell."

Jordan gave a harsh laugh. "You've been busy."

"Unfortunately. But the main point is that despite Bill's best efforts, we're alive."

"You do see why going into hiding is a good idea?" Lindsay asked softly.

Zach looked around the *Odysseus*. "I hate the idea of selling this boat. Maybe I can take it to a secluded location, repaint the name, and make believe we're somebody else. After I stage my own death," Zach muttered.

Anna's gaze shot to him. "You've been thinking about that?"

"Yeah. That might eliminate a lot of problems for me. Starting with my brother."

"Maybe," Lindsay agreed, but Anna didn't know if she was just trying to let him down easily.

Well, they'd cross that bridge when they had to.

Jordan looked across the deck toward the still-burning fueling station.

"Probably you should move the boat tonight. I hate to be a party crasher, but is there room for us to sleep here?"

"There's another cabin, almost as big as the master cabin. We can motor down the coast a few miles and anchor in one of the coves."

"Yes." Jordan turned to Zach. "I'd like to leave Lindsay here while I make a police report and pick up our clothes. So, could you come with me while the women stay here?"

"Yes," Anna and Zach both said immediately.

"And I'll get Anna's things, too," Zach said. He paused. "Hell, I don't even know where you're staying."

"The Palm Court Hotel. But what if they won't give you my stuff?"

"I think Zach and I can persuade them," Jordan added.

"We'll be back as soon as we can. Then we'll cast off," Zach said.

The two men exited the boat, and Anna turned to Lindsay. "I wish I knew my way around here better. Let's see where Zach keeps his linens." As she thought about beds, she flashed on what she and Zach had been doing earlier in the evening.

Lindsay laid a hand on her arm. "You don't have to wonder what I'm thinking about you. I know that you and Zach have a strong sexual relationship—like we do. It's part of the Darien package."

Anna nodded.

"Sex is a pleasure the two of you share. And it's a means to an end, because it opens your minds to each other." She laughed. "Jordan and I found you and Zach because we were practicing a new technique—Tantric sex."

"Oh." She joined in the laughter. "I guess we'd better not tell Zach, because he'll want to try it tonight."

Lindsay grinned. "He might not like it because it means postponing orgasm. Sometimes for hours."

"Impossible."

"Practice makes perfect."

Anna grinned.

They descended to the second cabin, and Anna checked the bunk. It had a comforter but no sheets. After opening a few drawers, she found the sheets, and she and Lindsay began to make the bed together.

It was such a normal activity. Yet she felt like everything in her life had changed.

Lindsay caught her mood. "If you and Zach are like me and Jordan, you probably didn't have a lot of close friends—because you had trouble connecting with people. Something was always missing, and it was that psychic component," she said.

"Yes," Anna admitted.

"Finding the two of you makes a tremendous difference to us."

Anna swallowed hard. Probably describing their feelings was never going to be easy for any of the Dariens, but she wanted Lindsay to know what was in her heart, so she laid her palm on top of the other woman's hand, and they stood silently for a moment.

"A friend like I never had before," Lindsay said.

"Yes."

They smiled at each other, then finished making the bed.

When Zach and Jordan returned, the women were up in the lounge relaxing over margaritas.

"Looks like we got here just in time for the party." Zach observed as he set down a bag on the deck, then went to the controls and started the engine.

JIM Stone looked at the news report from Grand Fernandino. He'd been keeping an eye on the island, looking for anything strange. Now he'd found something.

Picking up the phone, he made a call to a man he'd hired on a short-term basis.

"Check on the *Odysseus*," he said. "I want to know if anybody's aboard. If they are, keep them in port, and I'll give you further instructions."

A half hour later, he had his answer.

"Someone's on board, and they just pulled out of port."

Jim fought the urge to vent his anger and frustration. Instead, he carefully hung up the phone.

So he knew the freaks were alive.

Well, he'd keep looking for them, and sooner or later he'd find them.

ZACH piloted the boat out of the harbor, then along the coast to a small cove he'd discovered the week before.

They seemed to be the only craft in the area, and Zach dropped anchor in the darkness. In the distance, frogs chirped. And when insects began buzzing around the boat, Zach lit a couple of repellent candles.

As the boat gently rocked in the waves, Anna handed Zach a drink, and he joined the others in one of the comfortable deck chairs.

"This life has a lot of appeal," Jordan said in the darkness.

Zach slid his chair close to Anna and draped an arm over her shoulder. "I can't imagine myself not doing physical work," he said.

"You got a chance for plenty of action in the past few days." Jordan looked around the deck. "And you know, if you didn't want someone to find you, traveling from port to port on a nice comfortable boat would be a good way to go."

"It's a great boat, but it would be a little cramped for four people," Anna said.

"We could sell it. And add some of my trust fund money," Lindsay said. "That way, we could get something a lot bigger."

"You have a trust fund?" Zach asked.

"Yes. I mostly lived on my salary when I was a staffer on Capitol Hill. So I only dipped into my inheritance to buy my condo. Jordan and I both sold our places in D.C. and moved to a farm in West Virginia. But we're only renting. So we've got the real estate money, too."

"What about when we find other Dariens?" Anna asked.

"We get a big enough yacht, and that won't be a problem for a while," Jordan said. "And we'd all have to crew. So that should take care of the physical labor part. But we can also be on the lookout for several properties where we could live."

Anna swallowed. "What if we run into some Dariens who don't fit in with us?"

"We have to be prepared for that," Jordan answered, his voice turning gruff. Looking at Zach and Anna, he said, "The other couple we found tried to kill us."

Anna sucked in a sharp breath. "Are you going to give us details?"

"They were a twin brother and sister who bonded as children, and they had plans to take over the world."

"Bonded? You're not talking about like what happened with Zach and me."

"No, I'm talking about a physical relationship."

"They were in an orphanage, and they turned to each other for comfort. But they grew up warped, and they used their powers to establish a fake religious cult."

"Like San Donato," Anna whispered.

"But on a bigger scale, with richer patrons, in Florida. Where they could indulge the luxury lifestyle they craved. They'd gotten their hooks into a U.S. senator and were planning to maneuver him into the presidency when we encountered them."

"Jesus!" Zach swore.

He was silent as he stroked his hand up and down Anna's arm, then cleared his throat. "I guess we'd better ask—what happens to our kids? Do they have psychic powers? Or does it end with us?"

"We don't know," Lindsay answered. "And so far, we haven't been willing to take the responsibility of having children. Not when our lives are so . . . uncertain." She cleared her throat and turned to Anna. "I went on birth control pills. You have to decide what you want to do."

Zach knitted his fingers with Anna's. "Another important topic for discussion. But not tonight. It's been a long day."

"Very long," Jordan agreed.

"We can meet again in the morning. If it doesn't sound too mundane, I've got cereal for breakfast. And boxed milk. I hope you don't mind instant coffee."

Jordan laughed. "I can deal with that—on a short-term basis."

"If you get up before I do, maybe you can row the dinghy to shore and pick some bananas and breadfruit."

"Aye-aye, sir," Jordan answered.

It felt good to be joking around. And wonderful to have found these people who had so quickly become closer than family.

Anna rested her head on Zach's shoulder, and he wedged her against his side.

They stayed close together as they walked back to the master cabin. And as soon as they stepped inside, Zach closed the door and pulled her against the length of his body.

He was aroused, and when she tipped her head up, he brought his mouth down to hers for a hungry kiss.

"Did you ever picture this?" he murmured when they broke apart to drag in a breath.

"This? You mean love that reaches to the depth of your soul? Passion that burns you from the inside out?"

Uh-huh. And marriage. Don't forget we're getting married as soon as we can figure out how to do it safely.

Whether I have a piece of paper or not, I know I belong to you. Only you.

He kissed her again, and they swayed together, their passion building, and she wondered if they were going to get to sleep any time before dawn.

Well, maybe we can manage a couple of little naps, he whispered in her mind.

Turn the page for a special preview of
Rebecca York's next novel,

GHOST MOON

Coming soon from Berkley Sensation!

PROLOGUE

JUNE 1933

THE TWO WEREWOLVES were out for blood and too inexperienced to think of death—their own or the other's.

They had fought over a flirtatious little brunette. And neither one of them was willing to say she was just a temporary whim. So they met in a patch of Maryland woods, far from the haunts of men—each prepared to rip the hide off the other.

They had driven in separate cars to the dueling area, neither one of them bringing a second because this was a very private affair.

Back into the mists of time, the adult members of the Marshall clan had trusted no one besides their lifemates. Certainly not their fathers or brothers or cousins. They were all alpha males, all leaders of their own pack. And the only individuals admitted to that pack were their wives and immature children.

But neither had yet reached the age of bonding. And neither of them knew how to control the rage that flared in the animal portion of their spirit.

So they pulled their cars into the woods, each of them

going to a separate area to strip off his clothing and say the ancient chant that changed him from man to wolf.

Neither knew what the words meant. They only knew the ritual had been passed down from father to son through the ages.

Then they trotted into the clearing that they had selected and faced each other, eyes blazing and muscles tensed. One of them howled, then the other, before they circled each other, looking for an opening.

For a moment there was still a chance to back down. Yet pride and the violent instincts of their kind outweighed good sense. One sprang, knocking the other to the ground, and the fight was on.

They rolled across the forest floor, each trying to score a bite that would punish the other enough to make him back off.

Then one lost all sense of proportion and went for his cousin's throat, his teeth sinking through thick fur into vulnerable flesh. When he felt the other combatant go limp, he raised his head in alarm, then took a quick step away.

His opponent lay still, blood gushing from his neck, his expression as astonished as that of the wolf who had taken a fatal chunk out of his flesh.

The attacker backed farther away, saying the ancient chant in his mind, feeling his muscles and tendons contort as he changed from wolf to naked man. Ignoring the bite marks and scratches on his shoulders and ribs, he knelt beside the wounded animal lying on the ground.

"Caleb, Jesus. I'm sorry. I didn't mean . . ."

His cousin raised dull eyes. His jaws moved, and his face contorted, and then he, too, made the transformation.

The effort seemed to exhaust him. He lay breathing hard, then tried to push himself up, before falling back against the blood-soaked leaves, his fingers clawing at the ground.

"Jesus," Aden repeated, fear leaping inside his chest. "We've got to get you to a doctor. We can say . . . an animal attacked you."

But it was already too late. The life in his cousin's eyes flickered, then went out.

Aden looked around wildly, wondering what the hell he was going to do.

His heart pounding, he went back to where he'd left his clothes and swiftly pulled on his khaki pants and long-sleeved shirt.

It struck him, then, that he had killed a man. Well, a werewolf. His cousin. He had heard whispered tales in the family of werewolves who had disappeared over the years. And now there would be another one.

Caleb lived alone, the way they all did before they bonded with a lifemate. It might be days, weeks before anyone realized he was missing. And there was nothing to tie his disappearance to his cousin.

Somehow it seemed wrong to leave a naked body in the woods. So he went to the clearing where his cousin had taken off his clothes and brought the garments back. First he pulled the jeans up the limp legs, buttoning the fly before tackling the work shirt, and finally the shoes and socks.

As he worked, his mind churned, making feverish plans. He'd have to drive his cousin's Ford somewhere else. Maybe he should push it off a cliff into the river. That might be the best option. Or maybe not.

Well, he didn't have to figure out that part yet. But he'd better not drive too far, because he'd have to race back here in wolf form and . . .

Bury the body. He couldn't leave the evidence. Or could he? What evidence was that, exactly? That a man had been killed by an animal in the woods?

He shuddered, and a surge of family loyalty made his

throat tighten. He might have killed Caleb in a stupid fight, but he wouldn't abandon him out here in the open to be torn apart by forest animals.

He gritted his teeth. He had come out to the woods roaring mad over an insult. And now he was reaping the horrible consequences.

CHAPTER
ONE

PRESENT DAY

QUINN HAD COME through the portal between the worlds six times now, into this country so different from her own.

As she stepped into the Maryland woods, she took a deep breath of the air. In her universe, she would have caught the tang of wood smoke. Here, underlying the scent of pine trees, she could detect exhaust from automobiles and smoke from factories—even this far from the place called Baltimore, a city unlike anything in her world, where people walked around without fear of marauders swooping down from another city.

She had been there, riding in a car with Rinna and Logan Marshall—Logan from this world and Rinna from the other universe.

They had both taught her so much. Enough to get around here. She even had a driver's license, money, and credit cards.

She rubbed her arm, where an adept had removed the slave mark from her flesh. She was a free woman now. Yet she carried heavy obligations. And she must hurry.

She stood for a moment, sending her mind outward,

searching the woods for danger. In this place, it always felt like someone was watching her, yet when she looked around, she saw nothing. And after several moments, she put the feeling down to her own uneasiness.

Quickly she pulled off her leather tunic, the cool evening breeze tightening her nipples. With a shiver, she snatched up the clothing she'd hidden in a storage bin under a tangle of brambles.

The T-shirt had always struck her as obscene because of the way it molded to her body. But she knew it was perfectly acceptable here.

It was tempting to keep on her own leather pants, but she knew they would look primitive in twenty-first century America. So she shucked them down her legs as rapidly as she could before pulling on the silk panties and bra that were part of a modern woman's outfit.

When she was dressed in the T-shirt and worn blue jeans, she breathed out a little sigh.

Sitting down on a fallen log, she exchanged her sandals for socks and running shoes. After bundling up the clothing and hunting knife from her own universe, she took out a fanny pack and hooked it around her waist. Inside were her plastic ID cards—and a Sig Sauer. Logan had taught her gun safety and marksmanship, but she still hated the power of the weapon.

After returning the plastic box to the tangle of brambles, she started toward the Marshalls' stone and wood house, using a rough trail through the thick underbrush. But this time the familiar route was blocked by loose dirt and boulders that had tumbled down a cliff.

She stopped, running a hand through her mop of short curls as she considered climbing over the mess. But if the rubble shifted, she could get hurt. And out here, there was no one to help her. So she reversed direction, then took an alternate route toward her friends' house.

When she reached a small clearing in the woods, she

stopped short, her sixth sense tingling and her eyes straining to penetrate the shadows. Although she saw nothing,
she knew there was something hovering there. Waiting for
her.

Something she only half sensed. Yet she had the ability
to feel other people's emotions. Sometimes it was stronger
than other times. And it was working overtime now. She
caught the edge of deep pain and a gnawing hunger. Not
for food.

She shuddered and took a quick step back, ready to turn
and flee. Before she could escape, the air around her rippled, as though a being had stepped from nowhere into this
time and space.

Blinking, she tried to see into the spot where the air shim-
mered. The visual disturbance vanished as quickly as it had
appeared.

In the next moment, a man's strong arms grabbed her
from behind. The scream that rose in her throat was cut off
by a large hand clamping over her mouth.

She gasped and tried to twist away from the man who
held her. She knew it was a man because she could feel a
masculine body pressed to her back and feel his arm across
her middle just below her breasts.

Unable to break free, she kicked backward, trying to inflict some damage on his legs. But she couldn't make contact with his flesh.

He held her in place like a giant restraining a child, yet
when she looked down, she saw nothing.

And that was more terrifying than catching a view of a
powerful opponent. As the horror of her plight slammed
home, her heart skipped a beat and started up again in double time.

She had called him a man because he was holding her in
his iron grip. But she couldn't see him. Not because he was
hidden. There was *nothing* to see, although she felt the hidden substance of his energy body.

He wasn't human. Couldn't be human. And a feeling of desperation made her redouble her efforts to get away. Arms and legs pumping, she jabbed and kicked at the air. But she failed to connect with anything solid.

"Let me go," she gasped, even as she sensed that the plea was only a waste of time and effort. To fight a demon or ghost or whatever this supernatural being was, she needed cunning, not physical force.

As her strength ebbed, she wondered how she had gotten caught by this creature. Truly, she hadn't expected anything like this in Logan's universe.

Fighting the impulse to keep struggling, she forced her shoulders, arms, and legs to relax. And when she did, she thought she heard a ghostly sigh.

"Turn me loose." This time she said it softly, a plea, not a demand. Maybe that would work.

Because she hadn't expected an answer, hearing any words at all gave her as much of a shock as her captivity.

"Not yet."

His voice was deep and resonant and just a little rusty, like a man who hadn't spoken in a long time.

"Who are you?"

"I won't hurt you."

"Turn me loose," she repeated.

"You'll run."

He had that right. But she wasn't going to agree—not out loud.

At least he was willing to talk. Deciding she had nothing to lose by trying to gain his confidence, she closed her eyes and leaned back against him.

"Why did you grab me?"

"I want . . . company."

"Why?"

"I have been here a long time."

"Other people must have come through these woods."

"Yes. But they do not know I am here. They cannot feel me or hear me."

What luck! Her psychic talents had gotten her into this fix.

Was he a ghost? Or a demon? Or something else? She wanted to know, but she was afraid to find out.

While she was silently debating her options, she felt him stir, felt his hold on her change subtly.

One arm moved upward to clamp against her breasts. While she was reacting to that, she felt the fingers of his other hand stroking her cheeks, her jawline, in a pattern that could have been soothing—or sensual.

Then the feel of his fingers was replaced by his lips. His invisible body hunched as he slid his mouth gently along the line where her hair met her face. And he sighed as he found the curve of her cheekbone.

"Your skin is so soft. Like silk."

His voice had turned almost dreamy. Was this her chance to pull away?

She should seize the opportunity while his guard was down. But her resolve faded as his lips traveled to her neck. Her earlier fear was replaced by a buzzing in her brain . . . and a tingling sensation along her nerve endings. She hadn't noticed before, but he carried a very appealing, fresh, woodsy scent.

"Don't," she managed.

"Why not?" he asked, his mouth moving against her neck, then sliding lower, to her shoulder. His lips were warm on her skin. His breath exciting little tingles of sensation.

His breath? How could that be possible?

The question drifted out of her mind. He was standing behind her, so that his lips couldn't reach hers, even when she arched her neck and threw her head back.

"You're beautiful. I love your dark hair." He ran his fingers through the springy curls that covered the top of her head. "And your little nose. And your sensual lips." As he spoke, he touched each feature he mentioned.

He still seemed to be standing behind her. Could he really see her face?

A thought struck her, and she stiffened.

"What?" he murmured.

"Were you watching me undress?"

"You gave me a beautiful view of your body. Your breasts. Then that sweet, dark triangle at the top of your legs."

She felt her face heat.

"I was too far away to touch you."

"But not too far away to make those rocks block the path!" she accused.

He chuckled. "That wasn't easy. But I did it."

"Why?"

"Each time you came from . . . the other place, I tried to contact you. You sensed me, but you didn't hear my voice—or feel my touch."

The finger at her lips stroked back and forth. "Open for me."

She tried to resist. But somehow he had bent her to his will. After a few moments, she did as he asked, and his finger slipped inside, tenderly playing with her inner lips and sliding along the line of her teeth.

In some corner of her mind she was shocked at what she was doing—allowing herself to respond on such a basic level.

Yet she had stopped fearing him. He was no devil. Or if he was, he knew how to give a woman pleasure. Was he an incubus, trapped here in this patch of woods? That would explain the effect he was having on her.

Or was she simply so starved for a relationship with a man that she welcomed the attentions of a phantom?